"I have to leave," Anna responded lamely, scarcely hiding her disappointment. "My mother is looking for me. It was a pleasure to meet you, Mr. MacLaughlin."

He didn't look as though he believed her, but Ewan nodded. "The pleasure was mine." Even though they were strictly courtesy, his soft words sent a tingle down Anna's spine. "And thank you again for allowing me the book."

She smiled, delaying leaving even though she could hear her mother's heavy footsteps coming closer. "Enjoy it."

"Anna," her mother's voice boomed from behind the next stack of books.

Anna started toward it, not wanting her mother to see this perfect young man. She wanted to keep him just for herself. Casting one last glance his way, she committed his image to memory so she would never forget the five incredible minutes she spent in his company.

"Good-bye, Mr. MacLaughlin."

He tipped his hat at her. "London's not that large, Miss Welsley, so I won't say good-bye just yet."

DON'T MISS A SINGLE
AVON TRUE ROMANCE

AN AVON TRUE ROMANCE

Anna
and the
Duke

KATHRYN SMITH

AVON BOOKS
An Imprint of HarperCollinsPublishers

FIND TRUE LOVE!

www.avontrueromance.com

To Elsa

With many hugs and thanks

Love, Aunt Kathryn

CHAPTER ONE

Scotland, 1818

"Why don't you just pick one, then?"

Standing waist deep in the chilly waters of Loch Glenshea, Ewan MacLaughlin slicked his wet hair back from his face and stared dumbly at his cousin Jamie. "Pick one what?"

With a sigh and an expression of exasperation, Jamie jerked his head in the direction of the shore. "One of *them*."

A crowd of girls from the village had gathered to watch the boys swim. Some of the girls were trying to goad the others into joining them, for the day was sunny and hot and they'd all been working since sunrise. None of the girls was actually brazen enough to wade in, however.

Ewan scoffed as the sound of giggling drifted across the water. "What would I want to pick one of them for?"

Jamie scowled, drawing his dark auburn eyebrows together. "Are ye daft as well as stubborn? So the rest of us might actually have a chance of choosing one as well!"

Ewan truly had no idea what his cousin was talking

about, and he was certain he was neither stupid nor stubborn, but as he studied the girls on the shore he noticed that most of them were watching *him*. An uncomfortable realization settled in his chest. He'd never thought of himself as much of a catch before, but as an eligible, landowning young man of twenty-four, he realized that he was definitely seen as a catch.

"I don't want one!" he blurted with absolute certainty, his heart pounding in his chest. The idea of spending the rest of his life with one of those girls— any girl—filled him with dread.

Wanting to put a stop to this ridiculous conversation, he dove under the surface of the loch, each powerful stroke of his arms taking him farther away from his cousin and his absurd questions.

Him, a husband? The very thought filled him with horror. While many of the girls of his village were bonny, to be sure, there was not one who caught his interest more than the others. Not one who set his heart pounding or made his palms damp. He couldn't imagine spending the rest of his life with a single one of them. What would they have in common? And what would they think of a husband who sometimes stayed up half the night reading or painting? A sensible Scottish lass would think him as daft as Jamie seemed to think him.

Lungs close to bursting, Ewan broke the surface of the

lake, only to find Jamie coming up behind him, his long chestnut hair trailing like seaweed behind him. His cousin's fair skin had finally started to tan rather than burn, but he was still several shades lighter than Ewan. Jamie's complexion was the only delicate thing about him. He was pure Scot through and through—as strong as an ox and just as stubborn as one too. He had to be. It was the only way his family had survived the Clearances. They'd been kicked off their land by the wealthy landowners, and Jamie came to his cousin Ewan looking for work to support his family—and work he did. It was Ewan, the lord of the land, who wasn't a true Scot. No matter how hard he tried, he couldn't change the fact that English blood also ran in his veins.

"What do you mean, you don't want one?" Jamie demanded, treading water beside him. "You'll not find a more bonny lot anywhere—not even in the court of King George himself." The statement wasn't meant to be insulting, of that Ewan was certain, but it stung all the same.

Ewan averted his gaze so his cousin couldn't see the guilt there. He was certain it was his father's blood—*English* blood—that made him want to taste the world beyond his tiny village of Loch Glenshea, beyond Hadrian's Wall to the southern lands of England. He had no good reason to feel such a pull toward his father's homeland. In fact, he resisted it violently. His father had deserted Ewan and his mother years ago, leaving his mother to waste away and eventually die broken and in much lowered circumstances. Ewan had been very young, but memories of his mother were burned into his mind.

Ewan's one memory of him was of his father leaving after his mother's funeral. It was fuzzy, for he'd been just a wee lad of three. At the time, Ewan was glad to stay in Scotland with people he knew, but as he grew older he wondered why his father hadn't taken him with him, why he had left his son to struggle to keep his home standing and his people prosperous. He also wondered why he still thought about his father after all these years. He deserved none of Ewan's curiosity. He certainly didn't deserve the small bit of his son's heart that still ached at the thought of his father not wanting him.

"I have no desire to take a wife, Jamie," he replied softly. He'd seen what marriage had done to his mother. He had no desire to afflict anyone with that kind of suffering—nor have it put upon him for that matter.

But even as the bitter thoughts ran through his head, they were chased by memories of the kind of marriage his grandparents shared—one of hard work, love, and laughter. He knew that his mother and father's marriage hadn't been a normal one.

Jamie snorted. "You don't have to marry her, Ewan. Just pay more attention to her than the others so they'll give up hopin' you'll pick one of them and start lookin' at the rest of us."

It didn't seem right to Ewan to pretend to court a girl he didn't want, and he didn't like having the success of his cousin's love life placed on his shoulders. He already had enough to worry about. Winter was only a few months away and there were repairs to be made before the snow fell. He and his grandmother weren't impoverished yet, but they were close.

"Why don't you just pick one *you* like, Jamie, and then try to court her?" That seemed like a much better idea than Ewan having to do all the work.

Another frown. "And just how am I supposed to do that when they're all pinin' for your pretty face?"

Ewan flushed with embarrassment, but he met his cousin's gaze evenly. "Just be your usual charming self," he teased with a smile.

Jamie growled and lunged toward Ewan. Laughing, the two cousins wrestled in the shallow water like two young otters. The two were well matched: while Jamie was the bigger of the two, Ewan was more agile. As long as he could avoid getting shoved under the water, he could hold his own. The girls on the shore cheered them on, and Ewan couldn't resist rubbing it in his cousin's face that most of the cheers were for *him* and not Jamie.

"Ewan MacLaughlin!"

Trained by years of instantly answering when his grandmother called or getting a rod across the back of the legs, Ewan released his hold on Jamie's shaggy head and turned toward shore. He felt his cousin's hands come down like anvils on his shoulders, ready to push him under.

"I see you, James MacLaughlin! You stop your tomfoolery this instant!"

Lilian MacLaughlin stood with her fists firmly planted on generous hips. She'd been pretty once, but years of struggle had hardened her features. Hers was a stern, handsome face, one that a young man easily obeyed. Usually, her eyes sparkled with good humor. From this distance, Ewan couldn't tell if they sparkled or not, but he could hear uncertainty in her voice. It shook a bit, sending a shiver of dread down Ewan's spine. Nothing scared his grandmother. Or at least he hadn't thought anything could.

"There's someone here to see you, Ewan," she called. "Get yourself to the house right away."

Mystified, Ewan swam toward shore. Who could it be coming to see him that his grandmother wouldn't identify by name? He knew of no one who could make her react in such a way.

Water streamed from his sodden breeches as he sloshed from the loch. He barely felt the tiny pebbles along the edge as they bit into the tough soles of his feet.

Since boyhood, Ewan and his friends had spent as much of their summers as possible barefoot and shirtless. But boyhood was behind him now. That was obvious in the appreciative stares the girls gave him as he strode to where his shirt lay on the grass. Suddenly, he was very conscious of how his breeches clung to his backside and legs, and that his chest, once smooth and thin, now threatened to burst the seams of his old shirts.

Inside he still felt like a boy, but outside he looked like a man, and the girls of his village, once friends, were suddenly seeing him as one.

The worn linen of his shirt stuck to his wet skin. Embarrassed by the girls' giggling, he kept his head bowed as he fastened the buttons. Jamie charged up beside him.

"What's goin' on?"

Ewan shook his head, spraying them both with droplets of water. "I've no idea."

"Do ye want me to come with you then?" Jamie's bright blue eyes were filled with concern.

Clapping him on the shoulder, Ewan flashed his cousin a bright grin. "Nae. You stay here and entertain the ladies. Angharad seems to be very interested in your . . . conversation."

Jamie glanced over his shoulder and flushed crimson from the tips of his toes to the top of his head when he caught the pretty redhead's frank stare. He turned back to Ewan, his eyes wide with fear. "What do I do?" he demanded in a strangled whisper.

"Talk to her, I suppose," Ewan replied with a grin, as he began to walk away. "And be your usual charming self."

Ewan ran the short stretch to Castle MacLaughlin. The castle sat on a small isthmus of land that jutted out into the

depths of Glenshea. It had been built two hundred years
ago by one of his ancestors. It stood proud and strong
against the rugged landscape like something out of a
legend. The tawny stone turned to gold in the afternoon
sun and the stained glass in the upper windows sparkled
like gems. The castle was the jewel of the MacLaughlin
lands, and Ewan longed to restore it to its former glory. Just
the sight of it made his heart fill with pride.

Little changes had been made to the outside, though
the inside had been renovated half a dozen times over the
years when the MacLaughlins had the funds to do so. As
lord, it was Ewan's job to see to the necessary repairs, but
his father had robbed him not only of his birthright, but
of the money required to fulfill his duty. He managed to
keep the castle warm and dry, but there were other things
that needed to be done, such as new carpets and draperies,
and fresh paint. It had been a good year for sheep and
crops; perhaps there would be enough money to purchase
some new carpets after everything else was taken care of.

Maggie, the housekeeper, met him at the servants'
entrance with dry clothes, boots, and a slab of freshly
baked bread dripping with butter. Ewan's stomach
growled.

"Get yerself dressed behind the screen there," she told
him with affectionate brusqueness. "And then you can eat."

One whiff of the fragrant bread was all the urging
Ewan needed. He slid behind the screen and quickly

changed his clothes. Located in the bottom of the castle, the kitchen was cool despite it being early June. Warmed by the dry clothes, he draped his wet garments over the rack by the fire and crammed his feet into the boots. He grabbed the steaming bread from Maggie's hand with a grin and a kiss on her cheek and set off down the hall to find his grandmother and his mysterious visitor.

When he stepped inside the front drawing room, he found a tiny bald man sitting on the sofa across from his grandmother. The little man's posture was so rigid he looked as though he had been carved from stone.

He jumped to his feet when Ewan said hello.

"My lord!" he cried, stepping forward to shake Ewan's hand. "It is a pleasure to meet you, although I fear I bear bad tidings."

Ewan's heart seized in his chest. No one *ever* called him by his title unless they were a bill collector or someone looking to gain something.

"Good day, Mr. . . . ?"

"Chumley, my lord," the man replied, still pumping Ewan's hand. "Alfred Chumley."

Alfred Chumley was English, a fact Ewan was hard-pressed to hold against him when he looked like a gnome and the top of his head barely reached the middle of Ewan's chest.

He pulled his hand free. "Please sit, Mr. Chumley. May I offer you a drink?" Vaguely, Ewan realized his own accent was almost as crisp and as *English* as Mr. Chumley's.

His mother's final wish had been that he be educated like his father's folk, and for a while, young Ewan had ached to be more like the man who had deserted him. He'd tried so hard to be as English as the tutors who guided him. Now he felt a measure of disgust at himself for trying to be anything like this little man from a country he'd never seen but that had been the cause of his mother's unhappiness.

"A brandy would be lovely, if you have it, my lord." Flicking out his coattails, Mr. Chumley again seated himself.

"Brandy it is, then." Crossing to the oak cabinet in the far corner of the room, Ewan poured two glasses of brandy before crossing back to seat himself on Chumley's right. Ignoring his grandmother's disapproving stare, Ewan took a sip of the fortified wine.

"What brings you into Scotland, Mr. Chumley?"

Mr. Chumley pulled a large leather satchel into his lap and opened it. "It's about your father, my lord."

Ewan choked on a mouthful of brandy. His eyes watered and his nose and throat burned from the liquor. Neither his grandmother nor the barrister moved to assist him, but only Mr. Chumley seemed concerned. No doubt his grandmother thought he deserved to choke. She despised strong drink.

"What about my father?" Ewan demanded once the

coughing stopped and he could speak again.

Mr. Chumley's expression was one of pity and sympathy. Ewan didn't want either. "I . . . I'm afraid he's dead, my lord."

Ewan experienced more surprise than any kind of sorrow. He'd expected the old man to live forever—a constant reminder that neither Ewan nor his mother had been able to earn his love.

"And what has this to do with me?" How he managed to keep his voice so low and controlled he had no idea. For twenty-one years he'd waited for contact of any kind from his father and had received nothing. Was he expected to dress in black and weep now that he was dead?

How could he mourn someone he'd never known? And why had anyone even bothered to tell him? How could it possibly make a difference now?

Mr. Chumley's entire head flushed scarlet. "Y-you're in the will, my lord."

A fist in the face couldn't have surprised him any more. What could his father have possibly left him? More importantly, how could he have believed Ewan would possibly want it? He'd married his mother for her title and her fortune and then deserted her when he'd inherited his own title.

He'd returned to Scotland for his wife's funeral—not to mourn her but to make sure she was dead. He'd taken one look at his son and then left Ewan behind. He hadn't even given Ewan's mother the respect of a full year of mourning. He remarried not even two months after her death. He no doubt had other children to name in his will. Why bother with his forgotten oldest?

Ewan fought to keep his expression calm. "There's nothing that man could possibly have had that I would want," he replied.

Mr. Chumley looked from him to his grandmother and back again. His grandmother fixed him with a strange expression that told Ewan she understood something he didn't—something that made his stomach clench with unease.

"Well, I'm n-not sure that you have much choice but to accept this, my lord." Mr. Chumley cleared his throat.

Scowling fiercely, Ewan rose out of the chair to his full height of six feet four inches. Mr. Chumley's Adam's apple bobbed as he swallowed hard.

"What do you mean I have no choice?" Oh yes, Ewan was very capable of playing the role of lord of the manor when necessary. If Mr. Chumley meant to intimidate him, Ewan would show him who was truly master.

The little Englishman shuffled through some papers with visibly shaking hands. Finding what he wanted, he held it out to Ewan.

"Might I remind you, my lord, that you are your father's oldest child."

Ewan snatched the papers from Mr. Chumley's hand

but didn't look at them. He kept his puzzled gaze locked on the man's round face. "So?"

Mr. Chumley pushed his spectacles up on his nose and tried again to make Ewan understand. "You're his oldest son, my lord. His oldest legitimate son. His heir."

Understanding blossomed like fire to dry tinder inside Ewan's stomach. "You mean . . . "

Mr. Chumley nodded. "Yes, my lord. I mean that you are now one very, very wealthy and powerful young man. You're the new Duke of Brahm."

Five minutes to herself. That was all she wanted. Five minutes away from her mother's endless prattle about fabrics and dresses and wedding plans.

Especially wedding plans.

Ducking into the bookshop, Anna Welsley knew she had at least five minutes—maybe even seven—in which to soothe her frazzled nerves and forget her mother even existed. Just the smell of paper, ink, and leather bindings was enough to calm the raging headache that threatened behind her right eye.

The store was quiet, blocking out the sounds of the busy day outside. In here, Anna could lose herself for a few moments, escape her life and become the heroine of a novel or poem. She could pretend to be that woman and forget about the girl she was.

She loved books like most girls loved new dresses. No

doubt her mother would have some kind of seizure if she knew that, so Anna kept her passion for reading a secret. Even Richard didn't know.

A man should know of his fiancée's passions, shouldn't he?

But then, Anna found it difficult to discuss her passions with Richard. In fact, she rarely knew what to say to him at all. He was so confident, so poised and charming that she felt positively tongue-tied in his presence, afraid that she would reveal what a boring ninny she was if she dared to open her mouth.

It made her nervous just to be around him, and she often caught herself wondering what he even saw in her. She was quiet and bookish—not the kind of vivacious, sparkling girl a young man would want as his betrothed. But Richard didn't seem to notice that they were ill matched, or perhaps he did not care. He was always the perfect gentleman—a fact that made him a model to other young men, made him desirable to other young women and sought after by their mamas.

So why was Anna feeling so unsure of him and that he had chosen her to be his wife? Richard was everything she ever dreamed of having in a husband. When he noticed her last season, Anna couldn't believe her good fortune. There she was, just another debutante in just another white gown, and *the* most handsome, charming young man of the *haute ton*, London's cream of society, had singled her out for not one, but *two* dances. One of those dances had been the waltz—a dance her mother had thought scandalously indecent and refused to let her practice until Richard asked permission to whirl her about the floor.

That had been the most glorious night of her life. All the other girls had been terribly envious, and when Richard sent her a huge, sweetly scented bouquet of roses the next morning, Anna's heart sang in joy. She knew she was the luckiest girl in all of London to have garnered the attention of such a young man during her first Season, and she appreciated it, she truly did, but when Richard had come to her parents just a few months ago and asked her father's permission to ask for her hand, Anna had been overwhelmed with myriad unexpected emotions. One of which was alarmingly close to panic. Why would a gentleman of his quality want to wed a girl such as her? A girl who could barely string a sentence together in his presence.

Perhaps it was just a bad case of bridal nerves, as her mother insisted. After all, Richard didn't seem to mind that she was quiet around him. He seemed to like it. The problem was that Anna wasn't quiet by nature. Surely she would overcome her shyness before the wedding? And there were other things for them to do than talk.

Kissing, for example. Anna blushed furiously as she remembered how Richard had kissed her the night before, after the Whitman-Holt ball. It gave her butterflies just to think about it. Her mother would *not* have approved.

Peering out the window, Anna saw that her mother had yet to notice her disappearance. She was still talking to Mrs. Cole, no doubt boring the poor woman with every detail of Anna's upcoming nuptials.

"Good day, Miss Welsley."

Anna cast a sheepish smile at the elderly man behind the counter as she turned away from the window. "Good day, Mr. Hornsby."

"I take it your mother chose not to accompany you into the shop this morning?" Mr. Hornsby's pale green eyes sparkled with amusement. It was a running joke between them—Anna's mother *never* entered the store except to collect her daughter and demand to know what she was doing in such a "dirty, dusty place." Somehow, Marion Welsley never figured out that her daughter was actually looking at books.

"She is talking to Mrs. Cole in front of the dressmaker's," Anna replied with equal humor. The same dressmaker's where she had spent the last two hours being pinned and prodded and talked about like a fashion doll rather than a person.

"Ah. You have plenty of time to browse, then."

Anna chuckled. "A few minutes at the very least. Do you have anything new in?"

"I just shelved a new edition of Wordsworth at the back."

Anna wrinkled her nose. Poems about nature might

please the minds of others, but she wanted something more . . . meaningful.

"Nothing else?"

Mr. Hornsby laughed at her expression. "There's a new volume of Byron back there as well."

Now *that* was more to her liking! Her mother would certainly not approve of her daughter reading poetry written by someone as scandalous as Byron, but that had little to do with the excitement fluttering in Anna's stomach. There was something about the way Byron wrote, something about the way he made her feel. He made her want to experience life and all its glories. She wanted to travel, she wanted to see the world, but most of all, she wanted to feel that sweeping passion Byron so often talked about in his poems.

No doubt her mother—even her friends—would think her terribly silly for wanting someone to burn for her like the subjects of Byron's poems. All her life she had lived within the social structures of London, the order of her mother's household, the misfortune of being born female. What she truly wanted was to experience something wild and untamed, to break the rules and stomp upon the circumstances. Of course, to do so would mean social ruin, and while she might be fanciful, Anna Welsley was not a fool. Still, just once, it would be nice to have someone spout a little poetry in her honor.

As dear and sweet as he was, Anna couldn't imagine her

fiancé using verse to express his deeper emotions. Maybe she was just too romantic, one of those weak-minded girls her mother claimed novel writers preyed upon. If only she knew how Richard truly felt for her. He kissed her as though he loved her, but she had yet to hear the words. Maybe then she wouldn't suffer this anxiety all the time.

Anna walked briskly to the back of the shop. She must hurry if she was going to find anything before her mother came looking for her. Dear Mrs. Cole would listen to her mother talk for only so long before making some excuse as to why she must leave. Her mother had no imagination and therefore her conversation tended to always entail the same subjects. For the last six months, she'd been able to talk of nothing else but Anna's engagement. After all, it wasn't every day that the firstborn son of a duke deigned to marry a mere nobody.

Not that Anna was a complete nobody—she was distantly related to both the Earl Spencer and the Duke of Wellington, but her father held no title and he was a man of business, which was looked down upon by society's chosen few, the *ton*. The only thing that truly saved Anna from being a social outcast rather than one of its darlings was her huge dowry. She was heiress to her father's shipping company—something relatively unheard of for a daughter. And whoever married her would gain a foothold in that shipping company, a fact that had made Anna much sought after during her London debut.

Aside from his considerable charm, the fact that Richard, heir to a duke, had money of his own made Anna feel as though he was truly in love with her.

At least she hoped he was, because she didn't care how large *his* fortune was. If he loved her, truly loved her, it wouldn't matter if he was rich or poor.

Suddenly, Anna realized she was not alone. There was a man standing with his back to her in the poetry section. A very tall, very large man with quite possibly the broadest shoulders Anna had ever seen. He wore a long, gray greatcoat over buff-colored breeches and shiny black Hessian boots. The gray hat perched on his head added several more inches to his height. The man was a giant!

And he should have been frightening, but all Anna could do was stare at him in awe. She'd never seen a man so . . . so . . . *commanding* before.

He didn't hear her approach, so intent was his attention on the book in hand.

"'She walks in beauty, like the night / Of cloudless climes and starry skies, / And all that's best of dark and bright / Meet in her aspect and her eyes: / Thus mellowed to that tender light / Which heaven to gaudy day denies.'"

His voice was deep and melodic, with a slight burr to it that only made Byron's words all the more effective.

"You read very well, sir," she remarked, her voice annoyingly breathless. She shouldn't have spoken. It was highly improper, but there was no one around to hear her speak other than him.

He started. Snapping the book shut, he whirled around to face her, and the full effect of him was like a blow to the stomach.

He was without a doubt *the* most incredible-looking man she had ever seen. What she could see of his hair was light brown liberally streaked with gold. And his features were rugged and solemn. He wasn't exactly handsome, but incredibly captivating. And he was young—although a few years older than her own eighteen years.

"Th-thank you," he replied, his hazel gaze hesitant as it met hers. "Miss—"

Oh, where were her manners? It might have been shocking for her to speak to him, but it was even ruder of her not to introduce herself. Extending her hand, Anna smiled, hoping she didn't look like a complete fool. "Miss Welsley. And you are?" *Other than completely magnificent, that is.*

He took her hand, dwarfing it in his much larger one. "MacLaughlin. Ewan MacLaughlin." He pronounced it like *Lock*lan rather than the softer *Loff*.

"Well, Mr. MacLaughlin," she responded, marveling in the strength of the fingers clasped around hers. "You have a lovely voice for poetry—and good taste in it as well."

He held up the book, a slight smile curving his lips. "I've never read Byron before. I've heard so much about him, I decided I should at least see what all the fuss is about."

"He's one of my favorites." Gazing toward the shelves, Anna discovered the empty spot where Mr. MacLaughlin had found the book. His was the last copy. Swallowing her disappointment, she smiled at him. "I heartily recommend you buy the book."

His gaze never left her face, bringing a blush to her cheeks. "It wouldn't happen to be the book you came here to buy, would it?"

"It was," she replied honestly. "But I already have some of Byron's work at home. I'd hate to deny you the pleasure of discovering his poetry."

He offered the book to her. "I couldn't enjoy it knowing I took it from you."

How sincere he sounded! Anna's blush deepened. "Please. I insist." She couldn't explain it, not even to herself, but it was suddenly very important to her that he take that book.

He held the book to his chest with one large hand. "I've always been told it's rude to argue with a lady, so I won't. Thank you for your sacrifice, Miss Welsley."

Anna smiled. Was it warm in the bookshop or was it just her? "I'd hardly call it a sacrifice, Mr. MacLaughlin, but you're welcome. I hope you enjoy it."

"I shall think of you whenever I read it."

He made his declaration so forcefully that Anna could only stare at him in surprise. Surely her mouth was hanging open like a door on one hinge! No one had ever told her they'd think of her when reading poetry—and Byron no less!

Ewan flushed a dark red. "I-I mean I shall never forget your kindness."

Strangely, Anna's heart sank a little. What else could she expect? She was hardly the type of girl who inspired poetry. Maybe if she was blonde and blue-eyed—the quintessential English Rose—and the daughter of an earl, she'd have more young men gifting her with verses on the beauty of her face, but she had dark hair and dark eyes and no one but Byron seemed to appreciate that kind of coloring. And Byron was in another country— too far away to do her any good.

Anna's mother chose that exact moment to enter the shop. Anna could hear the sharpness of her voice from all the way at the back.

"I have to leave," she responded lamely, scarcely hiding her disappointment. "My mother is looking for me. It was a pleasure to meet you, Mr. MacLaughlin."

He didn't look as though he believed her, but he nodded. "The pleasure was mine." Even though they were strictly courtesy, his soft words sent a tingle down Anna's spine.

"And thank you again for allowing me the book."

She smiled, delaying leaving even though she could hear her mother's heavy footsteps coming closer. "Enjoy it."

"Anna," her mother's voice boomed from behind the next stack of books.

Anna started toward it, not wanting her mother to see this perfect young man. She wanted to keep him just for herself. Casting one last glance his way, she committed his image to memory so she would never forget the five incredible minutes she spent in his company.

"Good-bye, Mr. MacLaughlin."

He tipped his hat at her. "London's not that large, Miss Welsley, so I won't say good-bye just yet."

With her heart tripping in her chest and her feet practically tripping over each other, Anna rounded the corner, narrowly escaping a collision with her mother.

"Where were you?" Marion demanded. "Didn't you hear me calling?"

"I was reading a book on advice for brides, Mama, and didn't hear you at first." She linked her arm through her mother's much larger one and steered her back toward the front of the store. "I hope I haven't kept you waiting long."

Whatever her mother said in reply Anna didn't hear. She was too busy thinking about Ewan MacLaughlin and wondering if indeed London was so small that she might actually see him again.

CHAPTER TWO

All that's best of dark and bright meet in her aspect and her eyes. . . .

He'd never dreamed such a girl existed.

Standing in the window of the bookshop, Ewan watched as Miss Welsley and her mother stepped out into the street where an open carriage sat waiting among the fading puddles of rain on the cobblestones. The warm afternoon sun would have them gone in time for it to rain again.

Mrs. Welsley lumbered into the vehicle like a bear climbing a hill. Her gracelessness made her daughter's movements as she stepped up behind her seem all the more effortless. Delicately taking the hand the footman offered her, she lifted the skirts of her dark blue gown so she wouldn't trip and stepped up into the carriage. He caught a glimpse of a shapely ankle in a pale stocking as she did so.

Miss Welsley turned as the carriage jerked into motion. It was as though she had known—or perhaps *hoped*—that he would be standing there watching. She smiled in his direction, and even from that distance he could see the sparkle in her dark eyes. Ewan pressed his fingers to the window, wishing the cool glass was her warm cheek instead.

And then she was lost in traffic, and lost to him.

Ewan glanced down at the book in his hand. It was a frivolous expense, but according to his father's solicitor, he could well afford it. And what better way to spend his father's money than on something the old man would have no doubt turned up his aristocratic nose at? Ethan Fitzgerald hadn't been capable of appreciating beauty. If he had been, he never would have left Scotland.

He wouldn't have left Ewan's mother.

But Ewan didn't want to think about all the things his father had done to his mother, mostly because he didn't know just what his father had done. He'd been too young to remember it. He didn't remember his father living with them and he didn't remember much of his mother, except that she seemed to cry a lot. He remembered her rocking him and weeping as she sang him to sleep. He couldn't remember ever hearing her laugh, and for that he blamed his father.

His grandmother never said anything bad about his father, but he'd overheard her talking with other women when he was younger. She made it pretty clear that Maureen MacLaughlin had wasted away pining for her English husband.

And now here he was watching after an English girl. He should be disgusted with himself. His first full day in London and already his father's blood was showing. He'd be better off forgetting Miss Welsley and taking care of the business he came to attend to. The sooner he settled his father's estate, the sooner he could return to Scotland.

In the meantime, he would see as much of the city as he could.

He approached the counter and smiled at the man behind it. "I'll take this."

The older man took it from him. "Ah, the Byron. I'm surprised Miss Welsley allowed you to take it." He spoke with such fondness that Ewan was surprised. Obviously Miss Welsley was a regular customer. Perhaps if Ewan frequented the shop enough he would see her again.

"Actually, she insisted that I take it," Ewan replied, not wanting the man to think he'd forced Miss Welsley to allow him to have the book.

Wrapping the book in paper, the proprietor raised a brow. "Did she? Well, you must be a special man indeed for Miss Welsley to give up a new volume of Byron, Mr. . . . ?"

Ewan blushed to the roots of his hair. "MacLaughlin," he muttered, not bothering to use his title. He'd rarely used it in Scotland and it seemed pretentious of him to use it now.

The old man tied a neat bow in the string around the package and extended his hand. "Arthur Hornsby."

Ewan accepted the handshake with a grin. "Pleased to meet you." Releasing the other man's hand, he fished in his purse for a few coins and paid for his purchase.

Mr. Hornsby handed the wrapped book to Ewan. "Please come back again, Mr. MacLaughlin."

"I will. Thank you." Tucking the book under his arm, Ewan turned toward the door. It might be best if he didn't come back. It wouldn't do him any good to see Miss Welsley again.

He hailed a hackney coach without any difficulty and gave the driver directions to his father's house. There was no sense in putting it off any longer. The sooner it was done with, the sooner he could take his father's fortune—most of which had been stolen from Ewan's mother—and return to Scotland. He'd seen enough of the world outside of Loch Glenshea to last him a lifetime. He'd make the necessary repairs to the castle and his lands and spend the rest of his life as a wealthy landowner and lord. It was a life he was much better suited to than that of an English gentleman.

Perhaps one day he'd even take a wife.

Maybe a girl who likes poetry would appreciate the beauty of the Highlands, a voice in his head teased.

He sighed. So much for putting thoughts of a certain doe-eyed English girl out of his mind.

It was useless to even think of it. There was nothing saying Miss Welsley even had the slightest romantic interest in him, and nothing saying his infatuation would continue upon closer acquaintance. He'd probably never see her again. In fact, he would strive not to.

As the coach drove through the neighborhood known

as Mayfair, Ewan wondered how his father had ever entertained the idea of living in Scotland. Certainly, Scotland was not without its castles and grand estates, but Mayfair was the bosom of the English aristocracy, and each house seemed grander than the last. Great, sprawling walls of stone with Grecian columns and more windows than a person could count on both hands and feet drifted past. They taxed windows in England. Most of those taxes surely came from Mayfair.

Finally, the coach rolled to a stop and Ewan stepped out. He cast a brief glance at the house before turning to the driver. "Are you sure this is the right place?"

The driver nodded. "'Tis the address you guv me, m'lord."

Swallowing hard, Ewan nodded. "Thank you." He tossed the man a few coins in payment and started up the walk, the book of poetry still tucked under his arm.

How his legs managed to carry him to the door he'd never know. His limbs were shaking so badly he was surprised he could even stand, let alone move. This had to be a mistake. This house—this unbelievable house—could not be his!

The iron gate swung open at his slightest touch, giving him an unobstructed view of Brahm House.

It was huge, rising several stories above the ground in the Neoclassical style; a sprawling Grecian temple demanding awe from each and every person who gazed upon it.

Built with large blocks of golden-hued stone, it easily stood three floors high. High columns ran along the front between each window and flanked the large oak doors.

The gravel drive cut through a lawn of rich, verdant grass, so thick it looked like velvet. Not a weed or shrubbery to be seen anywhere except for the immaculately trimmed topiaries hedging the front of the house.

He was three-quarters of the way to the house when he heard the pounding of hooves coming up fast behind him. He whirled around to see a horse and rider bearing down upon him.

"Out of the way!" the rider shouted with the humor of a man used to having others do his bidding.

Ewan didn't have to be told twice. He dove to the side just as the horse thundered past. He landed on the grass with enough force to knock the air from his lungs.

Blasted fool! The idiot could have killed him!

Drawing breath, he rolled to his feet, dusted off his hat, and shoved it back on his head. He hoped the landlady at his lodgings knew how to remove grass stains, because he had a long, dark green smear down the right side of his brand-new greatcoat. His grandmother would have given the reckless rider a good tongue-lashing.

Obviously the fellow either worked at the house or was a guest there. As the new Duke of Brahm, Ewan would tell the hooligan exactly what he thought of nearly being run down in his own drive. He held an immense dislike for people who had no respect for others. He was raised to show courtesy.

His mood and expression grim, Ewan continued on to the house with a quickened pace. He banged the knocker on the door and waited with a barely simmering temper to be allowed inside.

The door opened, revealing a butler dressed in austere black. The man was a study in colorlessness. White hair, white complexion, pale eyes, and stark black clothing. He put Ewan in mind of a chessboard.

"Yes?" he intoned. His voice was as colorless as the rest of him.

"I'm here to see the duchess," Ewan replied as politely as a man who had almost been run over could manage.

The butler's cold gaze swept the length of him, taking in the grass stain on his trousers and coat. He obviously did not like what he saw.

"The duchess is not at home today. Good day."

The door had almost slammed in his face before Ewan realized he'd been dismissed. Thrusting out his hand, he managed to stop the door before it shut. The butler shot him a baleful glare.

"Kindly remove your hand, sir. If you have something to sell, take it around to the servants' entrance."

Ewan scowled. He might look a little dusty, thanks to the lunatic on the horse, and his clothes might not be the height of fashion, but he certainly didn't look like a common peddler!

"I'm not selling anything," he gritted out between clenched teeth.

"Then, unless you have a card to leave for my lady, I suggest you return at a later time." The older man shoved on the door.

Ewan's good humor quickly exhausted itself. What was wrong with this godforsaken country? Even the servants thought they were better than everyone else!

"*I*," Ewan growled, "am the Duke of Brahm and this is *my* house and unless you want to find yourself looking for new employment in the morning, you will let me inside *now*."

Well, *that* certainly got the man's attention. The door flew open and the butler stared at him with a mixture of horror and fear. "You're whom?"

Ripping his hat off his head and stepping inside, Ewan glared at the smaller man. "I'm Ewan MacLaughlin of Glenshea—the oldest son and heir of Ethan Fitzgerald. *Who* are you?"

"F-forgive me, my lord." He bowed. "I am Peters."

The butler was staring at him differently now. His light eyes glittered with what looked like tears. If the old goat started bawling, Ewan was going to hit him—right after he got over feeling guilty for causing the man to cry.

"My God, you look just like him," Peters whispered.

Ewan didn't need to be told who *him* was. "I do not,"

he retorted irrationally, his tone sharp. "Why don't you show me to where I might wait for the duchess?" Good lord, he had only just stepped foot inside the house and already he was acting like lord of the manor! Normally he would be heartily ashamed of using his social status to intimidate another person, but he was still too mad to care about snooty Peters and his feelings.

"This way, my lord." Peters crossed the hall with a brisk pace. "Might I say it's an honor to finally meet you, Your Grace."

"Mm," Ewan grunted, not trusting himself to speak.

The entrance hall of the house was just as impressive as the outside, with its smooth marble floor and lifelike statues of Greek gods and goddesses. Ewan was grateful Peters was in front of him and couldn't see his head turning from side to side as he gazed in wonder at the beautiful sculptures and paintings surrounding him.

And it was all his? It seemed too incredible to be true.

Peters led him into a small parlor decorated in pink and white. It was very feminine, very doll-like in its decor. It was obviously a room used exclusively by a woman.

Seated on a dainty sofa was a tiny woman with chestnut hair just beginning to gray. She wore a black gown, and a black handkerchief was crumpled in the fist of her free hand.

"Your Grace," the butler intoned softly, as though dreading disturbing her when she was so obviously distraught. "There is someone here to see you."

Ewan waited for the woman to lift her head. She didn't. It was as though she hadn't heard.

Peters flushed at her lack of response. "Your Grace?" He spoke loudly this time.

This time she heard him. Surprise registered on her features as she turned her gaze toward them.

"Yes, Peters?" Her tone was hopeful. Had she been expecting him? Ewan wondered. Or would any interruption of her sorrow do?

The butler moved to allow her a full view of Ewan. "The duke is here, Your Grace."

Perhaps Peters could have chosen a better way of introduction. The mere mention of "duke" lit the woman's face with pleasure—until that second when she realized the duke he referred to couldn't possibly be her husband. The disappointment and pain that shadowed her delicate features as she turned to gaze toward him tugged painfully at Ewan's heart.

She looked at Ewan as though seeing a ghost.

"Oh my dear Lord," she whispered, pressing the hand-kerchief against her bosom. "You're Ethan's son."

It was hard not to feel for this woman, who was so obviously distraught by his appearance. "I am, Duchess Brahm," he replied with a deep bow.

She rose to her feet and came toward him with her hands held out. "Oh, you mustn't call me by my title. You must call me Hester." She clutched his free hand. "After all, I should have been your stepmother."

Her use of "should have been" told Ewan that she knew something of his father's behavior toward him and his mother and that she hadn't necessarily approved—a fact that instantly made him warm toward her.

"I apologize if my arrival here has caused you any grief," Ewan told her as she led him to the tiny sofa. It looked as though it would break under his weight.

"Nonsense," Hester replied as she sat. "Needless to say we were very surprised. I'm afraid I knew nothing about you until just before Ethan died." She dabbed at her eyes.

Ewan was confused. "But just a moment ago—I mean, I thought you knew."

Shaking her head, Hester smiled sympathetically. "No. Ethan—your father—confessed everything to me on his deathbed. I was . . . greatly upset to discover that you had been kept from us all these years."

Kept from them? She made it sound as though Ewan hadn't been allowed to visit rather than just plain hadn't been wanted.

"Us?" Surely she didn't expect him to believe his father had actually wanted him?

"Yes. Myself and your half brother and half sister."

Brother and sister! Ewan could scarcely believe his ears! All his life he had wanted a brother or a sister, someone to share his mixed Scottish-English heritage and who understood him.

But his brother and his sister weren't like him. They were English.

"Yes. You have a sister, Emily, and a brother named Richard," Hester told him, smiling gently at his obvious surprise.

At that precise moment, the door to the parlor flew open and in ran a young woman of perhaps sixteen or seventeen years of age. She wore a pale lavender gown—a suitable color for half mourning—and her tawny-colored hair trailed down her back in a mass of heavy waves and pink ribbon.

"Is it really him?" she cried and froze when her gaze landed on Ewan.

It was like a blow to the chest when their eyes met. Except for the fact that her eyes were a startling shade of blue, there was no denying that this girl was his sister, for she looked as much like Ewan himself as a girl could and still be lovely.

He rose to his feet just in time to catch her as she flung herself into his arms with a joyful "Oh!" He had not expected this kind of reception. He had not expected their kindness.

Not quite certain what to do, he returned Emily's exuberant embrace with a rather awkward one of his own, and then stepped back so he could look at her.

"I'm so glad you are here," she gushed. "When Father

told us about you, I couldn't believe I had another brother, and a Scottish one at that! I do so love your poet Mr. Burns!"

A soft chuckle escaped Ewan. "We're rather fond of Robbie ourselves, thank you."

Emily's expression changed to one of sorrow, bringing out the dark circles under her bright eyes. It was a reminder to Ewan that although his sister seemed all smiles and laughter, she was still mourning her father. It had been only a few months since Ethan Fitzgerald died, but it had been a lengthy illness that had claimed him, softening the blow of his loss only a little.

"Well, well," came a voice from the far side of the room. "Unless I'm mistaken, I'd say my elder brother has finally arrived."

The voice was soft and cultured, rigidly polite, but something about it sent a shiver down Ewan's spine. He turned toward the door where a young man, a little younger and smaller than himself, stood staring at him with a resentful gaze.

Richard Fitzgerald had his father's blue eyes, but that was it. In all other respects he looked almost exactly like his mother—reddish brown hair and handsome features. Ewan wondered if that was the reason his brother's eyes narrowed when they took in his own appearance. As much as he despised his father, his mother had always told him he was the very image of him.

Emily skipped toward Richard, oblivious to the tension between the two young men.

"Oh, Richard! Isn't it wonderful?" she cried, snatching up his hand and pulling him toward Ewan. "And doesn't he look just like Papa?"

Hostility radiated off Richard and Ewan couldn't blame him. The boy had obviously spent his entire life thinking he was going to be the duke, only to have it taken away from him by a brother he never even knew existed.

As he came closer, Ewan realized that Richard had been the lunatic on horseback who had sent him diving into the grass. Any sympathy he felt for his brother died a quick death.

Obviously, Richard came to the same realization as soon as Ewan had. "I say," he said, the slightest edge of a taunt to his voice. "You're the fellow I almost ran down on the lane, aren't you?"

"What?" Hester cried, rising to her feet. "Richard, whatever were you thinking?"

Richard smiled at his mother, but it didn't quite reach his eyes, Ewan noticed. "I wasn't expecting anyone to be *walking* up our drive, Mama. Besides"—his gaze drifted back to Ewan—"no harm done, eh, old man?"

Ewan's lips stretched tightly. "None."

"Not like you can't afford a new coat now that you're the duke," Richard continued, his eyes as hard as stone while his voice remained light and jovial. "Still, I apologize for my shabby behavior." He extended his hand.

Ewan took it. "And I apologize for being born first," he replied, his tone equally as bright as his brother's had been, but he applied just the slightest pressure to his brother's hand, letting him know he wasn't fooled by the false politeness.

For one instant, Richard's mask slipped and Ewan saw just how hurt and angry he was. Oh yes, his father had a lot to answer for. Perhaps he and his brother would find some kind of truce over their mutual anger where their father was concerned.

"I took the liberty of having a room prepared for you," Hester remarked as Ewan released his brother's hand. "All you need to do is send for your belongings."

"I wouldn't want to intrude. . . ." Ewan's voice trailed off as both Hester and Emily insisted he stay. It was his house, after all.

He had to admit, he would like the chance to get to know them better, and there was a certain satisfaction in sleeping under that roof, knowing his father was probably rolling over in his grave at the mere thought of it.

"You *must*," Hester insisted. "I simply refuse to take no for an answer. It's your house and you must treat it as such, beginning with joining us for dinner tonight. Richard's betrothed and her parents will be joining us."

Richard looked decidedly uncomfortable. "I'm sure my brother has better things to do this evening, Mama."

"On the contrary," Ewan informed him with a broad grin, ignoring the niggling of guilt in his stomach. "I'd be delighted."

"Haven't you heard a word I've said?"

"Hm?" Turning from the carriage window, Anna met her mother's angry gaze. "I'm sorry, Mama. I thought you were talking to Papa."

That was a lie. Anna's father was snoring softly on the seat beside her mother. The man had only to look inside a carriage and he was sound asleep.

Her mother made a *tsk*ing sound. "You know what your father is like. You should have known I was speaking to you instead of woolgathering. La, I have no idea what you find to daydream about all the time."

Anna smiled humorlessly. Any other mother whose daughter was engaged would assume her daughter was thinking about her upcoming wedding, but not Marion Welsley. She always suspected Anna of having her head in the clouds.

Which was true for the most part. Thinking about her marriage always made her nervous, especially since Richard had moved the date from next April to the coming October. He wanted to have it even sooner, but Anna's mother had insisted on having enough time to prepare.

Surely his desire to marry her so quickly meant something, didn't it?

"I daydream about many things, Mama. Didn't you when you were a girl?"

"Bah!" her mother scoffed, her cheeks jiggling as the carriage hit a rut. "I never bothered with such frivolities."

That was because her mother had no imagination. "That's too bad."

Her mother snorted. "Too bad? Too bad? Gel, you spend too much time with your head in the clouds and not enough time thinking about the world around you. You should be happy with what you've got, not clouding your mind with flights of fancy."

"I enjoy flights of fancy," she replied peevishly. Oh, why was she even bothering to argue? Her mother would never see her point.

"You'll enjoy being the Duchess of Brahm even more," Marion retorted, jabbing the air with a pudgy finger.

Anna rolled her eyes. "Mama, you know very well that now that Richard has discovered he has an older brother he won't inherit the title."

"Fustian. You're too young to know about such things, but I know that half these 'over the anvil' marriages performed in Scotland are illegitimate. Richard assures me that this boy is no more the heir to his father's title than I am. All he has to do is prove it."

Anna doubted the late duke's marriage to his Scottish wife was such a sham. Hester and Emily certainly believed it was legitimate, as had the duke himself. She understood

Richard's disappointment, but really she didn't see that there was any way he could claim the title instead of his brother. And Richard, ever the gentleman, would never dare do anything to risk his own reputation, such as trying to prove his brother illegitimate. Would he?

She glanced out the window at the sinking sun as they rolled toward Mayfair. "Well, obviously the duke believed he was legitimate or he never would have named him as his heir."

Her mother waved a bejeweled hand in dismissal. "Then why had he kept the boy a secret all these years?" She tapped the floor of the carriage with her cane. "No, I believe Brahm named the boy as his heir out of spite. Didn't Richard say that he and his father had quarreled before he died? No doubt the old man was spiteful enough to want to cut his own son out of his rightful inheritance."

It seemed to Anna that the duke had been trying to ensure that his firstborn son didn't get cut out of his rightful inheritance and that's why he made news of the young man's existence known. Of course, her mother was terribly loyal to the boy she had chosen to be her son-in-law and nothing could be said to sway her.

"I don't know what's so important about a title anyway," she muttered.

A bubble of laughter welled up in her chest at her mother's expression of shock and outrage.

"What's so important about a title? I'll tell you what's

so important about a title—a title makes the difference between being a lady and being a tradesman's daughter. It's what will make you and your family acceptable. *That's* what's important."

Anna raised a brow but said nothing. What was important was her mother gaining a place in London society. Her mother might treat her like a child, but at eighteen Anna was old enough to know certain things, and one thing she knew for certain was that her mother was more obsessed with wealth and position than anyone had a right to be. She was also using her daughter to gain the social prestige she had never been able to achieve on her own. Despite what connections their family might claim, very few of those connections even bothered to speak to them.

Turning her gaze to the window once more, Anna watched the scenery pass by. Soon they would be coming up on Hyde Park where there might still be the odd person walking or riding, even though the fashionable hour of five o'clock had long since come and gone.

Had Mr. MacLaughlin gone for a ride in Hyde Park that afternoon? Or had he gone home and read Byron's poetry? Before her mother had interrupted her, she'd been daydreaming that was exactly what he had done. She pictured him so clearly with his shirtsleeves rolled up over tanned, muscular forearms. He'd read Byron's words of passion and his thoughts would turn to her as he'd promised they would.

But now she imagined him in Hyde Park instead. She imagined herself standing on the grass talking with a friend and spying him riding toward her, astride a giant gray stallion that he managed to control with little effort. Somehow he'd lost his hat and his sun-streaked hair was mussed by the breeze. His charcoal-gray coat hugged his broad shoulders and his biscuit-colored trousers clung to his strong, muscular legs. . . .

"Will you pay attention!"

Anna yelped and jumped. Her father bolted upright with a snort and series of incoherent syllables. And Marion Welsley stared at her daughter with eyes that glittered like little black gems and a face that was magenta with rage.

"You have not heard a word I've said," she seethed.

Anna didn't know whether to laugh or to jump from the carriage and run for her life.

She made a mistake.

She laughed.

If at all possible, her mother's face grew even redder, and in the dim light of the carriage, almost seemed to glow with anger. Anna had never seen her mother so upset.

"I can't believe you're laughing when all of our plans could very well be—"

"Oh, look," Anna's father said as the carriage rolled to a stop. "We're here."

Sighing in relief, Anna wrapped her light shawl around her shoulders. The carriage door opened and her father stepped out first, then turned to offer his hand to her mother.

"You're going to have to learn how to act pretty quickly there, missy," her mother hissed when Mr. Welsley left the carriage. "Your husband will demand much more than just a listening ear from you and you had better attend his wishes. There'll be no crawling back to us when you realize that you can't always have things your own way."

Anna stared at her, her expression blank despite the anxiety swirling in her stomach and her heart pounding against her ribs. "I've never crawled to you for anything, Mama. I don't expect to start anytime soon."

Marion Welsley's eyes narrowed as she shook her ringleted head. "Where did I go wrong? Haven't I always tried to do what's best for you? I buy you the best clothes, sent you to the best schools."

"What have you done other than dictate what I wear, who I'm friends with, and who I marry?" Anna demanded, her own temper rising. "So far, you have done *nothing* for me and everything for yourself!"

Her mother gasped in outrage, and for a moment Anna feared her mother might actually strike her. Cringing, she waited for the blow. It didn't come. Opening her eyes, she found her mother staring at her as if she were a stranger.

"Are you two coming?" Mr. Welsley asked as he stuck his head inside the door. "I'm famished."

Marion rolled her eyes. "Simpleton," she muttered and lumbered out of the carriage, ignoring the hand her husband offered.

As Anna moved to follow, her father seized her hand and gave it a gentle squeeze. "Don't worry, blackbird," he whispered, using his old nickname for her as he helped her to the ground. "Your mother just wants you to have what I could never give her."

Unexpected tears pricked the backs of Anna's eyes as she gazed up at her father. He knew more than she realized. She could see the hurt in his eyes, but there was love there as well.

"Thank you, Papa."

"I thought you were hungry," Marion's voice boomed and Anna winced. All those years of having people drill manners and social behavior into her daughter's head and Marion had never absorbed any of it herself.

They were greeted at the door by Peters, who seemed highly agitated. Usually the man was as controlled and emotionless as cold molasses, but not so tonight. He had a feverish brightness to his eyes and a nervousness to his movements.

There was an aura of excitement and energy inside Brahm House that was alien to Anna. When the old duke had been alive, the house always seemed happy and comfortable—less so, of course, as his illness worsened, but this was different. This felt like the entire house was on its toes, waiting and watching for something to happen.

Peters led them to the blue drawing room—the room the family always met in before dinner. Anna noticed there was an extra guest with them tonight.

A tall man stood against the mantel, talking in earnest with Emily, Richard's younger sister. The expression on his face was so near that on Emily's that Anna marveled at the resemblance. No wonder the whole house was abuzz—this was the mysterious heir! There was something familiar about him.

"Mr. and Mrs. Welsley. Miss Welsley."

The stranger started at the sound of her name, and the anxiety Anna had felt earlier blossomed into full-fledged panic when the stranger turned his head and met her gaze.

"You," she whispered as all eyes turned toward her.

Her fiancé's brother was also her Mr. MacLaughlin.

CHAPTER THREE

Ewan was amazed he could even find his voice. The one girl who managed to turn his head was his brother's fianceé. How bitterly ironic. "Good evening, Miss Welsley."

Richard, who had risen as soon as Anna and her family were announced, cast a suspicious glance in Ewan's direction. "You two have met?" He turned to Anna for verification.

Anna nodded. "We have. This afternoon, in fact. In the bookshop." She looked every bit as alarmed to see Ewan as he was to see her. "Forgive my loss of manners, Mr. MacLaughlin—I mean, Your Grace. I had no idea of who you were."

"Why would you?" Richard interjected brightly, looking closely at Anna. "It's not as though any of us have met him before."

Ewan's expression didn't change. Was it just his imagination or did his brother take every opportunity to slight him? He couldn't blame Richard for resenting him, but it wasn't as though Ewan had asked to be his father's heir. He'd be happy to still be a secret if it wasn't for the fact that the money would set his home and his people back on their feet.

"And why is it that the two of you have never met before, Mr. MacLaughlin?" Mrs. Welsley asked. Her tone was deceptively innocent, but Ewan didn't miss the sly glance she cast his brother. What the devil was going on?

Anna's gaze dropped to the floor. Her cheeks flushed a dark red. She was obviously embarrassed by her mother's behavior, and Ewan's resentment of the woman grew. He knew what she was getting at. She was questioning the validity of his parents' marriage, and therefore questioning the legitimacy of his birth! It was perhaps the biggest insult she could bestow upon him—upon anyone.

Angered beyond belief, Ewan held the woman's haughty gaze, clenching his jaw against the desire to put her soundly in her place. He sucked a deep breath between his grinding teeth.

"Because in accordance with MacLaughlin tradition, ma'am, the title passed through my mother to me. In such cases, the heir takes MacLaughlin as his surname to keep the name alive." He smiled coldly as her confident expression faded.

"And, incidentally, I'm not a 'mister.' Even without my father's title I am the Earl of Keir. You may address me by either title. I have several lesser ones as well, Viscount Dunkirk, Baron Kyne. You may take your pick." He'd tried to keep his tone light, but he couldn't keep a note of condescension from creeping in. How dare this woman question his birth or his rank! And how dare she insult the memory of his mother by doing so.

Marion Welsley's face paled. She dipped a small curtsy in his direction. "I beg your pardon, my lord."

Ewan nodded in acknowledgment of her apology. He believed her to be sincere. Of course she would be sorry to insult a peer of the realm. He'd found that many people in England went out of their way to please someone with a title. Part of him liked all the bowing and scraping from the English, ordinarily so disdainful of the Scots. Another part of him found it embarrassing.

He turned his attention to Anna, who still looked decidedly uncomfortable.

"Thank you so much for your suggestion, Miss Welsley. I'm quite enjoying the book—even though I haven't had the opportunity to read much of it in the last few hours."

Her head came up and her dark eyes seemed unnaturally large in her face. She wasn't as pale as most English girls, being a true brunette, and a delicate blush turned her complexion a marvelous mixture of honey and roses.

And all that's best of dark and bright meet in her aspect and her eyes. . . .

"I'm glad you're enjoying it, Your Grace." Her voice was soft—husky for a girl's—and just how he remembered it. Just the sound of it sent a shiver down his spine. He would like to hear her read some of Byron's poetry aloud.

"I am," he replied, staring deep into her eyes. "Every poem makes me think of beauty."

Her blush deepened, and Ewan knew she remembered him telling her that he would think of her whenever he read the book.

"What book is this?" Richard demanded, not quite succeeding in keeping his tone light. His intense gaze fell upon Anna. A stab of guilt mixed with regret hit Ewan in the stomach. He had no business flirting with Anna as he had been. She was his brother's betrothed. He had no business even thinking about her as he did, but he couldn't help what he thought, just as he couldn't act upon it. She was out of his reach, and he'd do well to remember that.

"Miss Welsley recommended I try your poet Byron, brother." Calling the younger man by such a familiar term felt odd, especially since he believed Richard despised him thoroughly. "I must admit to being completely enthralled by his poetry."

Mrs. Welsley gasped and Richard's jaw tightened. They both stared at Anna as though she'd committed a heinous crime. Instantly, Ewan regretted having said a word.

"Anna!" her mother chastised. "Tell me *you* haven't been reading such filth!"

So not only did Anna's mother question his birth, but now she questioned his morals through his reading material. Filth? To be sure, Byron could be a little naughty in his work. He was also incredibly passionate, and Ewan would hardly call such genius filth.

"Calm yourself, Mrs. Welsley," Richard advised, taking Anna's hand. "'Tis no serious offense. Although Byron is hardly proper fare for an unmarried girl, Anna will be able to read whatever she wants—provided it's not too shocking—once we're married."

The reminder that his brother—his unlikable, undeserving brother—was going to marry this beautiful girl made Ewan's blood boil. No doubt Richard believed he was doing Anna and her family a great service by bestowing his magnificence upon them.

"And who will decide what is too shocking and what isn't?" Ewan asked with false humor. The gall! As if Anna hadn't enough intelligence to choose her own books! The very idea of it was foolish. Unfortunately, there were many people—women included—who believed that certain novels and poetry could damage a young girl's delicate mind.

Richard smiled, but his eyes were filled with malice. Could no one else see it? Or was Ewan's guilty conscience simply running away with him?

"I will, of course," he replied. "I think a husband might safely choose his wife's reading material."

"Quite right," Mrs. Welsley agreed with a pleased smile.

Hester, who had remained silent throughout the entire conversation, fixed her son with an expression of disappointment. "Your father never dictated what I could and could not read, Richard."

The young man had the grace to look duly chastised, and Anna, who had seemed to retreat into her own little world out of shame and humiliation, appeared strengthened by her future mother-in-law's words.

With a defiant lift of her chin, Anna pulled her hand free of Richard's. "Thank you, Your Grace. I believe I will expect the same courtesy and trust from my husband." Her voice quivered as she spoke, as though speaking her mind in front of Richard was not something she usually did. She didn't even look at her fiancé.

Ewan wanted to applaud her show of backbone, but wisely kept his mouth shut as Richard scowled at her announcement. Mrs. Welsley, her face ruddy, opened her mouth to respond.

"Let's go in to dinner, shall we?" the dowager duchess spoke, cutting off anything the other woman might have said.

Hester came up to Ewan, her eyes sparkling with emotion. She didn't approve of Mrs. Welsley's actions— or Richard's for that matter—he could tell, but there was sadness in her gaze as well. She missed her husband very much, and Ewan was instantly contrite for contributing to the scene with Richard, Anna, and her mother. Mr. Welsley had seemed blissfully unaware of the tension. Of course, the older man had seemed to doze through most of it.

"Will you escort me, Ewan?"

He smiled. "I would be honored." It wasn't as though she had singled him out—the man of highest rank always escorted the woman of highest rank in to dinner, but Ewan felt as though she had chosen him. A little voice inside him told him he reminded her of his father, and although the comparison chafed, he realized she meant it as a compliment.

What wasn't so easy to accept was being expected to take his father's place at the table. Richard didn't look very happy about it either. No doubt he was used to having the head of the table as his seat since their father's death. He could keep it for all Ewan cared.

"Richard," he said softly, standing beside the high-backed oak chair. "I believe this is usually your seat. I would be happy to sit elsewhere if you wish."

Surprise lit his brother's features, followed by a bitter twist of his mouth. "Thank you, Ewan," he replied, his tone one of gentlemanly blandness. "But as head of the family it is your seat *for now*."

The slight emphasis on *for now* set off an alarm inside Ewan's head. Richard saw Ewan as an intruder, as a fraud, and he was going to try to prove it. The idea formed with such clarity in Ewan's mind that he was stunned by it. That's why Anna was so embarrassed for him, why her mother had been so catty. They all thought he was a bastard and were just waiting for Richard to uncover the truth!

Seating himself, Ewan tried to school his features into a cool mask as his gaze traveled over those seated before him. He couldn't believe Hester or Emily capable of any kind of deception, nor could he bring himself to believe it of Anna. He could, however, well believe it of his brother and Anna's mother, while her father he wasn't so certain of. Richard had spent his entire life expecting to be duke. It was understandable that he wouldn't give it up without a fight. As for Anna's mother, well, she was a greedy woman, that was obvious. She no doubt preferred her daughter to be a duchess rather than the wife of a second son.

It was so ridiculous, though! Perhaps *he* had been reading one too many novels or tales of fancy. He was losing his grip on reality. Richard and Mrs. Welsley couldn't possibly be plotting against him. Could they? Did Richard care that much about some foolish title that he would ruin Ewan's reputation—and his life—just to claim it?

Yes. Everything in the way Richard behaved indicated that he was a young man accustomed to being a duke's son and had fully expected to inherit the title. Their father should have told him the truth a long time ago. It wasn't right.

Richard spoke quietly to Anna, favoring her with a charming smile, no doubt in the hopes of winning her favor again.

He wondered if Anna even loved his brother. Watching her now, the color still high in her smooth cheeks, he believed she was still upset with Richard for announcing he would censor her reading material. Ewan couldn't blame her for being angry. His brother was a complete idiot if he wanted to change a single thing about Anna.

"So," he began when it became apparent that no one else was going to start conversation. "When's the wedding?"

It was the last question he wanted an answer to, but it kept his mind focused. He shouldn't be meditating on the allures of his brother's intended. He shouldn't begrudge his brother some happiness. He shouldn't be jealous over a girl he didn't even know.

Anna ladled soup from a silver tureen into her bowl and didn't meet his gaze. "October." She smiled softly at Hester. "On the duke's birthday." Catching herself, she turned her gaze to Ewan. "The *late* duke, of course."

Ewan smiled. He'd known to whom she referred.

"That's October tenth," Richard informed him, lifting his spoon. "In case you didn't know."

Ewan gritted his teeth at his brother's innocent expression. "Actually, I did know, thank you. I vaguely remember that my mother celebrated it alone after my father left us. She died shortly after." The minute the words left his mouth, he regretted them. He didn't want them to know how much pain his father's leaving had caused his mother, and he certainly didn't want to give them any more fodder against him.

Hester looked positively stricken. Ewan thought Richard and Mrs. Welsley looked decidedly pleased. He hated the two of them at that moment. His mother's suffering was not anything to smile over.

He glanced at Anna. She looked sad. Ewan didn't want her to be sad for him.

"Perhaps Richard's wedding will make the date a happier occasion for you, Ewan," Emily remarked in a hopeful tone.

Because she was so sweet, Ewan forced a smile. "No doubt you are right, Emily." Right now he couldn't imagine feeling even a thimbleful of joy at the occasion. It was like Beauty being married off to the Beast, but all of Richard's ugliness was inside. Of course, there was always the chance that Anna's beauty was merely skin-deep and that she and Richard deserved each other.

Rubbish.

"It must be wonderful to have found the perfect bride at your age," he commented to Richard. "You can't be any more than what, twenty?" He kept his voice bland, but he knew how old his brother was. He was almost exactly four years younger, having been born less than a year after their father married Hester. Not even a year after Ewan's mother was buried.

His brother cast a warm smile in Anna's direction.

"Yes it is," he agreed as she blushed. "Some people never find the right one and are forced to marry someone they cannot abide for money or connections."

Ewan fought the urge to sneer. "I can't imagine what it would be like to meet that woman I'd want to spend the *rest* of my life with. I mean, knowing that you're going to be spending the next forty or fifty years with the same person . . . It's awe inspiring."

Richard smiled, but it didn't reach his eyes. "Yes, it is."

Anna stared at him with an expression Ewan couldn't read. Had he insulted her in his attempt to rankle his brother? That hadn't been his intention at all. Chastised, he offered her what he hoped was an apologetic smile. She smiled back.

"When I marry I want it to be to a young man with whom I can spend the rest of my life," Emily announced. "I refuse to settle for anything less."

Ewan smiled at her youthful conviction, despite the tension at the table. "I've no doubt you'll find someone to love you for the rest of his lucky life, Emily."

Wiping his mouth with a napkin, Richard made a scoffing noise. "Marriages of the *ton* are built on more than such a silly notion as love."

"Oh?" Ewan cocked a brow. Hadn't his brother waxed about the merit of wedding his perfect match not even five minutes ago? "What else are they based on?"

"Yes, Richard," Anna rejoined softly with a lift of her

sharp little chin. "What else?"

"Respectability, connections, common interests, blood, and wealth, of course," Richard replied, sticking his spoon in his soup. "Obviously affection is important in a marriage, but good bloodlines are just as important. You want to know what you're getting into."

The poor sod didn't even know he was digging a hole for himself, Ewan realized. He couldn't figure out if he envied or pitied his brother being brought up to always believe himself right. It must have been their father who'd taught him such arrogance. Hester certainly hadn't.

Ewan sipped his wine. "Sounds more like a business arrangement than a marriage."

Richard's brows drew together. "*My* father taught me that the most successful men treat life like a business arrangement."

"His public life, maybe," Hester injected, "but *your* father never treated his family like a 'business arrangement.'"

Ewan longed to correct her, but remained silent. What had he been if not the result of such an arrangement gone wrong?

Richard ignored her. "He also taught me that a man who is ruled by his emotions is a fool."

"Did he?" Ewan took another drink of wine.

"Yes. He did."

He met Richard's challenging gaze. "Then how

fortunate I consider myself that he taught me nothing."

The air fairly crackled with tension as the two young men stared each other down.

"Roast pheasant, Your Grace?"

Ewan glanced at the platter Anna held directly under his nose. It wasn't subtle, but she'd managed to end the standoff between the brothers.

"Thank you, Miss Welsley." The footman had taken his soup bowl, so Ewan took the platter and helped himself to some of the tender meat.

"And how are you enjoying London?" she asked once he'd passed the platter to Emily.

With an inward sigh, Ewan allowed himself to be led into meaningless, polite conversation. By the time the dinner was over he was heartily sick of the sound of his own voice, but he was entirely grateful to Anna for putting an end to his embarrassing behavior. He should know better than to allow his brother to get to him. There was no excuse for rude or inconsiderate behavior, and Ewan's remarks about his father were certainly inconsiderate in regard to Hester and Emily.

After dinner, the entire party retired to the drawing room. Neither Ewan nor Richard were interested in drinking port and Mr. Welsley didn't seem to care either way, so the gentlemen followed the ladies to the blue drawing room where Emily and Anna entertained them at the pianoforte.

Anna played beautifully and Emily had a lovely singing voice. A dim memory of his father singing to him and bouncing him on his lap drifted into Ewan's mind, seizing his heart with icy tentacles. Why had he never remembered it before?

When the girls had finished, everyone applauded politely.

"Do you play, Ewan?" Hester asked from her seat beside him.

"We have no—what do you call them?—bagpipes, Mama," Richard joked. Mrs. Welsley laughed.

A tight smile curved Ewan's lips. "No matter, brother. I play the piano just as well as the pipes."

"Not a very gentlemanly occupation," Richard replied with false jocularity, folding his arms across his chest.

Hester fixed him with an admonishing gaze. "Your father played."

Richard flushed to the roots of his hair. The red of his cheeks was a sharp contrast to the bright white of his collar where it brushed his jaw.

Feeling sorry for his brother for being chastised so many times in one evening, Ewan attempted to draw the room's attention.

"My mother," he said with a grin, "taught me that a good Scotsman should be able to wield a sword with one hand and make music with the other—preferably at the same time."

The women laughed—even Mrs. Welsley managed a smile. Mr. Welsley was sound asleep on the sofa beside her, and Richard stared at Ewan with an expression that could be described only as snide superiority.

"What a charmingly barbaric notion!" he cried, his voice ringing with mocking laughter.

Shocked stillness descended over the room. Even Mrs. Welsley looked surprised by the outburst. She squirmed uncomfortably on the sofa. Hester paled.

Emily stared at the floor, and Anna stared wide-eyed at her fiancé, but no one looked at Ewan except for Richard. Ewan held his gaze. If Richard sought to intimidate or humiliate him, he'd chosen the wrong way to go about it. His mother was a saint as far as Ewan was concerned, and insulting her didn't hurt him, it just made him very, very angry.

He'd had enough, and the resentment and animosity he'd felt from and toward his brother all night exploded into an inferno of rage. How he managed to keep from strangling Richard, he'd never know.

Rising to his feet, he towered over them all, drawing their hesitant gazes like a carriage accident.

He wanted to rage, wanted to drive his fist into his brother's face, but that would only prove himself a barbarian, not only in Richard's eyes, but possibly Anna's as well, and Ewan was determined to prove himself the better man.

"And one I learned well," he replied, smiling brightly in

Richard's direction. "Would you care for a demonstration?"

Richard arched a haughty brow. "I'm afraid we're a little too civilized to have any swords in the house, but I would be happy to accompany you to a fencing gallery if you desire."

It was as close to a challenge as his brother could issue and still retain his tenuous hold on his gentlemanly façade.

Ewan accepted the dare with a cool smile and a slight incline of his head. "I would enjoy that." And he would. He would enjoy any opportunity to put this spoiled brat in his place. It was very hard to have any sympathy for his brother at all.

He held Richard's stony gaze, forcing the younger man to look away first. Richard crossed the carpet to the liquor cabinet with his back stiff. He poured himself a glass of port.

Ewan turned to Hester, who stared at him with tears in her eyes.

"I'm so sorry," she whispered.

What she was sorry for, Ewan had no idea. He bent and took her hand, squeezing it with silent affection.

"'Tis I who should apologize," he replied, emotion bringing out the Scottish burr in his voice. "Forgive me. I shall take my leave now." He straightened and started for the door without a glance at anyone else. He didn't want to see how they regarded him. He especially didn't want to see Anna's expression.

"You'll be here tomorrow, won't you, Ewan?" Emily

demanded urgently, as though his being there meant something to her. "For the reading of the will?"

Ewan glanced from his sister to his brother, his countenance fading to a scowl. Richard looked entirely too sure of himself, as though he expected tomorrow to prove Ewan a fraud.

"I wouldn't miss it for the world."

"What a rude, awful boy," Mrs. Welsley remarked as the carriage rolled down the lane. Mr. Welsley was already snoring in the corner beside her.

Anna, who was thankful to finally be leaving Brahm House, nodded in weary agreement. "Yes. Richard's behavior was inexcusably rude tonight." Her father snorted in his sleep, as though he agreed with her. Anna smiled.

"Richard!" Her mother's voice hit a pitch just short of glass-shattering. "I meant that dreadful Scot! What could Hester have been thinking inviting that barbarian into her house?"

Anna frowned. Barbarian was not the word to describe Ewan at all. "It's *his* house."

Her mother dismissed her with a wave of her bejeweled hand. "Rubbish. There's no way that creature is the Duke of Brahm."

Pressing her hands to her eyes, Anna fought the headache brewing behind them. "He is the duke. His father acknowledged him, the solicitor was sent for him.

He's in the will, and he looks just like his father. What more proof do you need?"

Her mother's eyes narrowed. "You're too young to know about such things, but just because he's Brahm's son doesn't mean he's the legitimate heir. We discussed this earlier, don't you recall? I wouldn't be surprised if Richard discovers this MacLaughlin character was born on the wrong side of the blanket."

Anna was very tired of all this drama. What difference did it make? Let Ewan have his title. After all, it wasn't as if he'd had the benefit of knowing his father.

"They were married, Mama. I'm sure a copy of Ew . . . the duke's birth certificate will prove he was born after their marriage."

"Ah! But if they were married in Scotland in one of those foolish 'over the anvil' ceremonies, there's a very good chance the marriage wasn't legitimate!" Marion smiled smugly.

Anna hated her mother at that moment. Hated her right down to her bones for trying to ruin this young man's life.

"What difference does it make to you whether or not he's legitimate?" But as soon as she asked the question, she knew the answer. "This isn't about Ewan or Richard. This is about you."

Her mother made a show of studying her rings.

Spurred by anger, Anna leaned forward. In the dim

light of the carriage, her mother's features were almost entirely in shadow.

"You want so badly to have a duke in the family that you don't care about anything else. You don't care if you ruin a young man's life, and you certainly don't care whether or not your son-in-law loves your only daughter. You just want your precious title, and you're afraid I'm engaged to the wrong son!"

Marion's hand came up and swung. Anna caught her by the wrist, bringing a surprised gasp to her mother's lips.

"Strike me and you'll have to find another way to get your duke because I won't be marrying anyone." Anna couldn't believe how she was talking to her mother! It was as though someone else had snuck into her body while she wasn't looking. For that matter, ever since Anna had agreed to marry Richard, her mother had been acting like a different person as well.

Marion jerked her hand free with a glare. "You'll marry whom I tell you to or you'll be thrown out without a cent!" Her threat was softened by the tremble in her voice. She was scared. Scared of what?

Now it was Anna's turn to be smug. "Papa would never allow it and you know it. Don't threaten me, Mama. I don't like it."

"You're an ungrateful child."

"Yes," Anna agreed sarcastically as she leaned back against the velvet squabs. "I'm such an awful daughter for not allowing you to treat me like one of your lapdogs. Actually, I think you treat your dogs with more affection and respect."

Her mother regarded her with a hurt expression. "What is the matter with you? Can you not see that I want what's best for you?"

An unladylike snort broke forth from Anna's lips. "I'm sure you do."

"Of course I do!" her mother snapped. "I'm not entirely without feeling, you know, no matter what you might think."

Anna raised a brow but said nothing. No, she knew there was goodness in her mother, but lately all she'd seen was greed and calculation. She didn't like it.

Sighing, her mother slumped back in her seat, not caring that she now held her sleeping husband's arm pinned between herself and the cushions.

"Do you not understand that I want a better life for you than what I had?"

What? "A better life?" Anna echoed incredulously. "What was wrong with your life? You have money, a good husband—"

"Before your father made his fortune we lived in two rooms above his office. Sometimes I worried that we might lose everything and end up in debtor's prison. I don't want you to ever have to worry about money or position."

Softened, Anna reached across and took her mother's

hand. "Don't you want me to be happy as well?"

Marion snatched back her hand. "I think I'd rather see you miserable and rich than happy and poor. Happiness does not put food in your belly."

"Or rings on my fingers," Anna sneered, feeling her mother's rejection as keenly as a knife in the ribs. "I'm not you, and no matter how hard you try, you cannot fix your past by dictating my future."

With a stubborn lift of her chin, Marion stared out the carriage window. There might have been tears glistening in her eyes, but Anna couldn't be certain—and to be honest, she didn't want to know. "I can certainly try. And I can make certain you don't make the same mistakes I did."

"Yes," Anna agreed, her jaw clenched. "May the good Lord forbid I turn out like you."

Her mother recoiled as if slapped. "Have I been that horrible a mother to you?"

Sighing, Anna massaged her temples. What had started as a minor discomfort had blossomed into throbbing pain.

"No," she replied. Once her mother had been her best friend, but that had been years ago, long before Anna had become a marketable commodity as a bride, and long before her mother had become totally dissatisfied with her own life. Perhaps if her father hadn't been in trade, her mother would have been happier with her life. Perhaps if he'd been a lazy landowner who threw lavish parties and spent his autumns in the country hiding to hounds with other bored rich men, her mother wouldn't have to work so hard for those connections she seemed to hold so dear.

But her father wasn't a landowner. He was wealthy, but he was a city merchant. He might be a little embarrassing socially—especially since he had the unfortunate habit of falling asleep wherever they went—but that was only because he worked such long hours so Anna and her mother could have all the finery her mother claimed they needed.

Maybe the gowns and jewels were just a substitute. Could that be the reason why her mother had become so greedy? Were the rings and silks her idea of motherly affection? If they were, Anna felt sorry for her mother. And for the first time in her life, she felt a little more than annoyed with her father.

Marion folded her arms across her ample bosom, her mouth set mulishly. "I've only tried to act in your best interest."

"But you're not," Anna informed her, a weary edge to her voice. "You're acting in your own best interest. Can't you see that?"

"How is wanting you to have money and security acting in my own best interest?"

"Because you haven't asked me if I want money and security!" Anna cried. "You haven't asked me what I want at all."

Marion stomped her foot, causing the floor to vibrate under Anna's slippers. Her father snorted from the corner. "Are you trying to tell me that you'd rather be poor and a social outcast? You didn't seem averse to all the money and security at Almack's the other night!"

Almack's was *the* place to see and be seen in the upper ranks of London society. One had to be granted a voucher by one of the patronesses to even get in the door. It was every young girl's dream to dance at Almack's.

"Of course I'm not averse to them." Sighing, Anna shook her head. "But there's more to life—more to marriage—than wealth and security. Don't you want me to marry someone I'll love and be happy with?"

"You will be happy with Richard," her mother insisted. "And you'll grow to love him. 'Tis a much better situation than marrying a man for love only to be disillusioned by the notion years later."

"Is that what happened to you?"

Marion averted her gaze. "Let's just say I had fanciful dreams in my youth as well—dreams that couldn't live up to a cruel and harsh reality."

Anna glanced at her father. He was slumped against her mother's left side, snoring softly. Even their arguing couldn't wake him. He was a simple man, but Anna couldn't imagine him ever being harsh or cruel. Of course, maybe if her husband would rather sleep than talk to her Anna would be bitter too. But her parents had loved each other once, hadn't they? What had happened along the way?

"Perhaps Papa had dreams as well," she murmured.

Her mother turned back from the window. "Hm? Oh, yes, he did. Big dreams."

Her tone was so bitter that Anna almost winced. "I'm sorry your life hasn't been what you expected, Mama, but you have to allow me the freedom to live my own life."

Marion smiled at her. "You can live your life however you want to."

Dumbfounded, Anna could only gape at her. "Really?" Was her mother finally ready to allow her to trust her own judgment?

"Really," her mother replied with a nod. "As soon as you're married. To Richard."

CHAPTER FOUR

"Why are you here?"

Startled, Ewan whirled around. So much for sneaking into the reading of his father's will unnoticed. He'd even asked Peters, who was now the very essence of servile humility, not to announce him. He hadn't counted on any of the family wandering about.

At least he wasn't as late as he'd feared he would be. It had taken him forever to decide what to wear—not that he had much to choose from. He hadn't wanted to attend the reading looking like a lumbering Scottish barbarian. And he didn't. Dressed in a dark-blue coat and biscuit-colored breeches, he looked like a lumbering dandy; he was perfectly dressed and perfectly styled. Even Richard wouldn't be able to fault how he looked. He didn't even want to think about why he should care what other people thought of his appearance.

Correction. What *Anna* thought of his appearance—not that she was likely to be there when they read his father's will.

"Good morning, Richard," he murmured, drawing back from the doorway so the rest of the family wouldn't see him. "I'm afraid I don't understand your question."

The younger man's face tightened. "You heard me. Why are you here?"

A humorless smile curved Ewan's lips. "A little bald man came to Scotland and invited me. Said something about me being in the will."

If Richard's face became any stonier they'd be able to stick him on top of the house and use him as a gargoyle.

"Yes, I know. That's why I want to know why you're here. We already expect you to take everything. Have you come to lord it over us? Do you plan to take your revenge on all of us and evict us into the street? Will you punish us all for how you feel my father treated you?"

Ewan stared at his brother in shock. He opened his mouth to speak, but nothing came out. How could Richard even think such a thing? Is it what he would do to Ewan were their roles reversed?

"I would never do that," he replied once he found his voice. "It's our father you're angry at, Richard. I'm angry at him too. We shouldn't take it out on each other."

Richard snorted. "What reason do you have to be angry? You'll get everything—the title, the house, the money. You'll have it all."

Swallowing his pride, Ewan met his brother's wounded gaze with a frank one of his own. "I never had a father, and that would have meant more to me than any title or fortune. At least you had him."

Richard stared at Ewan as though he had sprouted a third eye. "And what good will having him do me now? All my life I've been groomed to be something I was never going to become, and he knew it! He knew you would be the duke and he never told me. Never!"

Such raw hurt and anger was painful to look upon. Ewan didn't know what to say.

"I want to ask a favor of you," Richard said after a moment's silence.

"Anything," Ewan replied and regretted the word as soon as it left his mouth. It was awful of him, but he still didn't quite trust his brother and he couldn't help but think he was being set up.

Richard looked as though he'd just bitten into something very bitter, so distasteful was his expression. "I would ask you to take care of my mother and Emily in the event that I'm not able to. I would hate for them to suffer any more than they already have."

And they'd suffered because of him, Ewan thought grimly. They must all think him some kind of monster to believe he would toss them out into the street, but what did they know of him? He was a stranger to them, and they were intelligent enough to know how he despised his father, so of course they would wonder if he would avenge himself on them.

"I will look after them." And he would. They were welcome to remain at Brahm House for as long as they wanted. It wasn't as though he had any use for the place, and he planned on returning to Glenshea as soon as he could.

Richard gave a sharp nod. "Good."

"But I'm certain you have nothing to worry about. I'm sure you've been well looked after." Ewan didn't know much about his father, but he knew that Hester, Emily, and even Richard had loved the man—he wouldn't leave the family he'd wanted without a penny.

His brother didn't reply, just looked at him with a strange expression Ewan couldn't read. He couldn't shake the feeling that Richard was playing with him, that he was up to something. But before he could read any more into it, Richard turned his back to him.

Ewan's gaze followed his brother as he walked away until he became aware of the oddest sensation of being watched. He was.

His heart flipped over in his chest as his gaze met Anna's, and a shiver of awareness ran down his spine. Dark and frank, her eyes seemed to stare right into the very soul of him. *Did she like what she saw there?* he wondered. He surely liked what he saw when he looked at her.

She was dressed austerely today. Her glossy dark hair was pulled high up onto her head in a simple knot. She wore no jewelry and a gown of a blue silk so dark it was almost black. Her only adornment was the soft rose of her cheeks and a single lily pinned to her breast. She stole his breath, she looked so lovely.

Who would have thought that he would feel such excitement at the sight of an English girl? It should bother him that he was so attracted to her, and the fact that it didn't filled him with a sense of guilt. His English blood was showing.

What was she doing here? Other than the odd servant, and Mr. Chumley, there wasn't a person in the room who wasn't family. It was unlikely that she was named in the will. He couldn't imagine Richard admitting to being vulnerable enough to want moral support, but as Richard's fiancée whatever was written in his father's will would affect her future as well.

The truth be known, Ewan didn't expect to inherit any more than was required by law. As the heir, he would get the title and any houses, land, or money that went with it. He didn't imagine his father would leave him—the son he hadn't wanted—anything else voluntarily.

It was he who looked away first. The scrutiny of her gaze made him blush and he didn't want her to know what effect she had on him. He didn't want this *English* girl to get under his skin as she did.

Purposefully he seated himself away from the family. Alone, and off to the side, he reminded himself of just how much of an outsider he was. The feeling was uncomfortable to say the least, but he'd do well to remember his place. Hester and Emily had tried to make him feel welcome, a kindness that had touched him deeply, but whether or not he could trust their sentiment would be proven by the outcome of the will.

Hester glanced at him. Inclining her head, she smiled a little and he could almost hear her unspoken question. Why was he sitting so far away? Understanding flickered across her features and her smile saddened, but she didn't appear hurt by his decision. She seemed . . . disappointed.

"If everyone is here, we will begin," Mr. Chumley said, his voice cutting through the hushed conversations humming about the room.

Ewan's gaze caught Anna's again as he turned toward the tiny solicitor, but she looked away before he could even smile. A coil of unease unwound in his stomach. She wouldn't be a duchess now because of him, and he wondered if she blamed him for it. Or was she just happy to be marrying the man she loved? He found it hard to imagine anyone loving Richard, but, then again, he had yet to see his brother's good side—if he had one.

He barely heard as Mr. Chumley began to read. The words from his father's hand seemed sad and full of regret, not what he had expected to hear at all. Ethan Fitzgerald had always seemed so removed from his life that Ewan was surprised at the pity he felt. His father hadn't even been fifty when he died—still a young man. He spoke of his wife, his children. And he spoke of Ewan.

"I ask my oldest son, Ewan, whom I have seen but once

since leaving Scotland, not to think too harshly of me or to think that I ever forgot him. I have watched over him his entire life, and although he might not believe it, I have always been proud to call him my son."

A hard lump lodged in Ewan's throat. He felt the weighty stares upon him and lowered his head to hide the tears burning the backs of his eyes. He didn't want to know his father thought of him. What good did telling him now do? Where had his father been when he needed him?

He let the anger wash the tears away. His father would have done well to save his pretty words. Nothing could make up for his desertion of Ewan and his mother. Nothing at all.

"As my oldest son and heir, Ewan MacLaughlin inherits the title of Duke of Brahm and the property of Brahm House in London and Brahm Park in Derbyshire, and the smaller estate of Featherington Keep in Yorkshire. The incomes from both estates equal some one hundred thousand pounds per annum. I also bequeath to Ewan the sum of fifty thousand pounds, the exact amount given to me by his mother, Maureen MacLaughlin."

At the mention of his mother's name, Ewan's blood ran cold. His father had destroyed her and no amount of money or power could ever make up for that. But what did he mean, "given" to him by his mother? He'd taken the money. Ewan's mother hadn't actually given it to him. Had she?

"I also ask my oldest son that he not hold the sins of

his father against his stepmother and his brother and sister and that he look after them as he would if he'd grown up with them."

Ewan braved a glance at Richard to catch his reaction. It was the same request he had made—except that their father had included Richard. The younger man was not impressed with his father's words. No doubt at twenty, Richard believed himself more than capable of looking after himself and the family, as well as being a good husband. Ewan himself was only four years older and didn't think he could possibly succeed at either task.

Mr. Chumley read through the rest of the will, which entailed money and a dowry for Emily, a house and money for Hester, property and money for Richard, money for a few favorite and faithful servants—it was fairly standard.

There was also something for Anna—a small painting that she apparently admired. Ewan's throat tightened when he heard the solicitor mention it. It was a painting of Loch Glenshea. Why had his father kept it all these years? Was it possible Ewan and his mother had meant something to him after all?

"The duke also left letters for some of you," Mr. Chumley said when the reading was finally over. He withdrew two thick folds of vellum from his satchel. He took one letter to Hester. The other he brought to Ewan.

Ewan stared at it as though it was crawling with maggots.

"He labored over this letter to you, Your Grace," Mr. Chumley informed him in that soft tone of his. "He was very hopeful that you would read it."

Slowly, Ewan's hand rose. Numb fingers took the letter from the solicitor's hand. The sheaves of paper trembled like leaves in the wind and Ewan crushed them to his lap so no one else could see how his hand shook. He didn't want it, and he most certainly didn't want to read it, but he would. He would because he wanted so desperately to think that his father cared for him, no matter that life had taught him differently.

A chair crashed to the floor and Ewan jerked his head up to see Richard storm from the room. Ewan leaped from his own chair and, tucking the letter from his father inside his coat pocket, hurried after his brother. Already he was assuming the role of head of the family.

He wasn't sure what he was going to say. He didn't even know why Richard was so angry. Ewan had been so young when his mother died, he hadn't grieved for her as an adult, and he didn't grieve for his father at all—not in the traditional sense. He hadn't really known either of his parents. All he had were the fuzzy memories of a toddler. He felt loss for what might have been, or should have been, but he had no idea how it felt to lose someone who had been there to watch you grow up.

Richard might have gotten a head start, but Ewan's legs were longer and he caught up to his brother in the empty hallway that led to the servants' stairs.

"What do you want?" Richard demanded as he whirled around in midstomp.

"I thought you might want to talk," Ewan replied lamely. Truth was, he'd been so intent on catching Richard that he hadn't given much thought as to what to do with his brother once he caught him.

"Huh," Richard jeered. "And what makes you think I'd want to talk to you? *You* are the last person I want to talk to. If it wasn't for you, my life would be what it should have been."

"Meaning you'd be the duke now." Ewan's tone was far from sympathetic as he lifted his gaze to the landscape paintings lining the walls. Lord, as much as he resented his father, even he hadn't been waiting for the old man to die!

"*Meaning*, you great lumbering oaf, that *I* would have been my father's oldest son—his only son—and that I wouldn't have spent my entire life wondering why he always seemed to be comparing me with some invisible rival."

Ewan's gaze shot back to his brother. "Invisible rival?" What the devil was he talking about?

"*You*." Richard sneered as he jabbed a finger in front of Ewan's chest. "Growing up, I could never figure out why I always felt as though I was competing for his affection. When he died, I went through his things to decide what to pack up and what to keep. I found letters. Letters written first by your mother and then by your grandmother telling every stupid little detail of your life."

Stunned, Ewan couldn't speak, couldn't even seem to think. All his life he'd believed that his father had left Scotland and never looked back. He'd stolen from his mother and left them there to practically starve. His mother had written to him? His *grandmother*?

"I-I don't understand."

Tears shimmered in Richard's bright eyes. "He might never have spoken about you, but you were always first in his heart. You took him from me and I will *never* forgive you for that." With that, he spun on his heel and bolted down the hall, running as though the hounds of hell were at his heels.

Ewan was dumbstruck. He couldn't believe what Richard had just told him. *He'd* been first in their father's heart? How could Richard even think such foolishness? Richard had been the one who'd had the benefit of knowing the man. Ethan Fitzgerald hadn't even waited the correct mourning period for his first wife before marrying Hester and starting a family. How could Richard possibly think that Ewan had ever meant anything to their father?

But how could he explain the letters? Letters his own mother and grandmother had written. He could see his mother clinging to some small hope that his father might return, but not his grandmother. His grandmother wouldn't have bothered with him at all unless she'd wanted to, or unless she'd promised his mother. Yes, that had to be it. She'd promised his mother to write to his father, but it hadn't been because Ethan had wanted to know about him.

So why had he kept the letters?

Oh, this was madness! Throwing his hands up in exasperation, Ewan turned and strode back to the study, resolving to not give the matter another thought.

He had a letter of his own to read.

The first thing Anna did when Ewan came back into the room was study his face and then his knuckles. No marks on either. Good. That meant that he and Richard hadn't come to fisticuffs.

It didn't mean they hadn't hurt each other, though. Anna could tell just by looking at Ewan that he was upset. She didn't know the entire situation, but she was smart enough to deduce that as difficult as it was for Ewan to realize that the father he believed had deserted him had been thinking of him, it was perhaps even more so for Richard to grow up thinking he was the heir. Both of them must be very confused and hurt, and their mutual dislike made it all the worse. Of course, from what Anna had seen, the gulf between the brothers was more of Richard's making than Ewan's. Not that Ewan wasn't capable of being just as churlish from what she had observed.

"Did you speak to him?" she asked, approaching him when he did not join the rest of the family.

Ewan's head snapped up. He'd been staring at the unopened letter in his hands. Anna couldn't help but wonder what it said. How did a father explain missing out on his son's entire life?

"Yes," he replied in an absent tone. "We . . . talked."

"Would you like to talk about it?" She shouldn't get involved and she knew it, but she couldn't stop herself from asking. She didn't know what it was about him that drew her to him, but her concern for him was stronger than any common sense she might possess.

His expression was dubious at best. He didn't trust her not to repeat their conversation to Richard. Why should he? She was Richard's fiancée, after all.

"I promise that whatever you tell me will be kept in the strictest confidence." She touched his coat sleeve. "I should like us to be friends."

Ewan stared at her hand so strangely that Anna could almost feel the weight of his gaze. She was tempted to snatch the offending appendage away and hide it in the folds of her skirt. Instead, she withdrew it slowly, bringing it to her side, as his gaze followed.

He raised his gaze to hers. The hazel depths were so open and searching that Anna caught her breath. She'd never met someone who needed a friend so badly. And how could he not? In England, he was surrounded by strangers, no matter that the Fitzgeralds were his family. Her heart broke for him.

"We cannot talk here," he murmured, his gaze lighting on Hester and Emily, both of whom watched them from across the room, their expressions worried. He smiled reassuringly at them, as though they'd been family for years rather than just a few days.

"Perhaps you would be so good as to escort me and my maid home since Richard is unable," she suggested.

Ewan nodded, his smile fading as he turned to her. "Yes. That would be good."

Trying to hide her disappointment at that lost smile, Anna managed a tight one of her own. "I'll fetch my wrap."

She left him standing there, holding his mysterious letter as she walked across the floor to where Hester and Emily sat. Taking her light shawl and bonnet from the back of the settee, she bent down to kiss them both on the cheek.

"His Grace has offered to see me home in Richard's absence," she explained. "I will take my leave of you now, unless you wish me to stay."

Hester shook her head, catching Anna's hand in her own. "There's no need for you to stay, my dear. I must apologize for Richard's behavior. He's taken his father's death so hard."

The tears in Hester's eyes proved that her son wasn't the only one having a hard time adjusting to life without the late duke.

"I think everyone in the family is having a hard time," Anna replied meaningfully, squeezing the older woman's fingers.

Hester glanced toward Ewan. "Yes," she agreed softly. "I hope they might both learn to forgive Ethan for what he's done."

"I'm sure they will." But Anna wasn't sure at all if the two brothers could learn to forgive each other.

Sighing, Hester squeezed her hand. "He was a good and loving husband, and that is what I choose to remember about him. Not the secrets he kept from me."

A sad smile curved the older woman's lips as she met Anna's sympathetic gaze. "I was angry when he finally told me the truth. But it seems like such a waste to be angry now that he's gone. Right now all I can feel is just how deeply I miss him."

Anna's throat was so tight she didn't trust herself to speak. Poor, poor Hester. What was it like to love someone so much that losing him left you feeling so empty that there was no room for anything else?

Releasing Hester's hand, she turned to Emily. "I'll see you tomorrow night?"

Emily nodded, smiling. "I look forward to it."

It wasn't entirely proper, as Emily was in mourning for her father, but the late duke had declared on his deathbed that he didn't want the family running around in black for a year and acting as though they were all dead as well. As a compromise, the family agreed to dress in half mourning, wearing grays and browns and lavenders instead of black. Emily had avoided balls and parties for the remainder of the London Season, but now that it was over, she had decided to honor her father's wishes and attend a few small gatherings. Tomorrow night was to be the first of such outings. Hester and Richard had even decided to attend, and Anna and her mother would be there as well.

A footman came and handed her a package wrapped in brown paper.

"It's the painting," Hester told her. "I thought you might like to take it home with you."

Anna smiled, her eyes hot with tears. She'd been touched by the late duke's gift. She had always loved the painting of the dark blue lake surrounded by a riot of colorful trees and mountains.

She said her good-byes and draped her shawl around her shoulders as Ewan came to meet her.

He bowed to Emily and Hester. "I shall take my leave as well."

"You will return later?" There was urgency in Hester's voice. Ewan nodded.

"And you will bring your things?" Again the near-panicked tone.

Ewan's smile was uncomfortable to say the least, but his eyes were warm with emotion. "If you wish."

"We wish," Emily responded with what sounded like a sigh of relief.

With that settled, Ewan and Anna left the room and walked down the corridor to the entrance hall where a footman gave Ewan his hat and gloves. Waving the footman aside, Ewan held the door for both Anna and her maid, Jane, drawing a blush and a stuttered thank-you from the young maid with his gallantry.

They were silent until the front door closed behind them and they stepped out into the watery sunshine. It had rained yet again that morning and the sun had yet to dry the shimmering drops from the grass, or chase the puddles away. A cool breeze—the kind that always followed a summer rain—brushed against Anna's face and she breathed it deep into her lungs, savoring the odor of sweet, damp earth and clean horses.

Drawing her cream-colored cashmere shawl tighter around her so it wouldn't fall, Anna allowed Ewan to hand her up into the brightly painted open carriage before assisting Jane up as well. The front seat allowed just enough room for them to sit next to each other without being improper, but it also had a seat for Anna's maid—close enough to them to be proper, but not close enough to hear their conversation.

With a flick of the reins, Ewan started the horses down the drive, their hooves striking the gravel with a lazy rhythm.

"Hester and Emily seem very attached to you already," Anna observed when he made no move to speak first.

He didn't look at her, and the brim of his hat shaded his eyes from view. "Yes. I suspect I remind them both of my father. I confess, the comparison gives me little joy, but I am glad to bring them some pleasure in what has to be a very painful time."

She studied him intently, realizing with a bit of surprise that he was being completely sincere and honest—something she wasn't used to in people of his class. The aristocracy always seemed to hide behind a façade of politeness and say all the proper words and sentiments while often thinking something completely different. Allowing someone to see your true feelings was seen as setting oneself up to be ridiculed.

"You're a good man, Your Grace," she told him, her voice soft.

He didn't look at her, but his cheeks turned pink. "I try to be."

"What a rarity you are." And she meant it.

"I don't think I'm so very rare," he said self-consciously as a footman opened the gate for them. Expertly, he guided the horses and carriage out into the street. "Aren't you a good person? Isn't Richard?"

"Richard is very proper," Anna replied, watching as other carriages rolled past. She loved the sound the horses' hooves made against the cobblestones. "Sometimes I think people become so obsessed with giving the appearance of being good that they forget what it really means to be a good person."

He looked at her, his expression one of amusement. "I can't imagine you being so caught up in appearances. After all, you gave up the book you wanted to a stranger in a bookshop."

Warmth flooded her stomach at the thought of their first meeting. "I have never held a door open for a servant," she admitted even though it shamed her.

A grin lit his features, softening his face and brightening his eyes, which were a clear, bright green in the sunlight. "You're right. You're an awful person. I can't imagine why Richard is marrying you—your beauty aside."

"Yes," Anna replied, her tone a mixture of the lightness she wanted to project at his compliment and the sudden bitterness that engulfed her. "But my mother was beautiful once as well. Richard's taking a great risk by marrying me, especially if I inherit my mother's peerless manner."

Ewan faltered—ever so slightly, but Anna saw it. He'd heard the doubt in her voice, of that she was certain. Truth be told, she probably shouldn't be talking to him about her personal affairs at all. It was unseemly, but she didn't care. It felt good to talk about it.

"He's brave because he adores you," Ewan replied, his gaze fixed on the traffic in front of them.

Anna wondered if he deliberately substituted "adores"

for "loves." There were times when even she didn't know the true depths of Richard's affections. Being a gentleman, mindful of her "maidenly sensibilities," he showed great restraint in expressing his own more passionate emotions.

"I have no doubt that Richard has some affection for me, Your Grace." She stared at the passing perfection of Devonshire House, rather than look at him. "We get along fairly well, but sometimes I wonder if Richard is marrying me or my father's business. I have no idea if he adores me as you claim."

"He should."

The sun disappeared behind a cloud as he spoke, adding to the shiver that raced down Anna's spine. He was right. Richard *should* adore her. He should love her. Just as she should love him.

"Do you doubt your decision to marry him?"

Her spine stiffened. Had he read her mind? "That is none of your business, Your Grace."

"Stop calling me that!" he snapped, startling her. "My name is Ewan. If you can't bring yourself to call your future brother-in-law by his Christian name in private, then perhaps you could call me Lord Keir, but for the love of God, don't call me by *his* title!"

Anna stared at him, her mouth agape. Anger had made him lose control of the horses, causing them to speed up at an alarming rate. Clinging to the side of the seat with one hand and to her bonnet with the other,

Anna braced herself.

Just as suddenly, the horses slowed again. She glanced at Ewan. His jaw was still tight, but his shoulders had relaxed somewhat and he once again had the horses under control. He muttered an apology.

"But it is my business," he continued as she also relaxed. "As much as I would hate to see you trapped in a loveless marriage, I would hate even more seeing you love a man who does not love you. My mother loved a man who did not love her, Anna, and it destroyed her."

His wounded anger washed over her like a wave upon a stormy ocean. She didn't even care that he was calling her by her first name. "And you still hate him for it, don't you?"

Ewan stared straight ahead. "I hate him for many things, and yet I cannot bring myself to despise him completely. Richard says he always felt like he was being compared with me growing up—an 'invisible rival,' he called me." He made a scoffing sound. "He says I've taken everything from him. He doesn't understand that I'd gladly trade the title for the chance to know my father. *That's* what I hate—the fact that even though the man left us with nothing, I still wanted—*want*—his approval."

Anna's heart was breaking. She had wanted him to open up to her, to trust her, but never had she imagined that his pain would run so deep. The fact that he was sharing this with her was an honor she could not take lightly. But neither could she allow herself to read more into it than that he needed a confidante.

It didn't make her special.

"Perhaps once you read his letter you will feel better about things."

He shrugged. "Perhaps. Meanwhile I have to move into a house with two women who want to love me and a young man determined to hate me." He sighed.

Trying to lighten the mood, Anna quipped, "There are worse fates than having two women determined to love you, I imagine."

"Not if they're the wrong women," he replied with a small smile.

Ignoring the pounding of her heart his expression inspired, Anna made another attempt at humor. "According to most men, there are no *right* women. It's just a matter of finding the least wrong and making the best of it."

He took his eyes from the road long enough to look at her in surprise. "Where'd you hear such nonsense?"

She blushed. "I overheard two gentlemen talking at a ball one night."

Ewan shook his head and glanced up at the sky. Anna's gaze followed. It was going to rain again, blast it.

"They were idiots," he told her. "I'm sure Richard thinks you're the right woman, regardless of what you might say, and I'm certain there are at least a hundred other men out there who would agree."

Anna laughed, touched by his insistence, even though she knew different. "I doubt you'd be able to find one man in all of London who'd take me for a bride without my fortune, Your—Ewan."

His expression was suddenly very serious. "I'm certain I could find at least one."

The implication of his words was slow to sink in, but it set Anna's heart pounding harder than it ever had in her life. Something about the way he looked at her made it clear who that one man might be. Whatever this fascination, this feeling was, it was wrong. She was promised to Richard.

"There you go again," she replied, fighting to keep her strangled tone light. "Being kind when you don't need to be."

He didn't respond, but his expression grew shuttered, as though he realized he'd crossed a line.

They drove the rest of the way in silence. It was a fairly long drive, made even longer by the heavy traffic and the awkwardness between them. It began to rain just as the carriage pulled up to the door.

Stepping down, Ewan lifted his hand to Anna to help her down. Their gazes locked as Anna hesitantly placed her gloved hand in his. Even through the layers of cloth between them, she could feel the heat and strength of his hand. This wasn't the hand of some pampered *ton* gentleman. This was the hand of a man. The realization sent a tremor of awareness through her.

As she jumped to the ground, she miscalculated the distance and ended up landing practically on top of Ewan. Toe to toe, the only thing that kept their bodies from touching was the painting she held tightly to her chest. As it was, her forearm pressed heavily against the solid wall of his chest.

She stared at him. He stared at her.

"Do you mind if I run inside, Miss Welsley?"

The spell was broken. Turning to her maid, Anna shook her head. "Go ahead, Jane." It was highly improper for her to be alone with a young man, but Anna didn't think her reputation could be ruined in her own driveway.

The maid left them there, bobbing a quick curtsy to them both before running for the servants' entrance around the back.

"I should go in as well," Anna murmured, trying vainly to break free of his mesmerizing gaze. What the devil was wrong with her? She'd never reacted this way to any young man in her life.

She tugged her hand free of his.

"I meant what I said," he spoke as she finally found the strength to turn away. "There are many men out there who would count themselves lucky to have someone like you."

Heat filled Anna's cheeks, making the rain seem all the more chilly as the first drops struck her face.

"Thank you." She raised her gaze and there was that

blunt, trusting honesty of his again.

"But I sincerely doubt that any of them would deserve you. Not even *one*."

And with that he climbed back onto his seat and easily steered the horses back down the lane as the rain began to fall in earnest.

Anna stood on the steps and watched the carriage pull away. She barely felt the rain as it ran down her face, soaking through her shawl and gown. Not until the carriage and its driver were lost from sight did she realize she was standing in the rain like an idiot.

A guilty, tingly idiot who had no right to take such pleasure in the inappropriate remarks of a man who would someday be her brother-in-law.

CHAPTER FIVE

He was insane.

That was the only way Ewan could describe his behavior toward Anna. Obviously he was out of his mind because that would be the only reason—the *only* reason—he would tell his brother's fiancé that he found her attractive.

It didn't matter that he thought Anna to be the most beautiful girl he'd ever seen. It didn't matter that her kindness had touched him deep inside. He shouldn't allow himself to become infatuated with her. It would lead only to heartache—and deepen the gulf between Richard and him.

He didn't know if he and Richard could ever truly be brothers, but he didn't want to give the younger man any more reason to dislike him—or add Anna to the list of things he'd "stolen" from him.

If Anna wanted to be stolen, that was, and she'd given Ewan no indication that she was the least bit attracted to him. Of course, she hadn't given him any indication that she was attracted to Richard either.

Regardless, it was still Richard's ring she wore on her finger and that was what mattered. Ewan had no business feeling the way he did when she was around. He was going to have to get a grip on his emotions.

"More coffee, Your Grace?"

Ewan's head snapped up. He'd forgotten he was in White's gentleman's club and not his rooms back home in Scotland.

"Please," he responded. White's had been his father's club and the easiest for him to get into for that reason. He looked enough like the late duke, and had been the subject of enough gossip and speculation, that anyone with eyes and ears would know who he was.

And everywhere he went, people seemed to know who he was. London was a big city—much bigger than he'd thought that first day when he told Anna they'd meet again. It was only the social circle that was small, but that hadn't prevented every tradesman, every shopkeeper, from knowing who he was. He couldn't even cross the street without some acquaintance of his father's flagging him down.

Thoughts of his father reminded him of the letter in his coat pocket. He was terrified to read it, especially in public, but now that his belongings from the inn had been packed and sent to Brahm House, he had little choice. He couldn't read it at the house with all the servants and family there gauging his reaction, and being in a public place would force him to keep his emotions in check.

The wax seal on the letter was black, and Ewan could

just barely make out the outline of a falcon in flight pressed within it. It had been his father's seal and now it was his. His life had been so drastically changed since learning of his father's death. It all still seemed so unreal.

With trembling fingers, he broke the seal and unfolded the thick sheaf of paper. The handwriting was firm but shaky, indicating his father had been unwell when he wrote it. The date at the top revealed that it had been written the day before Ethan Fitzgerald died.

> *My dear son—*
> *How strange it seems to call you that after*
> *all these years, and how strange it must be for you to read*
> *it, but you are and always have been dear to me. That you*
> *are reading this letter means that I am dead, and I am*
> *sorry that I never had the strength or the chance to tell you*
> *the contents of this letter in person. I have missed out on*
> *so much of your life, been denied many of the joys of*
> *fatherhood, and yet I cannot blame anyone but myself.*

"You've got that right," Ewan muttered, his tone less bitter than he had hoped. He raised his cup to his lips and drank. The coffee was hot and weak, but it relieved the dryness in his throat and gave him a moment to combat the mixture of hope and anger mingling in his stomach. He must try to keep calm until he'd read the entire letter.

His father had obviously felt he owed him an explanation and Ewan would listen. He didn't know how much of it he would like or accept, but this trip to London had made him realize that there was more to what happened between his parents than what he had perceived as a child. Perhaps that was why his grandmother had insisted that he come—to finally learn the truth. He and his father both owed each other that.

> *I know I've no right to ask anything of you, but I beg you to look after Hester and the children for me. Richard and Emily aren't that much younger than you, but they have been sheltered and spoiled their entire lives. You, on the other hand, I fear have not been sheltered and spoiled enough. For that, I am mostly to blame, but only because your mother insisted I take the money when I left.*

Ewan's heart froze against his ribs. His mother had *given* him the money? She'd *insisted* he take it? But that made no sense. Why would his mother do such a thing? Why would she let her husband leave her and give him money to do so? Why would she purposefully relegate herself, her child, and her people to borderline poverty while her husband made merry in another country?

> *I'll wager you never knew she gave me that money. I bet you thought I'd stolen not only your mother's heart, but her fortune as well. Well, she gave me that money as freely as she gave me her proud and wild heart, and all I had to offer her was my absence and*

*gratitude. When I inherited the dukedom, it was drowning
in debt. I knew I could turn it around, make it profitable
again if I could pay off the former duke's—my uncle's—
bills. Your mother gave me the money and told me
to go fulfill my destiny.*

Ewan could scarce believe it. His mother hadn't just
given her husband her fortune, but she'd practically packed
his trunk for him as well! Why? If she'd truly loved Ethan
that much, how could she just let him go?

*How I loathed leaving you. You were my sturdy little man,
still unsteady on your feet but already showing signs of
living up to your warrior heritage. There wasn't an English
bone in your body except that you looked so much like me,
and if the sketch your grandmother sent me last year is a
valid likeness, then I'm pleased to see your looks haven't
changed. Although you looked like me, your heart and soul
were Scottish, and I couldn't take you away from that—
even if your mother hadn't been so determined to keep you
with her. I was angry, of course, that neither of you would
be coming to England with me, but I soon realized that
neither of you would have survived here. Society would
have crushed your mother's spirit, would have gossiped
behind her back, and you would have become one of those
pale, withdrawn children beaten and tormented by others
instead of the strong, strapping lad you are now. No, your
mother was right in staying behind, but in my heart, I'll
always wish she'd come with me, for then we might have*

had more time together. As it was she hid her illness from
me, never asking me to return, never allowing herself to be
selfish. You may never forgive me for leaving you, Ewan,
and I understand that, for I will never forgive Maureen
for leaving me.

Something inside Ewan screamed in protest, insisting that his father had been to blame, that everything—his mother's death, his own unhappiness—was all Ethan Fitzgerald's fault, but Ewan couldn't believe it anymore. He didn't understand why his mother had acted as she had. He supposed she saw it as a great act of love, letting her husband go off to fulfill his destiny while she wasted away, but Ewan saw it as a great act of foolishness. She should have gone after him. He should have come back. But who was he to judge the actions of two people twenty years in the past?

But he couldn't help but be angry. Because of his mother's pride and his father's willingness to put up with it, he'd never known his father and had barely known his mother. He was so young when she died, he had only fuzzy memories of her, and even then she had been ill. Perhaps neither one of them had ever meant to hurt him or each other, but it didn't change the fact that they'd sacrificed their happiness just so his father could save the title.

As though that could ever compare with what they'd lost.

And now the title was his. It was a title he'd despised

only days before, but now he felt a certain kinship with it. He'd always known he'd inherit his mother's family's title, there was nothing new in that, but his father's title was different. His mother and father had both sacrificed so much—Ewan had been denied so much—so that his father could have the dukedom that it was only right it should go to Ewan now. It was his by more right than just birth. Everything in his life had led to this moment, to him becoming the Duke of Brahm. And even as tears burned the backs of his eyes and tightened his throat, his heart swelled with a fierce pride and love for those two foolish young people who had given so much for him to have such a legacy.

It was also so very difficult not to be angry at them both. Their pride had cost them so much. It had cost Ewan so much. How could he not harbor some resentment? Had no one given any thought to how this would affect him? He grew up not knowing his parents, and his grandmother had kept everything a secret from him, no doubt believing it to be for the best.

None of them had the right to decide his life like that. If he'd known what had happened between his parents, he might have had the opportunity to go to England, to know his father. But he'd never been given the chance.

Blast it, someone should have told him.

He went back to the letter.

I had no idea how ill your mother was. Your grandmother wrote to me in London and I returned as fast as I could, riding nonstop, but I was too late. She was gone when I arrived. My heart was broken, I was numb with grief and there you were, not quite understanding what was going on and you didn't even remember who I was at first. You cried when I tried to hold you, weeping for your mother with such heart-wrenching grief that it nearly killed me to hear it. Your grandmother was the only one who could soothe you, and I knew then that I'd been gone too long and there was no place for me in your life. I had wanted to take you back to London with me, but that was impossible, so I left you with your grandmother and returned to London. I threw myself into work and society. Told myself I didn't care, that your mother hadn't truly loved me. Oh, Ewan, I was such a bitter man. I blamed myself for your mother's death, told myself she would have lived if I had only done one of several hundred things differently. I was so angry at both Maureen and myself. I married Hester as punishment——who I was trying to punish, I'm no longer certain. I swore to never let my heart rule me again. But Hester was too sweet, too good, and she healed my wounds. I couldn't bring myself to tell her about you or your mother, not when Hester had given me so much. I couldn't tell her she'd been a replacement for your mother, especially since I'd come to love her so very much.

When Richard was born, it made me think of you and how much your birth had meant to me. I started writing to your grandmother. I don't know why I was so

*scared to see you or why I wanted to keep you my little
secret. I can only beg for you to forgive me as Hester has.
My foolishness cost me not only your mother, but you as
well, and I know how angry and bitter you must have felt
toward me all these years. I've no doubt many of your
villagers have painted me as the worst sort of villain. And
no doubt, your fine grandmother let you draw your own
conclusions. I'll wager she's sitting in Scotland right
now, wondering if your heart has softened toward me,
speculating your feelings, knowing that your coming to
London will be what finally takes you from boy to man.*

Ewan chuckled at this. He couldn't stay angry at his
grandmother for never telling him about his father. She
was a firm believer in every man choosing his own destiny,
in making up his own mind, right or wrong. No doubt he
wouldn't have believed her even if she'd told him his father
still cared, and no doubt he would have found a way to get
a letter to the old man, and Lord only knew what awful
things he might have said. She'd hidden things from him,
but he couldn't say she'd been entirely wrong to do so.

*Know this, my dear, dear boy, that no matter what you
think of me now, I hope one day you are as proud of your
son as I am of you. You are as dear to me now as you
were the first time I ever held you in my arms. I only hope
you can find it in your heart to forgive me for being a
foolish, stupid man.*

All my love,
your father,
Ethan Fitzgerald, Duke of Brahm

A tear slid down Ewan's check and he swiped at it with his sleeve before anyone could see it. He was already at the center of too much London gossip, he didn't want to fuel any more fires.

"Will there be anything else, Your Grace?" the waiter asked as he approached.

Not daring to look up for fear the man would see the dampness clinging to his eyelashes, Ewan stuffed the letter back into his pocket and shook his head. "No, that will be all, thank you."

He swallowed the last mouthful of cold coffee in his cup and left. Outside, the air was damp and Ewan was glad for the excuse to pull his hat low on his brow. He didn't want to be recognized—didn't want any attention at all. He needed to be alone with his thoughts. And what thoughts!

He couldn't believe he'd been so wrong about his father. He didn't even know whether or not he could assume the letter was the truth, but his grandmother would be able to verify its validity. If his father was being truthful, his grandmother may very well have kept things from him, but she wouldn't hesitate to tell the truth if asked, Ewan was certain of it.

Ewan walked the rest of the way back to Brahm House,

his mind on his father and how this letter changed everything he'd ever believed. It changed his relationship with Hester and Emily and Richard.

And it had to change how he felt about Anna. He'd already taken enough from his brother.

"It really is a disgrace."

Anna tore her gaze away from Ewan as he danced with yet another giggling debutante and turned her attention to the woman on her right.

"What is a disgrace, Mama?"

Marion thrust her chin in the direction of the dance floor. "That *person* trying to pass himself off as the Duke of Brahm."

Anna didn't look. She didn't want to see that foolish girl smiling up at Ewan as though he hung the moon in the sky. And she most certainly didn't want to see him smile back, just as he had smiled at every girl who threw herself into his path that evening. It was really quite disgusting. She was embarrassed for him, that's all it was. She certainly wasn't jealous.

Not at all.

Why should she care whom he danced with? She'd danced twice with Richard and with several other handsome gentlemen. And she was certainly more graceful than Julianne Markby. Poor Ewan's toes must be positively bruised from the foolish girl tramping all over them.

"He's not trying to pass himself off, Mama," she replied with some exasperation. "He *is* the duke."

Marion smiled. It was a cat-who-ate-the-canary smile and it made Anna nervous. Her mother was up to something.

"Mama," Anna said in a warning tone, "what are you up to?"

"Pooh, child. Why must you think the worst of me?"

"Begging pardon, Mama, but you normally deserve it." She lowered her voice. "I certainly hope you're not still questioning the duke's birth. I think his father's will quite proves he is legitimate."

Her mother faced her with a slow, narrow-eyed smile. "My dear gel, it's not a question of whether or not he is legitimate."

Anna breathed a sigh of relief. "Well that's—"

"It's whether or not he can prove it." Snapping open her fan, Marion waved the delicate silk-covered sticks in front of her face with all the grace of a cow elephant.

The urge to bury her face in her hands and scream proved to be almost too much for Anna, but she managed to keep herself under control.

"Why should it matter to you whether he is legitimate or not? He's nothing to you."

"Don't be stupid!" Marion shot her a sharp glance. "It decides whether my daughter is the Duchess Brahm or just plain Mrs. Fitzgerald."

"It shouldn't matter if I'm either. It should only matter that I'm happy."

In an instant, Anna's mother went from scowl to a deceptively sweet smile. "Are you saying you wouldn't be happy to be a duchess?"

"Not at the duke's expense, no," Anna replied truthfully. Of course she'd dreamed of marrying a rich and handsome man. Didn't every young girl? But the older she became, the more she realized that love was more important than any title. She'd rather marry a poor man who loved her than the richest man in England.

And that was why she was having these doubts about Richard. She didn't know how he felt about her.

She didn't know how she felt about him.

"What about poor Richard?" her mother demanded as though reading her thoughts. "Don't you care that this . . . this *imposter* has stolen his birthright from him?"

"Of course I care about Richard." Anna sighed. "I think it was very wrong of his father to hide the duke's existence from his family, but it cannot be changed. He cannot be erased and Richard cannot claim the title."

Again that secretive smile. "He can if his brother cannot prove he was born within the laws of wedlock."

"Oh, you're impossible! I refuse to listen to any more of this nonsense!" Jumping to her feet, Anna planned to get as far away from her mother as she possibly could.

"You're not leaving, I hope, Miss Welsley?"

Mortified, Anna met Ewan's amused gaze. Her stomach lurched at the sight of him. Lord, but she hoped he hadn't heard any of her conversation with her mother!

"Actually, I was just on my way to get some . . . uh . . . lemonade."

"I'd be honored to fetch a glass for you."

Anna shot him a look of pure panic. She must have made quite an impression because his eyes sparkled with humor and his lips twitched as though he was trying to keep from smiling.

"Or perhaps I could escort you to the refreshment table?"

Anna almost sagged in relief. Finally, she could escape her mother. Of course, good manners required she take her leave of her infuriating parent.

"Do you mind, Mama?"

Tight-lipped, Marion shook her head, sending the feathers in her elaborate hairstyle bobbing in all directions. "Do not be long." She cast a hard look at Ewan. "Good evening, Your Grace."

He gave a slight bow. "Charmed as always, madam." If he was being sarcastic, Anna couldn't tell. Straightening, he offered her his arm.

Her fingers were stiff from having been clenched into fists during her conversation with her mother, but Anna laid them lightly on his sleeve and allowed him to lead the way across the floor to the refreshment room. Hopefully he would never notice the warm dampness of her palm through the fabric of his coat. What was this strange effect he had on her? Just being this close to him made her oddly dizzy.

She stood by the wall and waited while he went for drinks. It was so much quieter in there than the ballroom, but then, they could run a herd of buffalo through the room and Anna would still find it quiet without her mother's presence.

"Here you are." Ewan offered her a glass.

"Thank you." As she took it, their fingers brushed and even though they were both wearing gloves, a shock ran through Anna's body. She jumped.

He didn't seem to notice her bizarre behavior and for that she was thankful. Surely she could at least pretend she was unaffected by him.

Taking a sip of her lemonade, Anna resolved to do just that—act normally. As the cool drink hit the back of her parched throat, she closed her eyes in pleasure at the tart sweetness. It was good—much better than the weak dishwater they called lemonade at Almack's.

"I don't believe I've told you how lovely you look this evening."

She looked away, blushing under his scrutiny. The way he looked at her made her feel warm and breathless, as though she had suddenly entered a very hot room.

She had taken extra pains with her appearance that

night. She'd chosen a simple, short-sleeved gown of rose silk with matching gloves and slippers. The high waist emphasized her bosom and the dusky color complemented her dark coloring. Her hair was gathered up on the crown of her head to fall in a mass of ringlets down her back. Her only jewelry was a strand of pearls around her neck and matching ear bobs.

She had tried to convince herself her desire to look nice had nothing to do with the fact that Ewan would be there, but she couldn't deny that she had wanted him to see her at her best. Surely there was no harm in that, was there? It didn't mean anything—except to make her one of the vainest girls in all of London.

"Thank you," she replied, raising her gaze to his. "You look very dashing as well."

And did he ever. Some men weren't meant to wear black, and ended up looking more like undertakers than fashionable gentlemen, but Ewan was splendid in his stark evening attire. While other young men wore their collars up around their ears and tied their cravats in impossibly intricate knots, he wore his shirt points just below his jaw and his neckcloth in a very simple fashion. Beau Brummell, former paragon of the fashionable world, couldn't have looked better.

"And I must thank you for coming to my rescue."

He grinned. "Is that what it was? I must admit I had no idea I was performing such a service. You're most welcome."

He didn't pry, didn't ask why she should need rescuing from her own mother, for which Anna was grateful. She couldn't tell him the truth and she didn't want to lie, so avoiding the subject altogether seemed the best tack.

"Yes, but this lemonade won't last forever and then I must return." With a resigned sigh, Anna raised her glass.

"There's no hurry," Ewan assured her. "Finish your drink and then we'll dance."

She raised a brow. "Dance?"

He smiled. "It's when you move your feet in various steps set to music. Surely you've done it before?"

Laughing at his teasing, Anna nodded. "Once or twice, yes."

"Good. Then finish your lemonade and we'll dance and then we'll find something else to do so you won't have to face your mother until you're ready."

She couldn't believe her ears. "You don't have to do that, Your Grace. I don't want you to feel responsible for me."

"I don't," he replied bluntly. "But since Richard's off somewhere discussing business, I'll stand in his stead. And my name's Ewan, remember?"

Anna felt an odd sense of disappointment at his words but smiled anyway. "Yes, I remember."

He nodded at her cup. "Then drink up and we'll dance." As if to hurry her along, he drained his glass in one gulp and gazed at her expectantly.

"I can't drink that fast."

"Sure you can."

"No, I can't."

"Why?"

Smiling, Anna shook her head. "Because it's not lady-like, that's why."

The glint in his eyes was teasing. "Do you always have to be a lady?"

How could he even ask such a thing? No gentleman would even think of such a question—he would already know the answer.

"Yes," she replied. "I do."

Sighing in exaggerated aggravation, Ewan plucked the glass from her hand, drained its contents, and set it and his own on the tray of a passing footman.

"There. Now we can dance."

Speechless, Anna was caught somewhere between indignation and delight. "I can't believe you did that."

Leading her into the ballroom by the hand, Ewan grinned. "Neither can I."

"You had better be a good dancer," she warned with good humor. "That lemonade was the best I've tasted in quite some time."

"I am an accomplished dancer. I would not have denied your refreshment if I did not think it worth your while."

He was acting a fool, but his antics made Anna happier than she had been in months. It wasn't until the music started up that her good mood faded.

"This is a waltz." Glancing around at the other guests, Anna didn't know what to do. She'd been given permission to waltz during her first Season, but she'd danced it only with Richard. It was considered a scandalous dance because it required the gentleman to hold the lady so close.

The idea of being that close to Ewan frightened her.

Ewan placed a hand on the small of her back. "So it is."

Her heart sped up at his touch. "Are you sure we should dance? Is it proper?"

He must have heard the edge to her voice, because his smile turned from one of joviality to warmth in seconds. "Anna, we are soon to be related. As head of your fiancé's family, I don't think anyone will think it scandalous that we share one waltz."

When he put it that way, he made her reservations sound perfectly silly. Anna acquiesced, and the two began to dance. It was just that society needed so little evidence to base a rumor on. She would not want anyone in her family or Richard's to be harmed because she and Ewan were having fun.

Richard. Her good spirits dipped even more. He should be the one she laughed and joked with. He should be the one waltzing with her. Instead, he'd left her with her mother over an hour ago to go talk business with some "associates." He didn't even tell her what the business was.

"You shouldn't frown like that."

Ewan's voice jerked her back to the present. Suddenly,

Anna was very conscious of the warmth of his hand through her gown and the long fingers wrapped around her own. Her hand looked so little inside his. She felt so small next to him. The top of her head wasn't much higher than his shoulder. It had to be his Scottish ancestry that made him so tall and . . . broad.

"Was I frowning? I beg your pardon."

His green eyes were bright with concern. "Are you not enjoying the dance? We can stop. . . ."

"No. You're a wonderful dancer, but then you already knew that. I'm just feeling a little jilted."

He nodded in understanding. Anna didn't want him to understand. She didn't want him to realize he was behaving like her fiancé should. Richard should be the one dancing with her. Richard should be the one sending shivers down her spine just by touching her. It certainly shouldn't be Richard's brother making her feel things she'd never felt before.

"I'm sure Richard would rather be here dancing with you."

Anna shrugged. Ewan didn't sound like he believed that any more than she did.

Their dancing had taken them over by the balcony doors, and with a few expert twirls, Ewan had them outside in the cool night air, where the air smelled of flowers rather than sweat and perfume, and the music and voices were low and muted rather than in competition to be heard.

"We shouldn't be out here," Anna protested. If anyone saw them, there would be a scandal.

"We'll stay in the light. We're perfectly visible from the ballroom."

Anna doubted that. From where she stood, she could see the dancers as they twirled and dipped inside, but the light from the chandeliers made it almost impossible for anyone to see out into the darkness. She and Ewan were in plain sight, yet completely invisible.

He stood before her, so big and tall with just herself to compare him with. Instinctively she took a step back from him. Young women had been socially ruined by less than being alone in the dark with a young man. If anyone did find them, Anna wanted there to be plenty of distance between them. It didn't matter that they weren't doing anything wrong. Society would still gossip, and Anna did not want to be involved in a scandal with her fiancé's brother.

"If we're caught out here, they'll say I tried to trap you into marriage. They'll think I want you because you have the title now. They'll say I planned to jilt Richard for you now that he won't inherit." With each assumption her voice grew in panic and pitch, because she didn't know if she would really mind the scandal.

Ewan's expression was a mixture of concern and amusement. "Are you?"

Anna scowled. "Am I what?" Of course, he could treat the whole situation as a joke. It wasn't his reputation that would be ruined!

"Are you planning on jilting Richard for me?"

Her cheeks flamed. "Of course not!" But she couldn't say for certain that she was telling the truth. Oh! It was wrong of her to even think such a thing.

A sympathetic smile curved his lips. "I know, and so does Richard. Honestly, Anna, you're safe with me. Please, relax. I just have something I want to say to you and then you can go back inside before your mother misses you."

Anna's heart sped up. "What do you want to tell me?"

"I'm sorry."

Her stomach fell. She wasn't sure what she'd hoped to hear, but that wasn't it. Cursing herself for being such an idiot, she frowned again. "For what?"

Ewan stared at his feet for a few seconds before raising his gaze to hers. "I know Richard resents me for inheriting the title," he said softly. "I know I ruined a great many of his plans, and I assume I probably ruined a few of yours as well. I've tried to apologize to him, but I don't know if he believed me. And now I want to apologize to you as well."

Anna shook her head. "You want to apologize for ruining my plans? What plans?"

Clearing his throat, Ewan straightened his shoulders like a soldier being confronted by a superior officer. "I imagine you were looking forward to becoming a duchess and having the kind of life that entails. I'm sorry that my existence denies you that life."

A spark of anger flared low in Anna's chest. "So, you're sorry I won't be a duchess?"

He nodded. "Yes."

Hands on her hips, Anna moved toward him, no longer caring if anyone found them out there alone or not. "Do you think the only reason I accepted Richard's proposal is so I'd be a duchess?"

"Isn't it?"

"No!" She was close enough now that she could poke him in the chest with her finger, but she didn't dare touch him—not when she felt like punching him. "I can't believe you'd think so ill of me."

"I don't." His voice was void of emotion. "But having a duchess for a daughter would make your mother very happy, wouldn't it?"

There was no point denying it. Anna didn't care to defend her mother. She was too busy defending herself.

"Yes, it would make her very happy, but that's not why I'm marrying Richard."

"No? Why are you marrying Richard then?" he demanded, folding his arms across his wide chest.

Anna opened her mouth but nothing came out. She couldn't think of a single reason.

"Do you love him?"

Shock jolted Anna like a bolt of lightning. "How I feel for Richard is none of your business!"

His expression went grim. "If you don't love my

brother, then you shouldn't marry him."

Oh, that was it! "How dare you! What do you know of it? You wouldn't know love if it hit you on that thick head of yours!"

A muscle ticked in his jaw. "I think I know a bit more about it than you do."

She snorted—a definitely unladylike sound. "Oh, do you? And what do you know?"

He towered over her, his face just as angry-looking as she felt, but she wasn't frightened of him, not in the least.

"I know that Byron was right. I know that love should inspire passion and poetry."

Anna shivered as he leaned closer, and it wasn't because of the breeze that whispered against the back of her neck. It wasn't right for them to be out there. She shouldn't be listening to her fiancé's brother talk about passion; it wasn't proper.

"Does Richard make you think of poetry, Anna?"

She sputtered in rage—not because he was wrong, but because he was right! He was oh so right! Richard didn't make her think of passion or poetry, and she was too ashamed to admit that to the one person who *did* make her tremble whenever he was near.

"You don't know anything!" She was dangerously close to losing what little control she had left over her emotions. If she didn't get away from him soon, she would hit him, or burst into tears. She couldn't decide which was worse.

Tears. Tears would be worse.

His hands cupped her face. She tried to jerk away, but he refused to let go, and held her so that she had no choice but to meet his gaze.

"But I *do* know, Anna," he told her, his voice suddenly little more than a whisper. "I know because 'all that's best of dark and bright' meet in *your* aspect and *your* eyes."

She stared at him, her heart pounding painfully in her chest. How could he tell her these things? How could he quote Byron and make her feel so beautiful when she was supposed to marry his brother? And yet, at the same time, her heart thrilled at his words, because she'd always dreamed that someone would feel that way about her— someone she could feel that way about in return.

Tentatively, she reached up and placed her palm over his heart, and spoke the first line of the poem that came to mind. "'A heart whose love is innocent.'"

And then his lips were on hers and Anna was too surprised to think of anything, let alone poetry. Warm and soft, his mouth moved against hers, making her tense and tremble all at once. Richard's kisses had never been like this!

"We can't do this," he groaned, pulling away after a breathless moment. Dazed and disappointed that he had stopped, Anna could only stare at him as he backed toward the balcony doors. His face was white in the pale moonlight and his guilty expression did more to break Anna's heart than words ever could. She supposed she should feel guilty too for kissing her fiancé's brother, but she just couldn't.

"Ewan, wait!"

Pausing by the door, he couldn't even look her in the eye. "I'm so sorry, Anna."

"I'm not," she responded. And she wasn't.

But he was already gone.

CHAPTER SIX

Her mother had company for breakfast.

"Richard," Anna said, guilt shoving her heart up into her throat as she entered the dining room, "what are you doing here?" Had Ewan told him about the kiss? Had someone else seen them go out onto the balcony? And why did that thought fill her with more hope than horror?

Her fiancé, who had risen to his feet at her entrance, sat back down. "I've come in hopes that I might persuade you and your mama to dine with us tonight at Brahm House."

"Of course, it did not take much persuasion," her mother replied jovially—more jovial than Anna had seen her in quite sometime.

"Your mama and I have also been discussing plans for the wedding." The smile Richard flashed her mother struck Anna as cunning and secretive rather than truly happy. What were the two of them up to? Somehow, she just knew it involved Ewan.

"Wonderful," she replied, forcing a bright smile as she crossed to the buffet where a breakfast she no longer felt like eating awaited. "Anything you'd care to share with me?"

"Oh no." Marion shook her head. "It's nothing that you

and I haven't already discussed, dear."

It was so easy for both of them to lie to her, Anna realized, spooning coddled eggs onto her plate. If either of them set out to harm Ewan in any way, she would wash her hands of them both. It would be difficult to turn her back on her mother, but she wasn't so certain she even knew her mother anymore.

The idea was appealing even if they didn't harm Ewan. For the first time, Anna considered crying off the engagement. She could do it.

Then she could marry Ewan.

The thought startled her so much she almost dropped her plate.

"Are you quite all right, my dear?" Richard asked. He sounded genuinely worried and Anna wondered if he meant it.

"I'm fine," she lied. "I'm just a little tired, that's all." She couldn't very well tell him that she was considering jilting him for his brother, now could she? And other than that one beautiful kiss, she had no idea if Ewan would even want her.

And instead of Ewan's kisses, she should be thinking of Richard's. But he had never kissed her as Ewan had. Perhaps she should ask him to? How else could she know if it was Ewan alone who made her feel this way, or if she was just fickle?

"Tired?" Richard's tone was one of amused censure. "It's after eleven. How could you possibly be tired?"

Because I spent half the night thinking about what a divine kisser your brother is.

"I didn't sleep well last night. I had a headache." That was all the explanation he needed.

She didn't dare look at either one of them for fear they'd see the distrust, or worse, the guilt, in her eyes. A footman held her chair as she seated herself at the table.

Richard sipped his coffee. "I was hoping you and your mama might want to visit some warehouses today to shop for household items—our household."

"I'm afraid I'm really not feeling all the thing today, Richard." Anna hoped she looked as apologetic as she sounded. "Why don't you and Mama go? I'm sure I'll love whatever you pick out."

There wasn't much chance of that, but it would give her an opportunity to express her fears to Ewan. Perhaps she was wrong in her suspicions, but she knew how much her mother wanted a titled son-in-law, and she knew how much the title had meant to Richard. Neither one of them would give up that easily.

Her mother looked positively thrilled with the turn of events, deepening Anna's suspicion. Normally her mother would insist she come along, but today she obviously wanted Richard all to herself.

"If you're unwell, dear, perhaps we will go on

without you. After all, it's only fabric and furnishings we'll be looking at. You can approve the choices before they're purchased." Marion smiled.

Richard reached out and took her hand. It was all Anna could do not to jerk it back. What was wrong with her? It was the kiss. Somehow, that kiss had changed everything, and now the touch of her fiancé, which at one time had at least been pleasant, made her cringe.

It was the guilt. It had to be the guilt that was responsible for this sudden aversion to the man she was supposed to marry.

"Are you certain you will be all right if we leave you?"

Anna managed a tight smile. "I'll be fine. I'll have Betsy bring me a headache powder and lie down. By the time we join you for dinner tonight, I'll be right as rain."

That seemed to appease them both and conversation turned to different matters. Keeping her responses to a minimum, and focusing her attention on her food, Anna managed to make it through the next half hour until they left. Then, as soon as they were out the door, she penned a note to Ewan that simply said:

I must speak with you. Please come at once.

She couldn't fight her suspicions any longer. She was convinced her mother and Richard were scheming against Ewan and she couldn't keep silent any longer.

She would never forgive herself if they did something to ruin his life—something she might have prevented.

She sent Jane with the note rather than a footman, knowing her maid could be trusted to secrecy, and within half an hour Ewan was standing in the blue drawing room, his hat in his hands.

"I'm glad my message found you at home," she said, breaking the silence.

He regarded her solemnly. "I was trying to think of an excuse to come see you. Anna, about last night . . . I apologize if I offended you in any way."

"Offended me?" He thought he had offended her?

He nodded. "Forcing my attentions on you was very ungentlemanly of me and I'm sorry."

"Oh." What else could she say? That he shouldn't be sorry because she enjoyed it? Well, that was just too brazen, even for her! And when he made it sound as though kissing her had been a mistake—which she knew it *should* have been—it made her reluctant to speak her feelings. A young lady never told a young man how she felt about him unless he made a declaration first.

And it usually helped if the young lady in question knew just what her feelings were.

"I didn't, did I?" Both his tone and expression were hesitant. "Offend you, that is?"

Anna shook her head, too bewildered to do much else. "No, you didn't offend me."

Ewan's face brightened somewhat. "Good. I am very happy to hear that. I hardly slept at all last night. I kept replaying it over and over in my head—" He flushed deep crimson and Anna's heart flipped in her chest.

So she hadn't been the only one who'd lain awake last night.

"I mean, I felt so awful about it," he insisted, and Anna wasn't certain which one of them he was trying to convince. "I had no right to take such liberties. You're engaged to my brother."

She didn't need to hear him repeat all the things she'd already thought. She knew all the reasons why the kiss had been wrong, but that didn't change the fact that it had felt so *right.*

It also didn't change the fact that her mother and Richard were up to no good.

Reaching out, she grabbed Ewan's hand to keep him from saying more. She tried to ignore the thrill that shot through her as her bare fingers clasped his much larger ones. Was it her imagination or did he seem as shocked by the contact as she was?

"Ewan, right now we have something more important to discuss than a kiss."

He frowned, as though he had difficulty believing her. "Such as?"

Anna took a deep breath. If her heart didn't soon slow down it was going to play itself out. "I suspect my mother and Richard are plotting against you."

He laughed. Not a chuckle, but a big, booming laugh.

Anna fought the urge to kick him. "This is not funny!"

Sobering, Ewan stared at her. "You're serious."

"Of course I am! Did you think I would send you such an urgent summons if I wasn't?"

"I thought . . . I thought you were just being coy," he answered sheepishly.

"Coy!" Anna had to laugh at that. "I've never been coy in my life." But she had been coy at the ball last night, hadn't she? Well, she would just blame that on Ewan. He brought out the flirt in her.

Setting his hat on the table beside him, Ewan braced his elbows on his knees and leaned forward. "What do you believe Richard and your mother have in store for me?"

How to say it without making both Richard and her mother sound like the worst kind of people?

There wasn't a way.

"I've heard Mama speak several times about Richard wanting to prove you illegitimate."

"Illegitimate?" His tone was incredulous. "But my parents were married."

"Can you prove it?"

His face darkened, his expression hardened, and suddenly Anna found him terribly fierce and intimidating. "What are you implying?"

"I'm not implying anything," she assured him. "I have

no doubt that your parents were legally wed. But I fear Richard and my mother are going to try to make it look as though they weren't so Richard will inherit the title."

Ewan's expression was still dark. "If the title means that much to him he's welcome to it. I'd give it to him if I could."

"You would?"

He frowned at her surprised tone. "Of course I would! I don't need it. I've already got one title. What the devil am I supposed to do with another one? It's the money I need."

"You need money?"

He nodded. "The village surrounding my home in Scotland has always depended upon my family and their lands. When my father left us, apparently my mother gave him quite a large loan—one she wouldn't allow him to repay. Things began to fall into disrepair. She was so in love with him she neglected everything else. With the money left to me by my father, I can begin to restore the castle, and the village will be prosperous again."

Anna had never met anyone like Ewan MacLaughlin in her entire life. He was more concerned about his "village" than he was about himself.

"I have money," she announced.

He looked as though she had just told him she had a third leg. "What are you saying?"

Yes, what was she saying? Marry me and you can have my fortune? For someone unsure of her feelings, she was certainly talking like she knew what she wanted. Lud, she was practically throwing herself at him!

"Just that if I can help you in any way I will."

He didn't look as relieved as she expected. Was it possible he was just as confused about this . . . this *attraction* between them as she was? Never in her eighteen years had she been so willing to break every rule of society for someone, but she knew without a doubt that she'd dance a barefoot jig on the Prince Regent's supper table if Ewan asked her to.

"Thank you. Your friendship means more to me than you'll ever know." Their eyes locked and right there and then Anna knew that they *both* wanted to be more than friends.

The drawing room door burst open before either of them could say any more. They both jumped to their feet in surprise. Richard stomped into the room, followed by Mrs. Welsley, a mixture of anxiety and anger on his face.

"What are you doing here?" he demanded, pointing an accusing finger at Ewan.

Anna stepped forward, barely containing her own anger. "When did you become master of this house?"

Richard stared at her in shocked surprise. He opened his mouth to speak, but Ewan cut him off.

"I was here looking for you, brother."

Richard pulled himself together, but his expression was still one of shock. "For me?"

An easy smile curved Ewan's lips.

"Yes. Your mother told me where you'd gone and I thought I'd stop by and see if you'd care to accompany me to White's. As soon as I arrived, Miss Welsley told me you'd gone out with Mrs. Welsley and asked if I'd care to wait." He smiled at Anna. "I couldn't refuse my future sister-in-law, now could I?"

He was so convincing even Anna almost believed his story, but then noticed how he kept his hands behind his back and that they were knotted into fists. He did not like to lie, even to someone who sought to publicly destroy him.

Richard seemed to believe him as well. He looked positively sheepish. "I'm afraid I cannot join you at the club. I'm taking Mrs. Welsley out shopping. We just came back because I had forgotten my gloves."

"Then they would be in the dining room," Anna replied coolly. "Not in here."

Richard flushed and her mother sent her a scolding look, but Anna ignored them both. "Come, *Your Grace*. I shall see you to the door." It was petty, she knew, but she had intentionally stressed his title to annoy Richard and her mother.

Ewan offered her his arm. His eyes teased her without his having to say a word. He didn't disapprove of her lack of manners. He was amused by them.

"Good day to you, Mrs. Welsley, Richard."

Both Marion and Richard muttered an inaudible reply.

Anna led Ewan out of the drawing room and through the hall to the front door. Ewan looked around to make sure they weren't being watched before asking, "When will I see you again?"

"Tonight," Anna replied, enjoying the flicker of pleasure and surprise that crossed his handsome face. "Richard invited us to dinner."

Ewan grinned. "Let's hope I'm not to be the main course."

Anna chuckled, raising her gaze to his. The warmth in his eyes caused her heart to skip a beat.

"We have much to discuss," he told her. "Do you think you'll be able to sneak away?"

She didn't like all this secrecy, but knew it was necessary if they were to stay ahead of Richard and her mother's plotting. "I believe I can."

"Good. Until tonight then." He reached down and caught one of her hands, raising it to his lips. Softly, he brushed his mouth across her knuckles, sending a jolt through her entire body.

"Until tonight," she whispered, unable to tear her gaze from his.

He left just as Richard and her mother came into the hall.

"I'm going to go lie down now," she said, hurrying toward the stairs in an effort to escape them both. Despite her conviction that she had done the right thing in going to Ewan, she couldn't help but feel like a traitor.

"Anna!"

She stopped, gathering her strength as Richard bounded toward her.

She raised a questioning brow, but remained silent.

"Anna, dearest," he said, a wounded-puppy expression on his handsome face. "I'm very sorry about my behavior earlier. I hope you will forgive me."

He looked so sincere. Was she wrong about him? No. Underneath that smooth, gentlemanly exterior was a young man who couldn't stand to lose. Had all his sweetness toward her been just another part of the charade? Or did he truly care about her?

And could she honestly marry him now, knowing him as she did?

"I'm not the one you should apologize to, Richard, but yes, I forgive you."

In a pig's eye.

A triumphant smile brightened his face and Anna wondered if everything in his life was about winning. She felt sorry for him if it was.

"Excellent. Now, what are you going to wear tonight? I want to make certain we complement each other."

What difference did it make? Sighing, Anna replied, "I have a handful of new evening gowns. One's a very pretty shade of violet—I thought I'd wear that." Violet was a lovely color on her. She always felt good when she wore it.

Richard smiled. "So you want to look pretty for your special someone, hmm?"

She stared into his smug face and realized just how accurate he was.

"Yes, Richard." She smiled somewhat smugly herself. "I want to look very pretty for him."

Then she turned and started up the stairs, wondering if Ewan liked violet.

Ewan found it remarkably easy to lie to his brother, especially now that he knew his younger sibling was scheming to destroy him. He'd suspected Richard's dislike, and the younger man had admitted to being jealous, but how could he possibly stoop so low as to try to label Ewan illegitimate?

He watched his younger brother from his seat at the head of the dinner table. Richard was all ease and charm as he chatted with Anna and her parents. Only Anna appeared immune to his spell. Fortunately, Richard didn't seem to notice his fiancée's lack of enthusiasm. Ewan didn't want Richard to know they were on to him. Not yet, anyway. He wanted to find out exactly what his brother was up to before letting Richard know he was aware of his plans.

His gaze drifted to Anna and his heart sped up at the sight of her. She was easily the most beautiful girl he'd ever seen. The violet of her silk gown brightened her complexion and made her eyes seem like huge, dark pools. Her thick hair was piled high on her head, with a few wisps hanging down to frame her face. She looked elegant and composed, and when she looked at him, Ewan felt as though he were floating.

And he couldn't even care anymore that she was English. He was learning very quickly that the heart had no prejudice where geography was concerned. It knew no boundaries. His heart was drawn to Anna just as his mother's had been drawn to his father. There was no use fighting it.

But he would fight it because she was engaged to his brother.

"You're awfully quiet this evening, Ewan," Hester remarked as she sliced into the roast quail on her plate. "Are you unwell?"

Tearing his gaze away from Anna's, Ewan smiled at the woman he was quickly coming to think of as his stepmother. "No, ma'am. I'm quite well, I assure you. I was just thinking about the letter my father left for me." Out of the corner of his eye he saw Richard stiffen. It was a cheap shot at the younger man, but it gave Ewan immense satisfaction.

Hester smiled warmly. "Good thoughts, I hope?"

"Yes, ma'am. The best."

Richard's eyes narrowed. "How was your visit to the club?"

Ewan smiled. Obviously his brother hadn't believed his story. "It went very well, thank you, brother. You should join me next time."

Ewan looked as though he would rather swallow glass.

After leaving Anna, Ewan had indeed gone to St. James' Street—to White's—even though that hadn't been his original plan, and met several close acquaintances of his father's. Most had been amazed to discover Ewan's existence, but there had been one man, the Earl of Whitly, who'd been a friend of his father's for years and had known about Ethan's first marriage. He and Ewan talked for several hours and when Ewan finally left the club, he felt as though he had a better understanding of the man his father was. He also felt a deep and biting regret that he'd never had a chance to get to know him.

"I wish I had a club," Emily remarked after swallowing a bite of potato. "Gentlemen get to have all the fun."

"Young ladies have more important things to do than idle away the day at some club," Marion remarked crisply. "Such pursuits would be damaging to the female mind."

From the expression on Emily's face, it was clear she heartily disagreed with Anna's mother, but good manners dictated that she not argue and so she speared another bite of potato with her fork and jammed it into her mouth. Ewan smiled. Apparently he wasn't the only one in the family who needed help holding his tongue.

Taking a sip of his wine, Ewan turned his attention to the food on his plate. He wasn't very hungry but he forced himself to eat anyway. The weight of Richard's stare was heavy upon his shoulders, and Ewan did not want his brother to see that he was not as at ease as he tried to appear.

After dessert, the ladies rose and left the men to their port and cigars. Mr. Welsley was the only one who smoked, and Ewan spent more time staring at the strong wine in his glass than drinking it. He was eager to join the ladies—or at least one lady—in the drawing room and learn what had happened after he'd left the Welsley residence earlier that day.

They said little, as Mr. Welsley rarely spoke at all and every halfhearted attempt by Ewan at conversation was met with an even less enthusiastic and brief response from Richard. Obviously his younger brother was through even trying to pretend he liked him.

Finally, Anna's father finished his cigar and the three of them left the table. When they entered the drawing room, Ewan thought Anna appeared relieved to see them. Her mother was deep in conversation with Hester, and as her loud voice carried across the room, Ewan could tell she was discussing plans for the wedding.

Anna wasn't planning on still going through with it, was she? Could she, now that she knew what Richard was up to? What about him? Could she just turn her back on this . . . this . . . whatever it was between them? For that matter, could he?

Part of him said he should stay as far away from Anna

as possible, that he'd done enough damage to Richard's life already. Another, much larger part said curse Richard, and to pursue Anna with every last ounce of energy he had. He'd never met a girl like her, who liked to read poetry, who enjoyed long walks, and who had so much spirit.

The girls in Glenshea didn't understand him because even though he was half Scottish, he was also half English. They understood that wild and free side of him, but they didn't appreciate his love of books and music. He was certain that Anna understood, and that beneath her ladylike exterior, there was a heart as wild as any Scottish lass. She was his perfect match. He'd felt it from the first moment he saw her.

Instead of going to her as he wanted, Ewan turned toward the piano where Emily sat. He didn't want anyone to notice how eager he was for Anna's attention.

His sister looked up from the sheets of music with a happy smile. Her face was so much like his own—so much like their father's—only softer, prettier. They had formed an instant bond and were already completely at ease with each other.

"You said you could play, didn't you, Ewan?"

"A little," he replied, caressing the polished top of the Broadwood Grand pianoforte. It was exquisite.

Emily leaped up from her seat. "Then you must play for us!"

Caught. He had been well and truly trapped by a

young girl who was tired of playing and singing for company's enjoyment, he could see it in her eyes.

"One song," he informed her with mock severity as Hester and Anna insisted that he play. "I will play one song and then the instrument is yours again, brat."

Smiling at his teasing, Emily skipped off to the sofa where her mother sat and settled upon it like a queen on her throne.

Well, he'd done it now. He hadn't played for an audience in quite some time. Normally he played for his grandmother during winter evenings when there was little else to do but stay inside around the fire where it was warm.

Gently, his fingers trailed along the keyboard playing no one melody in particular until they were nimble and comfortable on the ivory keys. Then, concentrating on the music and not the fact that Anna was watching, he began to play the first song that came into his head.

The music was soft and simple, and as the words came flooding forth, he opened his mouth to give them voice.

"The water is wide, I cannot get o'er. And neither have I wings to fly. Oh, go and get me some little boat to carry o'er my true love and I."

He could feel all eyes on him as his voice rose and fell with the music. He was a fair singer, as music was in his blood just as it ran through the veins of every Scotsman he knew. And as he sang, he thought of Anna, though he dared not look at her.

"Where love is planted, O there it grows. It buds and blossoms like some rose; it has a sweet and pleasant smell. No flow'r on earth can it excel."

Someone cleared their throat. Faintly, a voice rose in conversation—not enough to drown Ewan's out, but just loud enough to let him know that Richard was not impressed with his musical abilities.

Ewan raised his head and saw his brother conversing openly with Anna's mother. It was terribly rude behavior, but Ewan was more amused than anything else. His pride didn't like the insult, however, and so he turned his gaze to Anna and sang the next verse.

"There is a ship sailing on the sea. She's loaded deep as deep can be. But not so deep as in love I am; I care not if I sink or swim."

And Richard, who was so busy trying to humiliate him, didn't even notice the earnest expression on Ewan's face as he sang, or the blush that bloomed on Anna's cheeks as she watched him. For one timeless moment, there were only the two of them in the entire world, and in that moment Ewan knew that neither of them would be able to simply walk away from this thing between them.

Fortunately, no one else seemed to notice how they gazed at each other, or that he was singing for her and her alone. Blast it all, he was going to have to be more careful about hiding his feelings if he didn't want Richard to find out about them.

Somehow he managed to make it through the

remainder of the song and the applause that followed. Only Hester, Emily, and Anna seemed sincere in their enjoyment. Mrs. Welsley and Richard barely clapped at all and glared at him with thinly veiled hostility. Mr. Welsley was sound asleep in a winged-back chair near the fireplace, snoring softly. Ewan smiled. Singing someone to sleep could be considered a compliment, he supposed.

"Who would like to join me at the card table for a game of whist?" Hester piped up, her tone bright. Ewan had no doubt she'd noticed Richard's objectionable behavior and sought to lighten the mood of the party.

His stepmother fixed her attention on her son. "Richard, Mrs. Welsley, won't you join me?"

Mrs. Welsley looked delighted at the prospect of being Richard's partner. "Anna, you will join us." It was a demand, not a request.

Anna shook her head, her pink lips curving in a rueful smile. "Pray, excuse me, Mama. I find I still have a touch of the headache and haven't the concentration for cards tonight. Perhaps Emily would be so good as to take my place?"

Ewan caught her quick sideways glance and instantly stepped forward. "I was just thinking about taking a turn about the garden, Miss Welsley. Would you care to join me?" He lifted his gaze to meet Richard's. His brother's eyes were cold. "That is, if it is all right with you, brother."

There wasn't much Richard could say without making himself look ungracious, and from the tightness of his jaw, he knew it. Ewan smiled sweetly.

"Of course it's fine with me," Richard replied, his tone stiff. "Don't stay out too long, Anna dearest. It looks as though it might rain."

It looked no such thing, but Ewan took the remark as the veiled warning it was. Giving his brother a sharp nod, he offered his arm to Anna. She rose to her feet and laid her hand upon his forearm, sparing not even a glance for her fiancé. Out of the corner of his eye, Ewan saw Richard frown. They would have to be very careful with how they treated Richard, lest he discover that Anna had betrayed his confidence by telling Ewan of his plans.

Outside, the night air was warm, if not a little damp. The scent of roses and jasmine wafted on the breeze, filling Ewan's lungs with the sweet, heady scent.

They were silent as they walked down the low steps from the terrace to the grounds below. The gravel path crunched beneath their feet—the only sound in the otherwise silent garden.

"He's becoming suspicious," Ewan announced once they were a safe distance from the house. "We must be careful, or he'll realize you've told me what he's up to."

Anna nodded, her delicate features grim in the moonlight. "It's just so hard to pretend. I find it difficult to pretend my feelings toward him haven't changed."

"You're not still planning to marry him, are you?" Ewan's heart twisted at the thought.

She shook her head, tendrils of hair sweeping her shoulders. "I don't know. My parents are very desirous of the match, but . . . there's no way I can marry a man I neither love nor respect."

Ewan hadn't realized he'd been holding his breath until it came rushing out of his lungs in a sigh of relief. "Surely they wouldn't force you to go through with the marriage if your feelings have altered so drastically?" He couldn't imagine any parents being so cruel. No, that was untrue. He could very well see Mrs. Welsley behaving in such a manner. Mr. Welsley might actually stay awake long enough to put up a fight where his only daughter was concerned, however. And he couldn't imagine anyone forcing Anna to do something she didn't want to.

Anna's eyes were wide and filled with regret as her gaze met his. "He wasn't always like this, you know. When we first met, he was different. Very kind and very charming. I was flattered by his attention."

This was not what Ewan wanted to hear. He didn't want to know that Richard was capable of being nice and kind. He didn't want to feel sorry for his brother, and he certainly didn't want to feel any more guilt where Richard was concerned.

She stared straight ahead as they drifted along the winding path. "He was always so attentive. He's always been stiff and proper, and very proud of his social station, but I'd never seen this conniving, greedy side of his nature before. Not until—"

"Not until me," Ewan supplied.

Her head whipped around to face him. "I was going to say that it wasn't until his—*your*—father's death that I first truly noticed it." She looked away again. "The idea of becoming the duke consumed him. It became all he thought of, the prospect of finally filling his father's shoes. Then he found out about you."

Ewan's stomach clenched, as did his jaw. "If I'd known . . ."

"But you didn't. How could you have?" Anna stopped walking and seized one of his hands in her much smaller ones. "Ewan, nothing that has happened is your fault. Richard alone is responsible for his behavior. You can't blame yourself for his deceit and greed."

He stared down at her earnest face. Her eyes were nearly black in the darkness. The icy light of the moon made her skin glow with a heavenly light, and her mouth . . . her mouth was so perfect and pink.

He wanted to kiss her. He *needed* to kiss her.

"And you're certain you don't love him anymore?" His voice was hoarse.

Anna shook her head, her expression somewhat sorrowful. "I'm not certain I've ever known what love is."

Ewan's heart sagged at her words. What did he expect?

That she'd toss his brother aside with one breath and declare her love for him with another? Of course she couldn't do that. It was unfeeling of him to expect it.

"Ewan?" The question was a timid one.

He stopped walking and turned to her. "Yes?"

Her eyes were wide and questioning. "Have you ever truly cared about a young lady before?"

His poor heart burst with the desire to tell her how he felt, but he couldn't find the words to describe it. How did you tell someone it hurt to breathe when she was near? That your heart ached at the mere thought of her? How could he say such things and make Anna understand that such agony was the sweetest thing he'd ever experienced?

So Ewan didn't even try to use words. In fact, he didn't say anything at all. He simply smiled.

And then he pulled her close and did what he'd been dying to do ever since the last time he'd kissed her.

He kissed her again.

CHAPTER SEVEN

Locked in Ewan's warm embrace, Anna felt as though she was floating. Her hand pressed against the broad expanse of his chest, and beneath the layers of his clothing, she could vaguely feel the beating of his heart against her palm. It was racing, just like her own.

Her body tingled where it touched his, as though electricity flowed between them. His warmth wrapped around her, and the scent of him filled her nostrils. He smelled of the freshness of soap, with just the slightest hint of spice from whatever he shaved with. It made her dizzy, it smelled so good.

Oh, she could get used to kissing him. In fact, she could happily spend the rest of her life testing that very theory. His breath was sweet; his lips were soft and warm. Anna's arms snaked around his neck, so he wouldn't pull away before she was ready to release him. And when his arms tightened around her, she felt as though they were the only two people in the world.

But they weren't.

"An-*na!*" It came from a distance, but still too close for comfort.

Blast it all.

She stiffened. Ewan went completely still in her arms. He lifted his head, and she missed the feel of his lips on hers.

"It's Richard," he whispered, dropping his hands from her waist.

Anna nodded. "Must have been a quick game of whist." She lowered her arms to her sides. "Shall we hide, or shall we face him?" She was all for hiding.

Ewan smiled. What a beautiful mouth he had! "I think we ought to face him. After all, it might be something important."

Linking arms, they walked in the direction of Richard's voice, his calls growing louder with each step. Finally, they found him by the fountain.

He did not look happy to see them.

"Did you not hear me calling?" he demanded as they leisurely strolled toward him.

"We heard," Ewan replied. "And we came. Now what the devil is the matter that you had to come out here cater-wauling like a fishmonger?"

Anna bit her lip to keep from giggling. Richard had rather sounded like someone calling out for people to buy fish in a market.

Richard's expression darkened. "I've come to fetch Anna." He turned to her and she struggled to put on a straight face. "Your mother has come down with a sudden and severe megrim and wishes to return home at once. She asked me to find you." He shot an accusatory glance at Ewan.

Megrim, my foot, Anna thought, mentally rolling her eyes. Her mother rarely suffered from headaches. Most likely her mother and Richard couldn't stand her being alone with Ewan for more than five minutes and had concocted the scheme to separate them. Little did they know that both Anna and Ewan were well aware of their schemes and wouldn't be fooled.

"Then I will return at once," Anna replied. There was no reason for her to remain behind—except for Ewan, and she doubted they'd manage to be alone again that evening.

Richard offered his arm with an expectant gaze.

Reluctantly, Anna pulled her arm free of Ewan's. Richard was still her fiancé, regardless of how confused she was about her feelings. She placed her hand on Richard's forearm, and pretended not to notice the smug look he directed at his brother.

As they walked back to the house, Anna could feel the heat of Ewan's gaze burning into her back. Knowing he was watching her was enough to raise goose bumps on her arms and shoulders. A thrilling shiver raced down her spine.

"Are you cold?" Richard asked.

She shook her head, not trusting her voice at that moment. Cold? Oh no, she wasn't cold. In fact, she was rather warm. Warm with memories of Ewan's arms holding her and how her heart had hammered wildly as he kissed her. Had it affected him so deeply as well? She was tempted just to turn around and ask him and put an end to this pretending, but she knew it would be a mistake.

Surely Ewan wouldn't kiss her if he didn't care about her? But Richard kissed her sometimes as well, and she didn't know the depths of his feelings either. Oh, what a mess! Caught between two brothers, both so different, and not sure which one was the right one for her.

She cared about Richard, she really did. She just wasn't certain how deeply. She hated thinking he would deliberately set out to ruin Ewan, but she couldn't deny her suspicions.

And she was coming to care about Ewan. Very much so. In fact, if she wasn't careful, she feared her infatuation with the young duke would quickly turn into something more. What she felt for him was something wild and uncontrollable. Her knees were like jelly whenever he was near, and her heart pounded like the hooves of a dozen racehorses. Was it love?

The thought startled her. Was she falling in love with Ewan? She couldn't be. Could she? Oh dear, it was certainly going to make a mess of things if she was.

Her mother and father were still in the drawing room when they entered the house. Her father sat beside her mother, simply holding her hand. Her mother had a cold compress held to her forehead as she lounged on a green velvet sofa like a woman on the verge of death itself. Only the furious glitter in her eyes revealed her as the actress that she was.

At that moment, Anna realized how much she'd come to dislike her mother.

As they left the room, Anna was once again on Richard's arm. It was he who took her light shawl from Peters and placed it around her shoulders. He pressed a chaste kiss against her cheek. It immediately reminded Anna of the passionate embrace she and Ewan had shared in the garden, and as she gazed into Richard's warm blue eyes, guilt washed over her.

She had no business kissing Ewan when she was engaged to his brother. She had betrayed her fiancé's trust—first by going behind his back to warn Ewan of his plans, and second by kissing another man. She should be heartily ashamed of herself.

But she wasn't. She wasn't nearly as ashamed as she should be.

They said their good-byes, Anna being careful not to put more feeling into Ewan's than anyone else's. She hated this pretending. She was so worried she was going to make a mistake, say something she shouldn't. Ewan didn't look nervous at all. In fact, he treated her as though she were nothing more than his brother's betrothed. If she didn't know better, she wouldn't have thought he cared for her at all.

"What the devil were you about, girl, going out into the garden alone with that barbarian?" her mother snapped as soon as they were seated in their carriage and rolling down the lane. "He could have taken advantage of your innocence, or God only knows what else."

Anna arched a brow. "I see your megrim has miraculously cured itself."

Her mother had the good grace to blush. "Don't change the subject. Do you want to risk ruining everything with the duke?"

"*Ewan* is the duke, Mama." Lord, but she was getting tired of reminding her mother of that fact!

Marion scowled. "He mostly certainly is not! And Richard's going to prove it."

"Oh?" Anna tried to make her expression as innocent as possible. "And just how does my fiancé plan to do that?"

Her mother clammed up like a miser's purse. "I'm not at liberty to say."

Not at liberty to say? Not at liberty to say! Obviously Richard already harbored some suspicions about her relationship with Ewan if he'd sworn her mother to secrecy.

Which raised the question, if Richard didn't trust her, then why did he want to marry her? He certainly didn't need to marry her, unless he was keeping both her and her fortune nearby just in case he couldn't prove

Ewan illegitimate. Could he possibly be that greedy? He had enough money of his own without adding hers to it.

Could it be Richard actually cared about her? Why didn't he tell her? Why didn't he make her feel like Ewan did?

Anna leaned back against the seat. "Fine," she said as the carriage hit a rut in the road, knocking her teeth together with the impact. "I'll just ask Richard what his plan is. Then he'll know that you've spoken about it in front of me before."

Her mother's reaction was not what she'd hoped for. Marion's hand whipped out and caught Anna's upper arm in a viselike grip.

"Ow!" Anna turned to her father for help, but he was sound asleep in the corner.

"You'll do no such thing!" her mother warned, her voice low and trembling. "I will not allow you to ruin all my hopes."

"Your hopes?" Her mother was cutting off the flow of blood in her arm, but Anna was too angry to care. "What about *my* hopes, Mama? Or do you even care what I want?"

The older woman seemed surprised by the question. Her eyes narrowed. "Are you telling me you've changed your mind about marrying Richard? Because it's a little late for that now, missy. You're going to marry him and that's that."

Oh no, she wasn't! And she was very tempted to tell

her mother that too, but somehow Anna managed to hold her tongue.

"You want to have a duke for a son-in-law so badly that you'd resort to threatening your own daughter? What's happened to you, Mama? I used to be more to you than something you could sell to the highest bidder."

Marion's expression softened, as did her hold on her daughter's arm. Anna gasped at the rush that tingled through her veins.

"It's because I love you that I want to see you well matched." Marion pouted. "Is it such a crime for a mother to want to see her daughter married to a peer of the realm?"

Sighing, Anna shook her head. "I think every mother would like to see her daughter married to someone in the higher ranks of society, but Mama, you're trying to ruin another man's life in order to get it!"

Marion waved a gloved hand. "Oh, pish. He already has one title; he's certainly not going to miss this one."

"But he'll miss—" She caught herself before she could blurt out "money."

Her mother jumped on it like a cat on a bowl of cream. "He'll miss *what?*"

"The . . . the connection to his father," Anna lied. "The title is all he has to remember him by."

Again her mother was unmoved. "I'm sure Hester would give him a portrait of the late duke, or some other token."

Anna stared at her mother, aghast. "You really don't

care that Richard is planning to ruin him, do you?"

Marion shrugged. "Why should I? The lad's nothing to me. Besides, Richard's confident that his father was not married to the Scot's mother, so he'd only be taking what's rightfully his anyway."

"Does Richard have any proof to support his claim?"

Her mother's lips tightened. "I'm not at liberty to say."

But Anna hid her smile. Her mother had told her enough. Richard didn't have any proof. Not yet. And he wasn't going to find any, of that she was certain. Ewan's parents had been married, even Hester said so.

So what would Richard do when he learned that? Would he leave Ewan alone?

Or would he try to find another way to destroy his brother?

Richard's door closed with a soft thud. Inside his room, his own door open just enough so that he could see into the hall, Ewan watched as his brother strode down the corridor toward the stairs.

Early as usual. Over the past few days, Ewan had learned that his brother liked to be early for everything— it tended to make others feel bad for keeping him waiting. No doubt Richard would be early for his own funeral if he could manage it.

But tonight, his brother's punctuality would be to Ewan's advantage. He still had a good fifteen minutes before the family was to gather in the drawing room to depart for Lady Markby's ball. It wasn't much, but it would allow him to do a quick search of Richard's rooms before they left.

He crept out the door and jogged down the hall so quietly that even he could barely hear his feet hit the carpet. Richard's door was unlocked and Ewan slipped inside, closing it again behind him.

Richard's room was fastidiously clean. Not even so much as a neckcloth or pair of stockings littered the intricately designed carpet. Not a wrinkle marred the bedspread on the high four-poster bed.

It was unnerving, really. What twenty-year-old bachelor kept his rooms so tidy? It just wasn't natural. There should at least be a pair of stockings lying about. Then again, Richard seemed to thrive on order. It was hardly normal for a young man that age to be engaged either. Usually men waited until their mid or late twenties before even contemplating the idea. Of course, for a girl like Anna, Ewan would gladly give up his bachelorhood as well, and he was only four years older than his brother.

Did Richard love her? Was he capable of such emotion? It was shameful for Ewan to think such uncharitable thoughts of his brother, but he couldn't help it. Richard was not equipped to give Anna the kind of life she deserved.

And you are? a voice inside his head asked. *What are you going to do, take her back to a crumbling castle and hand her a hammer?*

Why, yes. If she wished it.

But other than the fact that she responded to his kisses with a passion that matched his own, Ewan had no indication that Anna harbored any deep feelings for him. True, she'd warned him about Richard, but that could be the actions of a guilty conscience. It didn't mean she'd toss Richard aside for him. And it didn't mean she'd follow him back to Glenshea either.

He'd already sent word home to his grandmother telling her to begin the necessary repairs. He wasn't about to allow Richard to stand in the way of them either. Mr. Chumley had assured him that barring any unforeseeable circumstances, the accounts would soon be changed over into his name.

Which brought him back to why he was in his brother's room to begin with. He had only twelve minutes left.

He crossed the carpet to the desk and began going through papers on the top. Nothing.

He searched the drawers. Nothing there either.

"Come on, Richard," Ewan muttered, closing the last drawer. "Reveal yourself." Only four minutes before he had to meet the others downstairs.

Then he spotted it. The wastepaper basket actually had sheets of parchment in it. Ewan grabbed one and held it up to the lamp so he could read. It was a rough draft of a letter.

Dear Mr. MacCormack:
I am writing to you as the executor of the estate of the
late Ethan Fitzgerald, Duke of Brahm. . . ."

Ewan's temper surged. "What a liar!" he seethed. Only his brother would dare write to the clergyman in Ewan's hometown and pretend to be someone else.

It is of utmost importance for the settlement
of the late duke's will that I receive a copy
of the certificate of marriage between him and one
Maureen MacLaughlin, believed to have been married by
you in September of 1795. . . ."

Believed to have been married? They *were* married! Ewan had a copy of the certificate himself. His mother had kept it, right along with a copy of his birth certificate. Richard could have saved himself an awful lot of trouble if he'd just asked Ewan to produce proof of his legitimacy.

A door closed down the hall. Startled, Ewan checked his watch. Blast it! He was late.

Smoothing the paper on the desktop, he folded it into a small square and slipped it inside his coat. He might need it later, just in case Richard did manage stir up trouble.

Ewan was just about to leave when he spotted another slip of paper sticking out of a book on top of Richard's desk. Quickly, carefully, he opened the pages and lifted the parchment to the light.

> *My Dear Lord Richard. I trust you have not forgotten that I have in my possession your vowels for the amount of £5,000. Please reply in writing as to when you might be able to settle this debt.*

A gambling debt? Five thousand pounds was a lot of money to owe someone. And it wasn't the only such letter hidden within the book. There were several others of a similar nature, only the amounts ranged from smaller amounts to one of almost ten thousand pounds—more than most people earned in an entire year. In fact, the amounts of his brother's debts could feed and clothe every one of Ewan's tenants for several years.

So this was why his brother wanted the title so badly. It wasn't purely out of filial devotion. He needed the income that came with it. Lord only knew how many other debts Richard had. Was it possible he couldn't pay them all, even with his generous inheritance? If so, it would certainly explain his increasing animosity toward Ewan.

He tucked the notes back into the book and closed it, making certain it was just the way he'd found it. This required some further investigation, but it shouldn't be too difficult to discover how deeply his brother was in debt.

Ewan checked his watch. Blast! If he didn't hurry, someone might very well come looking for him.

He went to the door and opened it a notch. All clear.

Slipping out into the hall, he tugged on the cuffs of his black evening coat to get the wrinkles out and strode toward the stairs. He couldn't wait to show Anna what he'd found. He couldn't wait to see her again.

Not a day went by that he didn't think of her. It had been two days since he'd last seen her and he'd felt the loss painfully. He didn't really care for London and all its hustle and bustle. Anna had been the bright spot in the entire trip.

So to pass the days, he'd spent hours in his father's study, reading over the books for the estates that Ewan now owned. His mother's money had helped his father become a fantastically wealthy man. Pride had kept Ewan's family from telling Ethan how much their own circumstances had been lowered, and from accepting repayment when it was offered.

There was such a thing as too much pride.

Emily and Richard were in the drawing room when he entered.

"You're late," Richard remarked, with a glance at his pocket watch. Why was he making such a great show of flashing the watch around? Then Ewan realized the watch had been their father's and Richard wanted him to notice.

"Lovely watch," he remarked.

Richard smiled smugly. "It is, isn't it? It was Father's."

"I know. I have a gold one almost exactly like it at home. He had the date of his marriage to my mother engraved on it." Why he felt the need to make the dig, he wasn't certain. He shouldn't be giving his brother more reasons to despise him, but Ewan couldn't help it. He hated that Richard thought himself so much better than him.

Richard's smile faded. "We should be going."

"What about your mother?" Hester hadn't joined them yet.

"She's not coming," Emily informed him with a sad smile. "She said she's not ready to face society just yet. Anna's agreed to chaperone me in her stead."

Her reply shocked Ewan somewhat—not that Hester didn't feel like going out so soon after the death of her husband, but that Anna would act as chaperone to Emily. Why, the two girls were practically the same age! But Anna was engaged to be married, and that made a difference in the eyes of society.

"And, of course, you'll be there to chaperone us all," his sister chirped.

That was even more startling than her previous remark. Ewan was used to looking after his land and tenants, but being responsible for a family was something altogether different. And he was responsible for Hester and Emily—

even Richard. It was his duty.

So what was he going to do with Richard, then? Even more daunting was what to do with the scores of suitors Emily was sure to attract. They would be coming to him with marriage proposals. How the devil was he supposed to deal with that?

"Ewan? Are you unwell?"

He gazed down into his sister's worried face and smiled. "I'm fine. I just realized that I'm going to have to deal with all the young men who fall madly in love with you. I'm terrified."

Emily giggled. "Richard will help you. Won't you, Richard?"

Richard's nod was sharp. "Certainly. I won't have you married off to just anyone." His jaw was tight as his challenging gaze met his brother's.

"We're in perfect agreement," Ewan replied, smiling at Richard's surprise. Ewan wondered for a moment, if it weren't for the title, if it weren't for all the animosity, if he and his brother might have been friends.

"I've never had a sister," Ewan continued with a warm glance at Emily. "I fear I'm going to need all the help I can get."

Emily hugged his arm. "You have no idea."

Ewan laughed.

Clearing his throat, Richard consulted his watch again. "We really must be on our way. I told Anna we'd come for her at quarter past. We're going to be late."

And Richard hated to be late almost as much as he hated clutter, Ewan would bet.

The butler met them in the foyer with their outerwear. Taking his top hat and coat, Ewan thanked the elderly man and waited for his siblings before exiting to the carriage. He told himself it was only polite, but a part of him knew the truth. After finding that letter in Richard's room, he wanted to keep his brother where he could see him.

Anna had never been so uncomfortable in her life.

The Fitzgerald carriage was large and roomy enough for four average-sized people to sit comfortably, but Ewan was bigger than average. He had to remove his hat to keep it from getting crushed against the roof. He couldn't stretch his legs out because Anna and Richard were in the way, and he had to keep his arms tucked in close around him just to give Emily breathing room.

Obviously he was uncomfortable as well, but Anna's discomfort stemmed not so much from a lack of room, but from her keen awareness of the man sitting across from her, and the wish that she was in Emily's seat instead of sitting next to Richard.

No, if Anna was sitting beside him it would be impossible to keep from touching him. Perhaps it was just as well, for how could she touch him and still hide her feelings from Richard?

But sitting directly across from Ewan was no easier. It made it difficult to pay attention to conversation—to anything other than him, if truth be told. She stared at his shoes, at the long trousers he favored over formal knee breeches. They were becoming more and more fashionable, but only a man with his title could get away with wearing them at one of Lady Markby's gatherings. The viscountess was very big on old-school formality.

She tried staring at his chest, to avoid looking at his face, but all she could think about was how solid and warm it had felt beneath her hands that night he'd kissed her in the garden. Warmth flooded her cheeks and she lifted her gaze.

He was watching her with an expression so intense Anna found it difficult to breathe.

Oh it was awful, this desperate pounding of her heart, the quickness of her breath. Awful and fierce and oh so very sweet! She both dreaded and looked forward to it. It felt as though a thousand butterflies had been released inside her chest and the feeling made her panicked and overjoyed at the same time.

She opened her mouth to speak, knowing that if they were going to stare at each other they should at least say something so Richard and Emily wouldn't notice their strange behavior.

"Have you met Lady Markby before, Your Grace?" she asked.

"Yes," he replied in the same bland tone she'd used. "I've had that pleasure."

"You won't think it's a pleasure after this evening," Emily joined in cheerfully. "She'll try to have you married to one of her daughters before the night is out."

Anna swallowed against the lump in her throat. Lady Markby's daughters were lovely, petite blondes with blue eyes and perfect figures—very fashionable. Anna felt like a hulking, shapeless brown lump next to them.

Ewan had already danced with the youngest at a previous party. He hadn't seemed taken with her, but she wasn't the prettiest of the Markby daughters. The oldest, Kara, was. If she set her cap for Ewan and batted those big eyes of hers at him, would Ewan fall under her spell like every other young man seemed to?

She couldn't bear to watch if he did.

Ewan raised a brow. Could he see her anxiety?

"Lady Markby can try, but I believe I still have the final say in whom I marry." Something in his voice made Anna's entire body flush with warmth. Her fear subsided somewhat.

"The Markby chits are fine-looking girls," Richard remarked. "And their looks are the least of their attributes, brother. They all have fine dowries too."

It was an innocent enough statement, but somehow Richard managed to make it sound like an insult.

"I have no need for more money," Ewan reminded him.

His voice was light, but his eyes were dark with emotion. His expression was guarded while Richard's was goading. This, Anna decided, was the difference between a man and a boy. Ewan was a man.

Richard shrugged. "One never has enough money."

Anna glanced at him out of the corner of her eye, an earlier suspicion returning. She had an impressive dowry as well. Was that her deciding virtue? That she could expand Richard's fortune?

"The only thing a person can never have too much of is common sense," Ewan replied dryly. Richard took the insult as he was meant to and flushed a dark red. Thankfully, he said nothing.

Poor Emily glanced back and forth between her brothers in confusion. She had no idea what was going on but was very distressed by the situation.

"Why are the two of you being so hateful to each other?" she cried, her eyes filling with tears. "You're supposed to be brothers! Papa would hate to see you treating each other so badly."

Ewan's expression was sheepish. Since he was sitting right beside her, he wrapped his left arm around his sister's shoulders and pulled her against his chest. Richard reached forward and took both of her hands in his. For the first time since Ewan's arrival, the three of them looked like a family. Maybe there was hope for them yet.

Anna watched in fascination as both Ewan and

Richard apologized to Emily. They fussed over her and teased her at their own expense until she smiled and was happy again. Anna could only imagine what a difficult time her friend was going through. She'd just lost her father, was trying to mourn him in the way he'd requested—by not mourning him—and the bad feelings between her brothers would only make that loss worse.

They arrived at Lady Markby's Mayfair address at the same time a dozen other carriages did. The wait to climb out of the carriage and enter the house was longer than the actual drive as they sat in silence as the carriages ahead of them emptied and pulled away.

A footman opened the carriage door and assisted Emily and Anna to the ground. Ewan and Richard followed.

The night air was cool and Anna knew the breeze would be much welcomed as it drifted through Lady Markby's ballroom, especially since the lady had an annoying tendency to pack as many people as she could into her parties. They'd be lucky if there was even room to breathe. And with that many people in one room, the odors one breathed weren't always pleasant, even less so when some of society had yet to embrace the fashion of regular bathing.

Ewan escorted Emily, and Anna had to pull back on Richard's arm so he'd remember his place and allow his brother and sister to lead the way into the house. Richard seemed to have a hard time remembering that his brother was the duke and therefore he went first. Whether his faulty memory was intentional or not, Anna didn't want to know.

Inside the mansion, footmen took their hats and coats, and they made their way up the broad, winding staircase to where the ballroom was.

They were announced, and as heads turned to catch a glimpse of the new Duke of Brahm, they stepped inside. Anna felt Richard tense beside her. La, but it must sting to see his brother garner the attention he believed rightfully his.

They entered the ballroom. The chatter rose up like a dull roar around them, matching the sounds of the orchestra, hidden behind swaths of mauve gauze and silk in the far corner of the room. Ladies walked by dressed in the height of fashion, bright splashes of color in contrast to the gentlemen in formal black and white.

"It's beautiful." Emily gasped, gazing around at the sparkling decorations that reflected the light from the countless chandeliers just as brightly as the glittering diamonds and gems adorning the two hundred guests.

"Not half so lovely as you and Miss Welsley, sprite," Ewan replied with a grin. Anna blushed, even though his words were meant to be taken lightly.

Richard glanced at her. "Are you all right, darling?

You look rather flushed."

Anna's blush deepened as she realized Ewan heard his brother's question. He had to know his remark was what made her pinken in the first place.

"I'm f-fine, thank you, Richard. It's a trifle warm in here, isn't it?"

"Would you like me to fetch you some lemonade?"

Anna made a face. She'd rather drink dishwater than Lady Markby's lemonade. It was even worse than that vile stuff they served at Almack's—if such a thing was possible. "No, thank you. I'll be fine."

Some of the concern left his expression, but Richard's gaze was still far more scrutinizing than Anna liked. "Then you won't take offense if I leave you for a few moments to speak with an acquaintance?"

Offense? She'd be glad to see him go, if only for five minutes so that she might collect herself.

"Of course not. Lord Brahm and Emily will keep me company."

To his credit, Richard's expression didn't change when she referred to his brother by the title he so desperately wanted as his own. "I shall be back shortly. Save me the first waltz."

And then he was gone. And within minutes, a handsome young man came by to ask Ewan's permission to dance with Emily and was granted his wish, leaving Anna alone with the man who had occupied her thoughts constantly for the past two days.

She couldn't think of anything to say, and just staring at him made her feel like an idiot.

"I'm feeling a little overheated myself," he remarked. "Would you care to take a walk to one of the windows, Miss Welsley?"

Anna glanced up. To one of the windows? Yes, that would be lovely. There was hardly anyone along that wall and it would be the most comfortable place to stand. It would also give them some privacy to talk while remaining in plain view of the entire room. Utterly proper behavior. She wouldn't be tempted to let him kiss her in front of a window.

"I would love to, Your Grace. Thank you."

They picked their way through the crowd easily, as everyone stepped out of Ewan's path. Whispers followed them across the room. Some remarked upon how the old duke had kept his son a secret. Others commented on how much he looked like his father. A few women tittered over how handsome he was. Anna wanted to tell them to mind their own business, but she didn't.

When they'd arrived safely at their destination, Ewan plucked two glasses of champagne off a passing footman's tray and handed her one. "I'm not much for alcohol," he explained, "but I hear drinking Mrs. Markby's lemonade is akin to taking one's life in one's hands."

Anna laughed, enjoying the soft breeze that blew in

through the open window, tickling the hair on her nape. "You heard correctly. " She sipped the champagne. Bubbles tickled her nose.

"I found something tonight that you might find interesting."

She met his gaze, all humor gone. "Oh, what?"

"A letter Richard wrote to the man who married my parents. He told the man he was our father's executor and that he needed a copy of their marriage certificate."

Anna gasped. She'd known what Richard was up to, but even she could not believe he'd stoop to such a deception! "What—" She lowered her voice. "What are you going to do?"

Ewan shrugged his broad shoulders. "Nothing. All Richard is going to receive is proof that my parents were indeed married. I could have given him that. Once he discovers that they were wed, and long before my birth, he'll have to give up this silly idea of proving me illegitimate."

He sounded so sure, so confident, but Anna wasn't so convinced. Her fears from two nights ago came rushing back with frightening intensity. Richard would not give up so easily. She knew him well enough to know that for sure.

"I found out something else as well," Ewan murmured.

Good heavens, as though discovering his own brother

wanted to prove him a fraud wasn't enough!

"What?" Anna was amazed she could even manage to speak. As it was her voice sounded like a door on a rusty hinge.

He steered her away from the window, as though worried someone might actually be on the other side listening.

"My brother has gambling debts. Rather *large* debts."

Anna knew she shouldn't be surprised, but she was. Her blood turned to ice water in her veins. She knew it. She knew there had to be another reason why Richard was in such a hurry to marry her. She knew there had to be more to it than affection, and now she was fairly certain that her fortune was a big part of it. What kind of trouble was Richard in?

A shiver ran down her spine when she thought of some of the stories she'd heard about men on the verge of financial ruin—or "dun territory," as many of the *ton* referred to it.

"Be careful, Ewan," she said softly, laying a tentative hand on his sleeve. "If Richard truly is deeply in debt, he might become desperate." And desperate men did desperate things to achieve their goals.

Ewan smiled, a smile that made her heart ache. "Anna, he can't do anything. Trust me."

Anna nodded. She could do that. She could trust him if not her own fiancé.

* * *

Outside, in the cool night air, Richard Fitzgerald stood deep in the shadows near an open window. An inch of ash clung to the tip of the cigar he'd forgotten about the minute he'd heard his name, spoken in his brother's voice, float out the window toward him.

Too bad they'd moved away from the window. He hadn't been able to hear their entire conversation. But he had heard some of it, and that was enough.

So Ewan had gone snooping, had he? Richard would have to be more careful in the future. As soon as he returned home, he'd destroy the other letters in the waste-bin in his room. He'd destroy any others he did not send from now on as well.

He wasn't all that surprised his brother was suspicious of him. As much as Richard hated it, they were related. It only made sense that they would have some kind of under-standing of each other. Ewan knew Richard resented him, just as Richard knew Ewan had fallen in love with Anna. No one else seemed to notice, but to Richard, it was as plain as porridge. Ewan wanted Anna as badly as Richard needed the title.

As for Anna, he supposed her duplicity would hurt more if he actually loved her, but instead her lack of loyalty only made him angry—and sad. He would have thought better of her, that she wouldn't fall for a pair of bright eyes and broad shoulders quite so easily. It hardly mattered, however. He needed Anna. He needed her fortune if he was going to pay his debts and maintain his lifestyle.

He hadn't meant for the situation to slip so far out of his control. He never set out to lose so much money; he just kept playing, hoping his luck would get better. There was always the chance he might win and so he kept betting—on horses, dogs, boxing, anything. Sometimes he won, but when he lost . . .

He wouldn't be in this mess if not for his father's betrayal. Richard had spent his entire life expecting to be duke. Everyone expected it—especially his creditors. They were more than willing to let him run up vast bills for boots and coats and trousers when they thought he was going to inherit the title. Now they weren't so keen on extending his bills. Now they wanted money. He'd even gone to a moneylender to borrow enough to keep the vultures happy. Now he needed even more money to pay the lender's high interest.

His inheritance from his father would pay them, but it would leave him nothing to live off of. That was why he needed to marry Anna. With her dowry and a share of her father's business he would be able to continue living in the style he required. He would save his reputation and keep the moneylenders from coming after their pound of flesh.

He and Anna's mother had an agreement. Anna would marry him and there was very little Ewan could do about that. Richard didn't doubt Anna would do as she was expected. She was a good girl, if naive. All he had to do was spend some more time with her, charm her a bit, and her heart would be his again.

But what to do about his brother? There was no way Ewan deserved that title more than he did. Just because he was the oldest did not mean he was cut out to be the Duke of Brahm. Richard had been preparing his whole life to be the duke and no . . . no *stranger* was going to take it away from him.

But first things first. He would have to destroy all the evidence of what he'd been up to. And then he'd have to think of a new plan.

A new plan to get rid of his brother.

CHAPTER EIGHT

His brother was suspicious. Ewan could tell by the way Richard looked at him as he crossed the floor to where he and Anna stood. Richard's "brief" conversation had turned into an hour. It was very shabby of him to leave Anna so long.

"Please forgive me for being gone so long, my dear," Richard said, taking Anna's hand. Ewan's instinct was to push him away, to tell him not to touch her, but Richard was still her betrothed and any interference from Ewan would only cause trouble. "Something of an urgent nature has arisen and I have to leave."

"Leave?" Anna echoed, her voice high with surprise and disappointment. And for one foolish moment, Ewan wondered if she was sorry to leave him, or if it was Richard she would miss. "But we just arrived."

Richard's shrewd, dark gaze met Ewan's. "There is no need for all of us to leave. I'm sure Ewan wouldn't mind remaining with you and Emily."

"Of course I wouldn't," Ewan replied, holding his brother's stare. "Do what you must do, brother." Why did everything he and Richard say to each other come out sounding like threats or warnings? It was stupid and childish of them.

"I shall see you tomorrow then, Anna dear." Richard brushed a quick kiss across Anna's cheek and Ewan's jealousy rose. His brother was goading him, he was sure of it. Richard wanted to make him angry. He wanted to mark Anna as his territory. He was telling his brother that he might have the title, but Richard had the girl, and that Ewan had better keep his hands to himself where Anna was concerned.

Not a chance.

"Don't stay out too late," Richard said softly to Anna. "You know how you get when you're overtired."

Anna's expression clearly said no, she didn't know how she got when she was "overtired" and that she didn't think Richard knew either, but she didn't press the subject. "I won't. Good night, Richard."

When he was gone, Anna turned to Ewan. "What do you suppose he's up to?"

"I haven't a clue," he replied honestly. "And I really don't care. All I know is that I can finally tell you how beautiful you look this evening without worrying about my brother overhearing or seeing your reaction."

Her reaction, of course, was a deep rosy blush. She glanced away. "You really shouldn't say such things."

"Why not? It's true. You're beautiful." He fought the urge to stroke her cheek, but if any of the dancers floating by them, or any of the numerous bystanders, happened to see, it would cause a scandal, and he had no desire to drag Anna or his family into a scandal just because he couldn't keep his hands to himself.

"Do you really think so?"

He nodded, his heart touched by the uncertainty in her voice. Did Richard never tell her how lovely she was? Lord, he'd gone from a boy who never wanted to marry, to a man who'd found a woman he could gladly spend the rest of his life with—and it was all because of Anna. She was more than just beautiful to him. She was the only woman in the world as far as he was concerned. It didn't matter that she was English.

"Dance with me." He didn't bother to wait for her reply before leading her by the hand out onto the dance floor. It was a waltz—the only way he could hold her and not have tongues wagging about it the next day.

Her hand went to his bicep. One of his went to her waist; the other caught her free hand and lifted it high. Even though he wanted nothing more than to crush her against him, he made certain he kept the required twelve inches between their bodies.

Stupid rule.

"I've finished the Byron," he told her once they were caught up in the flood of other dancers.

Her eyes lit up. In the soft light of the chandeliers, they were almost black. "Really? Did you enjoy it?"

"Very much. He's very . . . passionate." Passionate didn't even begin to describe some of Byron's work, but it certainly stirred the senses.

Another blush. "Yes. Byron is no stranger to the stronger emotions."

Ewan didn't bother to comment that Byron's "stronger emotions" were what had led to his self-exile from England two years ago. Lord Byron was now living somewhere on the eastern side of Europe, indulging in whatever sins he saw fit. Whatever the man chose to do with his personal life was his business. Ewan might not agree with it, but it didn't change the fact that Byron was still a gifted poet.

"I love poetry," she admitted. "Most girls my age can't stand it. They'd much rather read one of those 'horrid' novels with young girls being chased by dark and sinister villains." She made a face. "I'd much rather read about love than such nonsense."

Ewan smiled. He'd have to take her word for it. He'd never read a novel like the ones she described.

"Have you ever read any poems by Robbie Burns?" As he said the name, his accent slipped to a more Scottish burr.

Anna shook her head, smiling. "I don't believe so, but I've heard Emily mention the name before. I take it he's Scottish?"

Now it was Ewan's turn to blush. "He is, yes."

"Recite something he's written."

Staring down into her dark, dark eyes, there was one of Burns's poems that came to mind so quickly Ewan was frightened of it. It was foolish to feel so much for one person so soon after meeting her, but he couldn't help it. He was hers to command.

"'Oh, my Luve is like a red, red rose, / That's newly sprung in June. / O, my Luve is like the melodie, / That's sweetly played in tune.'"

Anna's smile grew. Whether it was at the poem or the thickness of Ewan's accent, he wasn't sure. "That's lovely."

"There's more," Ewan said before he lost his nerve. "'As fair art thou, my bonie lass / So deep in love am I, / And I will love you still, my dear, / Till a' the seas gang dry.'"

Anna's forehead creased in a frown. "What's he saying? What do 'bonny' and 'gang' mean?"

Ewan cleared his throat. "*Bonny* means beautiful and *gang* means go. He's telling her how beautiful he thinks she is and that he will love her until all the seas go dry."

Eyes wide, Anna stared at him. "Oh. Oh, that's beautiful!"

He couldn't kiss her, couldn't touch her outside of the movements dictated by the dance, so Ewan had to content himself with tightening his fingers around her hand and pulling her a little bit closer. As it was, there was still a good six inches between them.

"That's the way it should be, don't you think?" he

asked, his throat tight with emotion as their gazes held. "Love should last forever."

Anna's fingers tightened on his arm as a delicate pink crept up her neck and cheeks. "Yes," she murmured, her voice barely audible above the music. "Till all the seas go dry."

It was hardly a declaration, but Ewan felt as though it was. He was certain Anna felt the same way for him that he did for her. She wasn't the kind of girl who'd kiss someone she didn't care deeply for. In fact, he'd wager that aside from Richard, he was the only man she'd ever kissed. And he'd be willing to go one step further and bet that Richard hadn't kissed her the way he had.

He hadn't kissed anyone the way he'd kissed Anna either, for that matter—with such intense emotion, with his heart.

It was easy to imagine himself and Anna spending evenings by the fire at Castle MacLaughlin, reading poetry aloud or simply talking—and kissing. He could see her working beside him to restore the castle to its former splendor. And he could imagine getting old with her—even raising a family.

She scared the sense right out of him and he didn't mind one bit. Either this was true love or he was going mad. Either way, he didn't care.

They danced once more that evening and that was all. Anything more would have been improper and fodder for the gossip mill. Still, it was frustrating not being able to do what they wanted, not being able to let on that they wanted each other.

Even more frustrating was watching Anna dance with other men. Did it bother her watching him dance with other women? He couldn't imagine her having anything to be jealous about. The few girls he danced with, when he wasn't keeping an eye on Emily, spent more time giggling than talking. His cousin Jamie would probably like them better than he did.

Finally, it was time to leave, and Ewan was glad for it. At least in the carriage, he could have Anna almost entirely to himself. Emily looked so exhausted he doubted she would even stay awake for the drive home. It wasn't the same as being truly alone with Anna, but it would do. It would have to.

They left the ballroom ahead of most of the others and managed to get their wraps before the rush. It might be June, almost the end of the Season, but no gentleman or lady would dream of attending a social function without the ladies wearing an outer garment of some kind and the gentlemen in top hats.

Even with the wait for their garments, they had to weave their way through a crowd gathering in the foyer, out the door, and down the steps to where the carriage sat waiting.

Ewan handed both his sister and Anna up the step,

and climbed into the carriage to find both young women sitting on one side, leaving the other for him. Blast! He'd stupidly thought Anna would sit with him, but Emily would definitely take notice of such a thing. Or at least she might if she could keep her eyes open.

It was slow going for the first fifteen minutes as the carriage got behind a few others as it crept down the drive.

"Did you have a good time?" Ewan asked his sister.

"I did," she replied with a tired smile. "My feet are sore from dancing."

Ewan grinned. "I suspect the house will be overrun with suitors fighting for your attention tomorrow."

"I doubt it. " His sister stifled a yawn behind one gloved hand. "I'm so sleepy, it shan't matter anyway. One look at the bags under my eyes and they'll all run screaming for their mamas."

"Why don't you stretch out?" Anna suggested. "At this rate, it's going to be awhile before we arrive home. I can sit beside the duke and you can nap until you get home."

The light in the carriage was so dim that Ewan couldn't tell if Anna was blushing or not, and he didn't care. He could kiss her for being so sneaky!

"Do you mind?" Emily asked, turning to her brother.

"Certainly not," Ewan replied, hoping he didn't sound as eager as he felt. "You go ahead and rest. There's room for us both over here."

Smiling her thanks, Emily lifted her feet onto the seat

as Anna stood. Within seconds, Emily was curled up against the padded cushions with her eyes closed and Anna was settling in beside Ewan. Unlike the trip to the ball, when Ewan had taken pains to make certain his out-stretched legs didn't brush hers, he made no effort to keep from touching her.

Their legs pressed together from hip to ankle; their arms from wrist to shoulder. With a discreet flip of his coat, Ewan managed to cover their hands as he entwined his fingers with Anna's.

His heart hammered in his chest, his mouth was dry, and a mixture of joy and anxiety danced in his stomach. It was thrilling, this daring secrecy between them. He felt as though every hair on his body was standing on end while a thousand pinpricks of excitement dotted his skin. Unable to do anything else for fear Emily might open her eyes and see them, Ewan contented himself with stroking Anna's fingers. Rubbing her palm with the pad of his thumb, he caressed the length of her hand, which was so very much smaller than his own.

They sat in silence as the carriage rolled along the cobblestone streets. They didn't dare to even glance at each other. In fact, anyone looking at them wouldn't think they even noticed each other, except that beneath Ewan's coat, their hands and fingers were indulging in the slow, soft kisses their lips couldn't dare share.

All too soon they pulled up the drive to Anna's house.

Their gazes locked as their fingers slid apart. Funny how he felt the loss of her touch almost as keenly as if he'd lost something precious and dear.

"Thank you for seeing me home," she said, her voice soft.

"I'll walk you to the door," Ewan whispered so as not to wake his slumbering sister.

He stepped out into the cool night and held out his hand to assist her down from the carriage. Aware of the coachman watching, Ewan instructed the driver to take the carriage farther up the lane and turn around so they wouldn't have to do it as they were leaving.

With the driver gone, there was no one to see Ewan pull Anna into the shadows and kiss her until they were both breathless and dizzy.

"I've been wanting to do that all evening," he confessed, releasing her.

Anna's eyes fluttered open and she smiled. "I'm so very glad you got what you wanted."

He brushed a tendril of hair back from her face with his fingers. Her cheek was as soft as velvet. Was it just Anna who had skin so delicate? "Will I see you tomorrow?"

She ran a hand down the lapel of his coat. She seemed as eager to touch him as he was to touch her. How could he not be eager? No one had ever felt as good as she did. "Hester has invited Mama and I for luncheon."

Ewan smiled. Even the idea of spending more than an

hour in the company of Marion Welsley couldn't dim his joy at the prospect of seeing Anna again.

"I shall count the minutes," he teased as he reluctantly drew back into the moonlight. "Pleasant dreams."

Her smile was warm. "I'll be dreaming of you."

That she even said such a daring thing made Ewan's heart slam against his ribs with joy. "Good night, then."

"Good night."

He watched as she entered the house and closed the door, then he walked back into the lane to wait for the carriage. He saw the coachman's light in the near distance and heard the horses' hooves as it drew nearer.

Suddenly, something struck him from behind. Pain exploded behind his eyes, knocking him to his hands and knees on the gravel. Before he could stagger to his feet, a kick to the stomach sent him sprawling to the ground, gasping for breath.

"Get 'im up," a man's voice commanded above his head. "We 'aven't much time."

There were two of them that he knew of. One grabbed each of his arms and hauled him to his feet. Ewan lunged at one, striking him in the face with his elbow. The man reeled back, releasing Ewan's arm. Ewan drew back a fist to strike out at his other assailant, but was caught by a blow to the jaw that made his head snap back like a broken twig. Another blow caught him in the eye.

So now he knew there were more than two attackers.

A feminine shriek pierced the air. Ewan and his assailants froze. It was Emily. With his one good eye, Ewan could see her hanging out the carriage window, screaming at the men to leave her brother alone. God love her, she looked more angry than scared.

If that wasn't enough to frighten off his attackers, the sight of the Fitzgerald coachman waving a pistol in one hand and a whip in the other was. The man still holding Ewan gave him a sharp shove and took off running.

How Ewan managed to remain standing he didn't know. What he did know was that Emily had jumped out of the carriage and was pounding on the door of the Welsley home. Any minute Anna and her parents would see him in all his battered glory. He didn't want Anna to see him like this.

But he wasn't certain he wanted to return home either. If for no other reason than the niggling suspicion that the person responsible for this violence was his own brother.

"Did you see their faces?" Anna asked as she wrung water from a cloth into a basin.

Ewan winced as she applied the cloth to the gash on the back of his head. "No. It was too dark and I'm afraid I was too busy trying to keep them from killing me to notice what they looked like."

Anna's hands shook as she cleaned the wound. Thank heavens it wasn't deep. Still, it had bled quite a bit and the sight of Ewan being held up by the coachman, all that blood on the back of his head, had scared her senseless. In that split second Anna realized that her life would be completely empty without Ewan in it. How had he come to mean so much to her in such a short time?

Anna was loath to rouse any of the servants, and her mother hadn't the stomach to nurse such injuries, so that left Anna to tend to Ewan.

She stood between his knees as he sat on the drawing room sofa. His forehead pressed against her ribs as she dabbed salve on the top and back of his head. They were alone in the room and she rubbed his back with her free hand. Even through the layers of clothing, he felt strong and warm against her palm.

"What do you think they wanted?" she asked as he lifted his head. "Money?"

He shook his head, then grimaced as though the simple movement hurt. "I don't know. If they simply wanted money, why not take your jewelry as well?" He met her gaze. "They said they hadn't much time. I think they were sent to hurt—possibly even abduct—me."

Anna scowled. "Who'd do such an awful thing?"

Ewan looked at her as if he thought the answer obvious. "Who do you know who wants me out of his way?"

She was horrified. No. He had to be wrong. "Surely you don't think Richard was behind this!"

He caught her around the waist before she could pull away. "I don't want to believe he could be capable of such evil, but don't you find it rather convenient that I should be attacked in your drive when the only person who knew I was taking you home left the ball hours before we did? He had ample time to set it up."

She slumped onto his lap, too shocked and tired to care how improper her behavior was. "I can't believe it, but it makes perfect sense." She stared at him, not caring if her fear was written all over her face. "Ewan, you have to go back to Scotland."

His jaw dropped. "I beg your pardon?"

Twisting herself to face him, Anna gripped his shoulders with both hands. "You're not safe here." He wasn't safe and neither was she—not if Richard was as mad as Ewan suspected. "You must leave."

"Oh no." His tone was firm. "I'm not leaving you here alone with him."

"But he's not trying to kill me!" She shook him as much as a girl her size could shake a man as large as he was. Didn't he understand the danger he was in? Richard wouldn't dare hurt her—not while he still needed her—but Ewan stood between him and something he desperately wanted.

The thought of Richard harming Ewan made her rigid with fear. And what would happen if Richard succeeded in getting rid of his brother? Would he decide his fiancée was just as expendable?

Ewan smiled. He couldn't possibly find this *amusing!* Reaching up, he caught her wrists in his hands and eased them from his shoulders. "And we don't know for sure that he's trying to kill me either. It's quite possible that he's just trying to scare me. For what reason, I'm not sure, but I intend to find out."

Anna shook her head, her fear rapidly becoming panic. "No, you can't confront him. That will only make things worse!"

He raised a brow. "I'm not afraid of him. I refuse to run."

"So you're just going to let him send his henchmen after you until they beat you to death, is that it?" She tried to stand, but he held her firmly.

"Anna, Anna," he shushed in a soothing tone. "I cannot believe my own brother wants me dead. I think he simply wants to scare me, force me to run so he can make it look as though I had something to hide and try to prove my parents' marriage false."

Could he possibly be so trusting? "Ewan, he's your heir! If anything happens to you, Richard inherits the title! I'd say he has every reason to want you dead."

His expression hardened, his jaw taking on a very stubborn set. "I can't believe he'd go that far. I'd much rather believe he suspects there's something going on between us and wants to warn me away from you."

Anna didn't particularly find one possibility more comforting than the other. "Then we'll have to avoid each other as much as possible. We have to stop caring about each other." Yes, that was it. She could do it if it would keep Ewan safe.

He looked at her with eyes so warm and loving she wanted to cry. "You might as well ask the sun not to rise." Raising her hands to his mouth, he kissed her knuckles. "Anna, I'm not going to give in to Richard, no matter what his intentions are—if it's even him behind this attack." He squeezed her fingers. "I'd really rather you supported me than fought me on this. I need you."

Her heart melted at his words. How could she refuse him? In truth, she thought it would be difficult to refuse him anything. If he said he wanted the world on a platter, she'd try to get it for him.

She loved him. Loved him so completely, intensely. It was the most incredible thing—to realize it so clearly as she had. And even though it set her nerves on edge and made it difficult for her to sleep at night, she wouldn't trade her life now for anything in the world.

She pulled one hand free of his grip and pushed his hair back from his forehead. "Promise me you won't do anything foolish."

His expression was one of such surprise she almost laughed. "Me? Do something foolish?" He paused as if in thought. "I've never done anything foolish in my life. Well, hardly anything," he said, looking at Anna meaningfully.

She moved into his arms, not caring that it would be scandalous if they were caught in such a position. She loved being able to feel his warmth against her, loved being so close she could feel the rise and fall of his chest. He seemed so strong, so much larger than real life to her. He made her feel little and safe just by being near.

"Were you really worried about me?" He slid his free hand around her hip to cradle her back, lifting her higher on his lap.

Her gaze snapped up to his. "Of course. I was terrified."

He smiled. "Good."

She swatted him on the shoulder.

"Ow!" he cried.

Anna's heart jumped into her throat. "Oh no! I'm so sorry. Did I hurt you?"

"No." Ewan grinned. "I just wanted to make you feel bad."

Anna couldn't help but laugh. "You're awful!"

"Kiss me," he commanded, his voice whisper soft and filled with laughter.

She did kiss him. Sitting up, she lowered her head to his. It felt odd to have his face beneath hers rather than above, almost as if she was in control of how their lips touched instead of him. His mouth was warm beneath hers, both demanding and gentle, and she kissed him with all the love she had in her heart and then some.

The choice was made. She didn't even have to think about it. There was no contest. Ewan was the one she wanted. Ewan was the one she loved. It remained only for her to find the right way to tell him. But first they had to deal with Richard.

Ewan's hand rubbed her back, pulling her closer. Eyes closed, Anna gave herself up to the sensations the kiss offered. Nothing else existed when Ewan held her in his arms. She wished they could stay like this forever.

The sound of her mother's voice sent her wish up in a puff of smoke. She jerked out of Ewan's arms and just managed to jump to her feet before the door flew open to reveal her mother's large, nightcapped form.

"Aren't you finished yet?" Marion demanded, eyes averted. The only reason she'd left them alone was because neither she nor Emily could stand the sight of blood. "I've tried to keep Lady Emily company, but the poor girl's falling asleep on the sofa."

"I'm done now, Mama," Anna replied, surprised that her voice wasn't shaking. "You can have the duke's carriage summoned."

She felt Ewan rise to his feet behind her. "Thank you very much for your kind hospitality, Mrs. Welsley. I'm in your debt."

Even her mother wasn't a hard enough woman to withstand that charming tone of his, especially when he let his accent deepen to a softer, huskier Scottish timbre. Anna much preferred it when he spoke in his native burr. In fact, she had a sneaking suspicion that he tried to sound more English in order to fit in.

"You're welcome, Your Grace. I'm glad your injuries weren't serious."

It was all Anna could do to keep her mouth from falling open. Her mother actually sounded sincere! Was it possible she was warming up to Ewan? Or did she also suspect Richard's involvement and didn't approve of such tactics? Anna couldn't be certain. And honestly, she didn't care so long as her mother continued to show Ewan the respect he deserved.

She walked Ewan and Emily to the door. Poor Emily could hardly keep her eyes open, but she clung to her brother as though she were afraid someone might try to take him from her. Poor thing. Did Ewan have any idea how he filled that empty spot in Emily's life? He looked so much like their father, and being older, and so reliable, he readily stepped into the void left by their father's death.

Anna couldn't help but wonder if Hester and Emily didn't fill an emptiness inside Ewan as well. He smiled at his sleepy sister, and wrapped an arm around her shoulders to keep her upright.

"Thank you for everything, Miss Welsley," he said, back to pretending there was nothing between them. "We look forward to seeing you again tomorrow."

Anna smiled, the perfect picture of ladylike composure. The perfect fake. "I'm afraid it is tomorrow already, Your Grace. I shall see you again in a mere few hours."

Warmth flared briefly in his gaze. "I shall count the minutes."

Anna smiled. It was all she could do not to grin like an idiot. "Good night, Emily. Good night, Your Grace."

Closing the door behind them as they left, Anna slipped the bolt into place and prepared to extinguish the wall lamp.

"I certainly hope you're not being foolish enough to fall in love with him," her mother remarked from behind her.

Anna whirled around, her heart pounding. But instead of panic, she felt joy. Pure, sweet happiness that neither her mother nor Richard could destroy. "No, Mama. I'm not falling in love with him."

I already am in love with him.

"Idiots!"

Pacing the length of his room, Richard crumpled the note in his hand. The men he'd hired had failed. Not only had they failed to abduct his brother, but they'd also beaten him—something Richard hadn't at all intended. All he wanted was Ewan out of his way. All he wanted was for his brother to give him the title.

He'd thought that maybe a few threats would do the

trick. All he had planned to do was threaten Ewan's precious Scottish kinsmen, forcing his honorable, disgustingly loyal brother to do whatever Richard wanted.

Or at least that's what Richard had been stupid enough to believe. Now he realized stronger methods would have to be used. But what?

He'd have to be more careful next time. Poor Emily had been there. She could have been hurt, and Richard would never forgive himself if anything happened to his sister. Nor would he ever forgive himself if anything ever happened to Anna. He might not love her, nor she him, but he cared for her and—

Ewan loved her.

He froze in the middle of the floor. Of course! Why hadn't he thought of it before?

Ewan was only human and Anna was a lovely young woman—not as lovely as that oldest daughter of Lady Markby's, but pretty all the same. And she had that same annoying love of poetry that his brother possessed. It was only natural that Ewan would be attracted to her.

In fact, his brother was probably the only person who could truly appreciate all those things about Anna that Richard didn't. In a perfect world, were it not for the fact that Richard himself needed Anna and her money, he'd be tempted to say that Ewan actually deserved a girl like Anna.

But he did not deserve to be Duke of Brahm. He hadn't worked as hard for it as Richard had.

Therefore, Richard saw nothing wrong with using Anna to get to his brother. Oh yes, Ewan would do whatever he wanted if Richard threatened Anna.

CHAPTER NINE

"Is His Grace going to be all right?"

Anna glanced up from her dressing table to the mirror in which her mother was reflected. It was the second time that day her mother had asked her about Ewan's condition, and Anna didn't know any more now than she had the first time. The fact that her mother had actually come to her room to ask showed just how concerned she was.

"I would think so." She sifted through her jewelry box. "His injuries weren't that serious." At least she hadn't thought they were. A shiver of dread raced through her at the thought of anything happening to Ewan.

Her mother sighed. "Thank goodness."

"Why are you so concerned?" Anna asked, fastening a delicate gold chain around her neck. A tiny cross nestled against her breastbone. The necklace had been a present from her grandmother before her death and it was one of Anna's most cherished possessions.

Turning in her chair, she faced her mother. "I should think you'd prefer to have him mortally wounded so that Richard could inherit the title."

Her mother paled. "I may not have been fair in my

earlier treatment of the duke, but I have no wish to see him dead."

Anna's eyes narrowed. "You suspect Richard was behind the attack last night too, don't you?"

"I'm not sure," Marion replied, sinking down onto the side of Anna's bed. She met Anna's gaze evenly. "I know you don't like what I've done, Anna. I know that trying to prove Lord Brahm illegitimate was not well done of me, but I never wanted to see him injured. I want you to know that."

Anna nodded. "I know." And she did. Her mother was many things, but evil wasn't one of them. "What do you know about Richard's plans?"

Her mother drew a deep breath. She truly did look shaken. "I'm not sure what he's up to now that he believes the duke's birth to be legitimate."

Anna started. Richard believed Ewan's parents had been married? How had he discovered that so soon? Ewan said his mother had a copy of the certificates. Perhaps his father had kept copies as well. Either that or Richard had overheard her and Ewan talking at the ball. No, that wasn't possible. He'd been talking to a friend when she and Ewan spoke.

"Did he happen to tell you just how he made that discovery? And exactly when did he tell you this?"

Marion flushed. "I received a note from him just this very morning."

Anna's blood chilled. Was it possible that Richard's

discovery was just a coincidence, or had he been listening on the other side of the window last night? Thank goodness Ewan had had the good sense to step away from it for the rest of their conversation.

"Anna, Richard is desperate," her mother continued when Anna remained silent. "He truly believes that title is rightfully his." The urgency in her mother's tone caught her attention.

"Ewan doesn't believe he's in any real danger from Richard."

Clasping her hands in her broad lap, Marion sighed. "I'm not certain if he's in real danger either, but like I said, Richard is desperate, and desperate men will do desperate deeds. You might want to advise the young duke not to be so certain where his brother is concerned."

Anna's heart tightened in fear. "Why are you telling me this?"

Her mother's cheeks grew even redder. Her expression was one of extreme discomfort. "Because I know how little you think of me and I didn't want you to think I supported Richard's violence."

"But you would have supported his ruining his brother?"

Marion nodded, her gaze downcast. "I would have, yes. I thought I was acting in your best interests, but then I saw the way you looked at the duke and it made me so angry that I realized I'd been acting in my own interests." She lifted her chin. "You've developed a *tendre* for him, haven't you?"

There was no sense lying; the truth was surely written plainly all over her face. "I have, but I have no idea if he returns my feelings. Are you angry?"

With a deep sigh, her mother wearily shook her head. "Despite my shameful behavior where Richard was concerned, I would rather have you happy than miserable." She smiled slyly. "And a happy duchess would be preferable to a miserable Mrs. Fitzgerald."

Anna laughed. She couldn't help it. That her mother could admit to her ambition was hilarious. That her mother could admit to actually wanting her to be happy was incredible.

"We'd better be on our way," her mother remarked, rising to her feet. "We don't want to keep the Fitzgeralds waiting."

No. Anna didn't want to keep Ewan and his family waiting. In fact, she could barely wait to see him again.

"When are you going to break the engagement with Richard?" her mother asked as they left the room.

She didn't even have to think about her answer. "When I'm certain Ewan is safe from him. I don't want to be what sends Richard over the edge. I think it might be for the best if you continue to go along with him as well. You don't have to encourage him, but let him think you're still on his side."

"I think someone should go to Bow Street and inform the Runners of what's going on—just in case."

Her mother's words sent a shiver down Anna's spine and she clung to the banister for support as they descended the stairs. Her legs trembled at the thought of anything else happening to Ewan, but she wasn't so certain calling in the Bow Street law officers was the right thing to do at the moment.

"We have no evidence to give them," she reminded her mother. "And even if we did, I would want to consult Ewan before going to the runners with it. When we arrive at Brahm House, I'll contrive to speak to him privately and ask him what he believes our best course of action to be."

A firm hand patted her shoulder. "It will be all right, my dear. You'll see."

At the foot of the stairs, Anna paused and turned to her mother. "You're very disappointed that things haven't worked out as you'd planned, aren't you?"

Marion raised a brow. She looked tired—more tired than Anna had ever seen her look in her life. "I've been wrong about a great many things, Anna. Terribly wrong. My foolishness could have made your life very miserable, and it almost resulted in His Grace being grievously injured. It's extremely difficult not to feel sorry for that. I'm heartily ashamed of myself."

It was an awkward moment because Anna hadn't tried

to hug her mother in a long time, but she wrapped her arms around the soft shoulders and squeezed anyway, smiling when she was squeezed back.

"All right, enough of this foolishness." Her mother sniffed and pulled free of her embrace. Dabbing her eyes with a handkerchief pulled from her sleeve, her expression firmed into one of fierce determination. "We're going to be late. And we don't want Richard to suspect anything. We shall have to make like Edmund Kean and give the best performances of our lives."

Edmund Kean was one of England's finest actors ever to grace the stage of the Drury Lane Theatre. He'd taken the entire city by storm four years ago. Anna smiled at the comparison, but if anyone could match Kean's talent for pretending, it would be her mother.

And pretend she did. When Peters announced them in the drawing room of the Fitzgeralds' mansion in elegant Grosvenor Square, her mother was so much like her former self that Anna wondered if what had happened back at their own home had been nothing more than her imagination.

It was difficult to greet Richard first and not just rush to Ewan's side, but Anna managed to play her part as well.

"Good afternoon, Richard," she said, her voice bright as she endured his lips against her cheek. "I trust your business last night was concluded to your satisfaction?"

From the corner of her eye, Anna saw her mother pause

in her conversation with Hester, but only for a split second. Ewan, on the other hand, didn't even appear to hear her question, even though he was too close not to have.

Richard also appeared oblivious to her dig. Out of all of them, he was perhaps the most worthy of replacing Kean as England's best actor.

"Not exactly, my dear, but I won't bore you with the details. It's hardly the kind of thing that would interest a young woman."

How would he know what would or wouldn't interest a young woman? Richard knew *nothing* about women. If he did, he'd realize his charm was lost on her, and that his insulting assumption that she wouldn't understand what he told her served only to lower her opinion of him even further.

Anna forced a smile. "Well, as long as you got what you wanted, that's all that matters, isn't it?"

Richard's smile faded. Bother it! She was going to have to learn to hold her tongue!

Taking her by the hand, Richard led her toward the far wall where tall windows overlooked the back garden. It was all Anna could do not to dig her heels into the carpet. She didn't want to be alone with him. In fact, she was just starting to realize how afraid she was of him. If he'd hired men to assault his own brother, what would he do to a mere fiancée?

"Anna, my dear. Are you quite all right?" He even

managed to look concerned about her.

For a moment, Anna was disconcerted. He seemed so sincere, even his eyes reflected tenderness and warmth. It was so very hard to remember what he was capable of. Quickly. She had to think of something to tell him. "Richard, I was there when the duke was attacked last night, and you've not even asked if I've recovered from the shock."

Oh dear Lord, she sounded just like those eyelash-batting, hair-twirling girls she despised. Girls who intentionally made themselves out to be weaker and less intelligent than the opposite sex.

Richard proved which one of them was less intelligent by falling for her ruse. "Oh, my dear. I'm so sorry. I'd for-gotten that you tended to his wounds." He gripped her shoulders. "Are you all right?"

"I'm fine, Richard. Thank you for asking." She pulled free of his hold, trying to keep her aversion to his touch from showing. "But it was awful. Has His Grace quite recovered?"

Richard's expression was perfectly blank. "I believe so."

"It's really quite rude of me not to ask him myself when he's sitting right over there with your sister. Would you excuse me so that I might inquire after his health myself?"

A muscle throbbed in his jaw. Perhaps he wasn't such a good actor after all. "Of course. We'll go together. I haven't had a chance to speak to him today myself."

While she wasn't too pleased about Richard accompanying her, Anna was happy to finally have the chance to speak to Ewan. She'd lain awake half the night worrying about him and was eager to find out how he was recovering.

And she was eager just to see him.

Ewan met their approach with a warm smile. A smile Anna knew was meant entirely for her.

"Miss Welsley, what a pleasure to see you again." One eye was swollen and discolored and there was a bruise on his jaw, but other than that, he was still her beautiful Ewan.

"And under much better circumstances today, Your Grace," Anna replied, her voice formal and polite. How she hated pretending he meant nothing to her! "I trust you've suffered no further ill effects from the attack?"

He gave his head a little shake. "I'm a little sore, but that is all." He smiled at his sister. "I'm very fortunate that I had Emily to rescue me."

Emily blushed under the lighthearted praise. "All I did was scream like an idiot."

Ewan glanced up at Anna. "And I'm also very lucky that I had you, Miss Welsley, to tend to me."

"Yes," Richard replied before Anna could respond. "It was very good luck indeed. You should be more careful when out and about in London, brother. Footpads are everywhere, it seems. Next time you might not be so fortunate."

He walked away, leaving Anna and Ewan staring at each other, and Anna knew that Ewan now realized that his brother was much more dangerous than they'd first thought.

They were afraid of him now. Richard could see it in the way they looked at him. Good. Things were going better than he'd expected. He would never actually do anything to seriously harm either one of them, but they didn't have to know that. It would make dealing with his brother so much easier. Ewan wouldn't hesitate to believe that Richard might harm Anna and would do whatever Richard asked. And Anna would do anything to protect her lover.

He had them exactly where he wanted them. It was perfect. Meanwhile, they had absolutely no incriminating evidence against him whatsoever—nothing Bow Street or any judge would believe, anyway.

If all went as he had planned—and he had planned it well—he would soon have his rightful inheritance as well as Anna's dowry and a share in her father's business. The idea of having to resort to going into trade like a commoner was a bit annoying, but the revenue would go that much farther to keeping him in the style to which he was accustomed.

And the money would pay off his creditors. That was the most important thing. Some of them were becoming quite insistent and if he didn't pay them soon, he risked complete financial and social ruin once word got out of his circumstances.

He would have to act quickly.

Stepping up beside his mother, Richard smiled at Mrs. Welsley, letting her know he was still in control. She smiled back. It wasn't her usual confident smile, but it was good enough. It wouldn't hurt for her to be a little bit wary of him either, just until he and Anna were married and he had control not only of Anna's fortune, but had his fingers in the family business as well.

And soon he would have his father's title as well, as it was meant to be. He'd make his father proud. He hadn't been truly proud of Ewan, otherwise he wouldn't have kept him a secret. He'd been wrong all those years growing up—it hadn't been that his father was holding him up against Ewan, it had been the other way around. Obviously, his father had hoped that his half-Scot son would turn out as well and as polished and as English as Richard had. Yes, that was it. He was the one born and bred to be duke. And all he had to do was to take back what was rightfully his.

Glancing up at the ceiling, Richard's smile grew. He hoped his father was watching.

After luncheon Marion cornered Richard into joining them at cards once again, leaving Anna and Ewan free to talk.

"Your mother's being very kind to me," he remarked as they seated themselves far across the room from the others.

Anna smiled, clutching the book of poetry she'd brought along to make it look as though they were discussing verse rather than her fiancé's dark plans.

"Apparently she's realized how wrong she's been about Richard. Seeing you last night made her rethink her loyalties." She blushed. "And she's realized that I . . . that I consider you a particular friend." To speak any plainer would be improper for a young woman, not to mention humiliating if Ewan didn't return the sentiment.

He didn't try to hide his surprise. "I would have thought she'd think that was a bad thing rather than a good one."

Anna's blush deepened. "She'd rather have me happy than miserable."

"And she thinks I have the power to make you happy?"

His tone was so incredulous, Anna's heart plummeted to her feet. Oh, this was awful, just awful! "Ewan, I swear to you that my mother has not entertained the notion of marriage where you are concerned. I would never presume—"

He caught one of her hands in his own, looking around to make certain no one noticed. "Anna," he murmured, wincing in discomfort as he leaned closer. He was in more pain than she had originally thought. "I would be honored to be considered worthy enough to marry you. Any man would."

Her eyes widened. Her heart swelled at his words. Was it possible? Could it be that Ewan's intentions ran toward marriage? Just the very thought of it tied her stomach into knots. "Do you think so?"

He nodded, a mischievous sparkle in his eyes. "And to think I only had to possess two titles, several houses, and a small fortune to garner your mother's approval."

Anna laughed. She couldn't help it. Trust Ewan to lighten the mood, to find the humor in the absurdities of their situation.

Ewan laughed too. They were soon laughing so hard they clung to their sides as their bodies shook. Poor Ewan alternated between chuckles and moans as their mirth jostled his tender ribs.

"What's so funny over there?" Hester demanded good-naturedly from across the room.

"Yes, what?" Emily piped in, laying down her cards. "Tell us!"

"His Grace was just reciting a Robert Burns poem," Anna lied with a bright smile. "I was laughing at his accent. I suspect he'd have me believe that all Scotsmen are nearly impossible to understand."

"I think Ewan's accent is charming," Emily responded with a grin at her brother. "I'd love to marry a Scotsman just so I could listen to him talk for the rest of my life."

Anna grinned at Ewan.

"Aye," Ewan spoke, intentionally deepening his brogue. "And talk for the rest of your life a Scot could too, lass."

Everyone laughed except for Richard. "I hope you're joking, Em."

The young girl shrugged. "I've yet to meet a Scot other than Ewan, but if a tall, fierce Scottish warrior tried to sweep me off my feet, I wouldn't be averse."

More laughter.

"You've just described my cousin Jamie," Ewan told her with a wink. "Perhaps I'll introduce you."

Richard's face was red with anger. "I will not allow my sister to marry some barbarian."

Awkward silence fell over the room as anxious glances darted back and forth between the brothers.

Ewan's face went so hard, his eyes so dark, that Anna worried Richard might finally have pushed him too far. "It's a good thing that it's my permission she needs and not yours then, isn't it?"

Richard jumped up so fast he knocked his chair over. He didn't say a word, he just flashed Ewan a look of pure hatred and stormed out of the room, slamming the door behind him like a child having a tantrum.

Poor Hester looked humiliated. "I'm so sorry for Richard's behavior, Ewan. He's still mourning his father."

"We all are," Ewan reminded her softly. "You don't need to apologize for him, Hester. He's a grown man and able to do it for himself if he feels like it." He didn't have to say he doubted his brother would be sorry—it was in his voice.

Marion laid a comforting hand on Hester's and spoke softly to her. Anna turned to Ewan. "I've never seen Richard look so hateful before," she murmured. And it was true. He'd looked like a madman.

Ewan inhaled a deep breath and paused for a brief second before blurting, "Come to Scotland with me."

Her eyes widened. He couldn't have shocked her more if he'd slapped her, but at least she managed to find her voice. "What?"

He scooted closer, taking the book from her hands and opening it as though he was looking for a particular poem. "You were right last night. I don't think it's safe here any-more—for either of us. Richard's remark about me not being so lucky next time was proof enough of that if his parting look wasn't." He turned his head to hers. His breath was warm against her temple. "Run away with me. I don't want to take the risk of Richard using you to get to me. We could leave for Scotland—and Gretna Green—tonight."

Anna could scarcely believe her ears. Run away? To Scotland? Could she do it? Could she leave England, her friends, her family? Could she run off to some strange coun-try where she knew no one but the man she loved? The scan-dal would be incredible, even if they did stop at Gretna Green, a small town on the Scottish border where marriages were often performed. But scandal couldn't touch them in Scotland, and like all gossip, it would eventually fade away.

He hadn't even told her how he felt about her. He said nothing of love, only of danger and protecting her from it. Surely his invitation to elope with him meant his feelings for her ran deep. Didn't it? And it wasn't as though she had declared her feelings either, but she knew how she felt about him even if she hadn't said it.

"Yes," she whispered. "Tonight."

He reached over and gave her frigid fingers a warm squeeze. "I'll come for you at midnight. Pack only what you need. We'll send for the rest after we've arrived at the castle."

The fog in her brain cleared. "Castle? You live in a castle?"

He nodded, his gaze searching her face. "Do you mind living in a somewhat shabby castle?"

"No," she replied honestly, still not sure that this wasn't all a wonderful dream. "I don't mind at all."

"You can do whatever you like to it—it needs quite a bit of work, but you'll love it as much as I do, I'm certain." He laughed softly. "Before I came here I couldn't wait to see the world beyond Scotland. Now I can't wait to return. I can't wait to show you my home."

And Anna couldn't wait to see it. "Will your family—your grandmother and Jamie—will they like me, do you think?"

"They'll adore you almost as much as I do."

It wasn't a declaration of love, but it was the next best thing. And oh! How he looked at her when he said it—like she was the most beautiful girl in the world. No one had ever gazed at her with such intensity before. Her mouth opened but no sound came out. How idiotic she must appear!

Ewan smiled at her expression. "Surely you're not surprised that I care about you? I'm not in the habit of asking every girl I meet to elope with me."

Still she stared at him. A faint blush crept up his jaw. "Since you've agreed to run away with me, I'm going to take that as a sign that you are not without feelings for me as well."

At least she could nod. This all felt like a dream! "Yes."

His smile deepened. "My timing is awful. All I want to do is kiss you but I can't." Even if they were officially betrothed it still wouldn't be proper to make such a public display of their affection—especially not with their unsuspecting relatives sitting across the room.

"Your Grace," she said loudly. "I would love to borrow one of those books you've told me about. Would you care to escort me to the library?"

Eyes sparkling in understanding, Ewan nodded and raised his voice to match hers. "I'd be delighted, Miss Welsley."

They rose to their feet and made their excuses to the

other ladies, promising to return momentarily.

They practically ran to the library. Giggling like children, they hurried into the room and swept the door closed behind them. As soon as Ewan turned to her, Anna threw herself into his arms.

"Kiss me," she demanded, laughing. "Kiss me now!"

But he didn't kiss her right away. In fact, his expression grew far too serious for Anna's liking.

"Anna, I want you to promise me something."

"Anything," she promised. "Now kiss me."

His smile didn't reach his eyes. "If anything happens to me before we leave tonight I want you to go to Bow Street with this." He handed her a piece of paper taken from inside his coat. "It's the letter Richard wrote pretending to be our father's solicitor."

As she wrapped her fingers around the crumpled paper, a shiver of dread ran down Anna's spine. "Ewan, you don't think he'll try anything, do you?"

He didn't reply. He crushed her against him and kissed her as though there were no tomorrow. Anna tried not to think about the fact that there might not be a tomorrow for them. All that mattered was that she was in Ewan's arms. Today was all that mattered. And tonight was as far ahead as she would let herself think.

Throwing her arms around his neck, Anna gave herself up to the kiss and forgot about everything else but the two of them together.

Forever.

She'd said yes.

Tossing a shirt into his trunk, Ewan still couldn't quite believe he'd even gathered the courage to ask her. He hadn't meant to. He'd meant it the night before when he told her his intention to stay and face Richard, but all that had changed when he saw the hatred on his brother's face. It wasn't just his own safety he was worried about, it was Anna's. And since he'd be forced to harm his brother if he so much as touched Anna, Ewan decided the best course of action was to leave England.

There was nothing to make him stay forever. The title and the money were his. He'd stayed on only because he'd wanted the chance to get to know his family better. He wished he could have had more time with Hester and Emily, for they'd come to mean almost as much to him as his grandmother did, but he would be happy to put some distance between himself and Richard.

And it would be so good to get home. He'd been gone too long—long enough to know that he had seen as much of the world outside of his village as he wanted. Long enough to know that even though he was half English, his heart was all Scot. He longed for his home and his land. He even missed Jamie and the giggling girls who followed them wherever they went.

He smiled and tossed a pair of trousers in the trunk. A wife would certainly put a stop to the giggling girls.

Anna would love Glenshea. He felt it in his bones. In the summers they could picnic by the loch and in the winters they'd snuggle by the fire and drink hot cider as the snow fell softly outside.

Just thinking about it made his heart ache. He packed faster. He had only a couple of hours before he had to leave to pick up Anna. Straightening, he sighed. In just two short hours, he'd be on his way home with the woman he loved.

But did she love him?

A voice in his head told him she must if she was willing to leave her family and friends behind in order to run away with him. But she had planned to marry Richard as well, and Ewan knew very well that she hadn't loved him.

No, Anna cared about him. She'd said so—and he saw it in her eyes. She was just as scared to say it as he was, but he knew she returned his feelings. He knew it as surely as he knew his life would be empty without her.

They could be married in Gretna Green, and then if Anna wanted a fancier wedding later, they could make a fuss over the occasion.

He always thought he'd be scared to get married. The idea had always filled him with fear, but the thought of marrying Anna had just the opposite effect. He knew she was the one, and the idea of spending the rest of his life with her made him smile in contentment.

He finished packing his trunk and hefted it up onto his shoulder. Quietly, so as not to disturb anyone, he crept out into the hall. Hester and Emily had gone to bed early and Richard hadn't come back after storming out earlier. With any luck it would be morning before anyone noticed he was gone. If anyone did think to come after them, they'd still be married by the time they were found.

The house was still and silent as he tiptoed down the stairs. The servants had retired as well.

Outside, the night air was damp and chilly. It had rained a bit earlier, but hopefully not enough to make a mess of the roads. The trip to Scotland would be long enough without muddy and rutted roads slowing them down.

The carriage was waiting in the drive already. He'd ordered one of the older vehicles so the family wouldn't be left without appropriate transportation. It was a little on the shabby side, but it was still more comfortable than a hired hack.

But where was the driver? Frowning, Ewan lowered his trunk to the ground and walked toward the carriage. "Hello?"

Gravel crunched behind him. He turned, expecting to see the driver, and instead ended up with a damp cloth pressed against his mouth and nose. He tried to step back, but someone else caught him by the arms, holding them behind his back so he couldn't strike out.

The sweet-scented cloth made his head swim. They were drugging him! Vainly, he struggled against his captors, but it was too late.

Darkness engulfed him.

He woke up on an earthen floor. It was damp and cold beneath his cheek.

Blinking, he pushed himself up onto his hands and knees, ignoring the sharp ache of his muscles as he did so. His head was heavy and his tongue was dry and he felt like the devil, but at least he was alive.

For now.

He heard a strange jangling sound as he staggered to his feet. Looking down, he saw the shackle around his ankle. The chain connected to it ran across the floor to the wall. He jerked it. It held fast.

"Unless you've the strength of Hercules, you won't be able to free yourself from that chain."

Ewan didn't have to turn to see who spoke to him. He knew the voice.

"What are you doing, Richard?" he demanded.

Footsteps sounded on the hard-packed dirt behind him. He still didn't turn. He wouldn't give his brother the satisfaction of thinking he feared him.

"I think I'm preventing you from running off with my

fiancée, brother dear." Richard's tone was mocking. "That was your plan, wasn't it?"

Now Ewan turned to face him. "She's not in love with you." Why he said it, he didn't know. It wasn't as if it would make Richard release him.

Richard smiled. "I don't love her either. But her parents are giving me a portion of their business holdings to marry her. Plus, she has a rather large dowry." He shrugged. "And she'll make a good duchess, don't you agree?"

"An excellent one," Ewan agreed through clenched teeth. Anna meant nothing to Richard. Nothing. "That's why I plan to marry her."

Richard's expression hardened. "You're not marrying Anna."

He shouldn't taunt his brother, who was obviously unbalanced, but Ewan couldn't help it. "Well, she's not going to become a duchess if she marries you. Unless you plan to kill me. Do you plan to kill me, Richard?" If he did, Ewan hoped he had a good plan, because if he got free, he was going to strangle his brother himself.

Richard grimaced. "No, I don't plan to kill you. That would raise too much suspicion."

"Then how do you plan to make Anna a duchess?"

The smile returned. "You're going to give me the title."

Ewan shook his head, uncertain he'd heard him correctly. "I'm going to what?"

"You're going to sign a letter stating that my father was never legally married to your mother and that I am the true Duke of Brahm."

Ewan stared at him. Now he was certain his brother was insane. "But *our* father was legally married to my mother."

Richard's smile slipped. "Documents can be falsified, Ewan. No one will doubt your word."

"I won't do it." Ewan shook his head. "I won't denounce my parents' marriage just for your greed."

Richard took a step forward and for a moment Ewan thought he might hit him. He was ready for it. As soon as the little lunatic got within reach he was going to give him the pummeling of his life.

Richard stopped just out of reach. "You will do it."

Clenching his jaw, Ewan stared his brother hard in the eye. "And how do you propose to make me?"

"That's easy." Richard folded his arms across his chest. "If you don't sign it, I'm going to make certain something very, very horrible happens to Anna."

CHAPTER TEN

At half past nine, Anna pleaded a headache and went up to her room early. Once there, she began to prepare for her adventure.

Her palms were damp and her heart pounded frantically against her ribs. She couldn't believe she was actually doing this! She was running away! It was like something out of a novel.

She didn't care that her reputation would be ruined. Society would forgive her once she became a duchess. There would be those who would think she wanted only the title and was marrying Ewan instead of Richard just to increase her own importance, but she didn't care. She loved Ewan, not Richard, and nothing else mattered.

Shortly after ten, she heard her mother and father come up the stairs to their rooms. Her mother, obviously not wanting to disturb her in case she was actually sleeping, hadn't even knocked on her door. Anna felt a little guilty over deceiving her parents, but she couldn't risk them trying to prevent her from going with Ewan. Her mother was finally beginning to comprehend the sort of violence Richard was capable of, but no one knew how far he'd go to claim the dukedom. Ewan's life was not something Anna wanted to risk.

She even felt a little guilty over jilting Richard, but only a very little. He deserved to be humiliated after all he had tried to do to Ewan.

Ewan. Just the thought of him unleashed a horde of butterflies in her stomach and made her skin prickle with a frisson of electricity.

She glanced at the clock. It was now almost eleven. In a little more than an hour she would be on her way to Scotland with the man she loved. It was as difficult to believe as a dream.

Standing in the middle of her bedroom, Anna gave the room a final look around. It would be a long time—if ever—before she saw the pale yellow wallpaper with its tiny rose stripes and flowers. She'd slept in the rose canopied bed her entire life, woken up in it almost every morning since her father had bought it for her. He'd even bought her the matching dressing table, even though she'd had little use for it at the time. It wasn't until her mother started taking her out into society that she'd had a need for the high mirror and all its dainty drawers. That was when she suddenly started amassing a huge collection of ribbons, bows, and other hair accessories, such as curling tongs, clips, and pins. It was where she kept all of her personal grooming items.

She supposed she would have another dressing table at Castle MacLaughlin.

A castle! She would be living in a castle! It seemed too marvelous to even believe. And it would be her home—hers and Ewan's. She could decorate it however she wanted, make it a real home. And the two of them would live there forever. Raise their own children and grandchildren. And they'd never have to return to dirty, smelly London again unless they wanted to.

And Richard couldn't hurt them there.

Ewan had told her to take only what she needed and so very few of her belongings were missing from their usual places. A brush, some face cream, lavender water, a few ribbons, and a bit of jewelry were all that she'd taken from the vanity.

Her trunk held enough undergarments and dresses to last her a week or a few days more before they would need to be laundered. She'd packed the most travel-ready garments she owned—things that wouldn't wrinkle easily or need much attention, as she wouldn't have a maid to take care of such things on the journey. She wanted desperately to take her pale blue satin gown to be married in, but it would be a wrinkled mess by the time they reached Scotland, and she'd rather marry Ewan in pale rose velvet than a gown of creases.

She glanced at the clock on the mantel. Only fifty-five

minutes left to wait.

Moving to the armoire against the far wall, she pulled a few more gowns from it and two pairs of heavier stockings—just in case Scotland was cool in the summer. It occurred to her that she knew relatively nothing of Ewan's homeland—only that it was beautiful and that he loved it.

She was certain that she would love it as well. How could she not when it meant so much to him?

Forty-five minutes.

Closing the lid on her trunk, Anna sighed. There was nothing more she could do. She'd checked and rechecked everything. Now all she could do was sit and wait for Ewan to come get her.

She tossed a cloak and a bonnet on top of the trunk once she'd locked it and strode to the window. Luckily, her room overlooked the quiet street where they lived. Her parents' rooms were on the opposite end of the house, so when Ewan appeared on the street below, Anna would easily sneak down and let him in. Then he could collect her trunk and the two of them would be on their way. It would be morning before her parents—or Richard—even realized she was missing. And by then, she and Ewan would easily have an eight to ten hour head start.

Curling up on the window seat, Anna leaned her head against the glass and stared at the street below. And waited.

Forty-two minutes . . .

Forty-one . . .

Forty . . .

"You wouldn't dare hurt her." Even as he said the words, Ewan pulled against the chain that held him captive like a wild animal.

Richard smiled. It was a sure, confident expression. Of course he could look confident—he wasn't the one chained to a wall.

"You don't think so? Anna's a lovely girl, but she doesn't mean as much to me as she obviously does to you." He took a step closer—still not enough to put him within Ewan's reach. "The question is, does she mean more to you than our father's title and fortune?"

Ewan glared at him in enraged silence. Richard laughed. "I see by that murderous gleam in your eye that she does."

Murderous didn't even begin to describe how Ewan felt. "You can't expect to actually get away with this."

Richard smiled. Oh, how Ewan would love to wipe that smile right off his smug face! "Of course I do. No one will question me, and as you'll be safe and sound back in your crumbling ruin of a castle, no one will suspect that I've manipulated you in any way. And since you're not very likely to return to England—especially once I've married the girl you love—everyone will assume you've gone back to the Highlands to hang your head in shame. It's perfect."

Ewan's leg was beginning to ache from tugging on the chain. "Anna will never marry you. She loves me."

His brother's amused expression never faltered. "How do you suppose she'll feel when you don't show up tonight?"

Ewan froze.

"Oh yes, I know what the two of you had planned." His voice was smug. "I saw you in the library the other night. It was pure chance, I assure you. The library is where I always go to be alone. That seems to be the one thing you and I have in common. Except that I went there to think and you went there to kiss *my* betrothed."

"If you were there, then you know she has no intention of marrying you." Ewan's mind was whirling. Had Richard also overheard him tell Anna to go to Bow Street? Had he overheard their plans?

Richard frowned. "She said that?"

Ewan almost sighed in relief. Richard hadn't heard that part of their conversation. He would have said something by now if he had.

"Well," Richard continued, "it hardly matters what she wants. She'll have no choice but to marry me once you're out of the picture. Her mother certainly won't allow her to jilt a duke."

"Our father would be disgusted by what you're doing,"

Ewan informed him with a sneer. If he couldn't bait his brother with the loss of Anna's affections, he would strike where he knew he could inflict some damage.

The bait worked. Richard took a step closer, his face taut with anger. "He would not! I wasn't the one he was too ashamed of to even tell his family about!"

The insult stung, but Ewan ignored it. "Really? That's funny. Not too long ago you told me how you always felt as though you were being held up against an invisible rival—me. He was proud of me and you know it, just as you know that you never quite measured up against me."

Richard took another step, his hands clenched into fists at his sides. "I was wrong. He loved me. He loved me more than you. He couldn't even stand the sight of you! That's why he left you and your mother!"

Now it was Ewan who smiled. "That's not what he told me in the letter he left me. In fact, he told me how much he always thought of me, how much he loved me right up until the end. What did he say in the letter he left you?"

Ewan knew full well there had been no letter. His brother had been fortunate enough to be with their father when he died. He'd been fortunate enough to have an entire life with him. Ewan hadn't, but he hoped that Richard was angry enough, insane enough not to think of it that way. The letter was just one more thing Ewan had gotten that Richard hadn't.

His plan worked. Snarling, Richard threw himself at

him, and Ewan, being bigger and stronger, caught his younger brother by the jacket, slamming his fist into the younger man's face before he even had a chance to realize what happened.

Richard's head snapped back like a rag doll's. "Give me the key for this chain," Ewan demanded, drawing back his arm for another punch. He was tempted to hit his brother again anyway as payback for the beating his thugs had given him.

Suddenly, he found himself staring down the barrel of a very shaky pistol. "Let go of me," Richard demanded in a voice that shook almost as much as his hand holding the gun.

Ewan did. He released his grip on his brother's coat without protest, stepping back with his hands up where Richard could see them. He seriously doubted his brother could shoot him in cold blood, but he didn't want to provoke him. Richard was mad, and his insanity made his behavior impossible to predict.

"Put the pistol down." How he managed to keep his voice level, he wasn't sure.

To his surprise, Richard did lower the gun. "Don't try that again," he warned, wiping blood away from his cut lip with the back of his hand. "Next time I'll shoot you, brother or not."

Ewan nodded. He was lucky his brother didn't shoot him anyway. It would be very easy for him to make it look like the work of thieves, and then Richard would inherit the title easily. But perhaps his brother suspected that Anna knew enough about his actions that Ewan's death wouldn't look like an accident. Richard was too smart to risk it, but that didn't mean he wouldn't lose his head and shoot Ewan out of a jealous rage either.

"This all could have been avoided if you'd just stayed in Scotland where you belonged, you know."

Ewan didn't think that would have made any difference at all. Chumley still would have known of his existence.

He tried to reason with his brother. "Richard, if it's the money you need, I'll pay off your debts."

Richard laughed at that, a dry, brittle sound. "It's not just the money, brother. I want what's rightfully *mine*. I want the title, I want my fiancée, and I want to pretend you were never born!"

Ewan flinched under the full force of Richard's hatred. He would not be able to reason with him. His brother was too far gone to listen to anything he had to say.

"Short of killing me, I don't know how you can make that happen." The moment he spoke, he regretted the words. He didn't want to give the younger man any ideas.

Richard reached inside his coat and pulled out several folded sheets of paper. Keeping the pistol leveled squarely on Ewan's chest, he set the paper on a nearby table where a quill and ink sat waiting.

He gestured to the table with the gun. "Come here. I

have some writing for you to do."

Slowly, so as not to make any sudden moves that might alarm his brother and cause him to shoot, Ewan inched toward the table. His chain just barely allowed him to reach.

"What am I to write?" he asked, loosening the lid on the ink.

"They're letters naming me the rightful duke and a letter to Anna explaining why you left her."

Ewan looked up, meeting his brother's gaze evenly. "And what is my reason for leaving her?"

Richard smiled. "You've decided you're not ready for marriage. You've realized you don't truly love her after all. You're sorry but you're already betrothed to a girl in Scotland."

Those are an awful lot of reasons, Ewan thought. And not one of them was one Anna would believe. Were they? Lord only knew what she thought when he hadn't shown up for her earlier. She was no doubt either sick with worry or irate—or both.

"She won't believe it."

Richard sighed. "We've already had this discussion. Stop stalling." He lifted the gun. "Write."

Ewan turned his attention back to the blank paper. He couldn't believe a title could mean so much to someone that he would ruin so many lives—and risk ruining his own—just to obtain it. In a way, he almost felt sorry for Richard for thinking the dukedom was so important. His obsession with it was obviously because it was all he felt he had left of their father. The poor fool. Even Ewan knew their father well enough now to know that he had left both his sons so many other ways to remember and honor him.

But even though he knew it, Ewan didn't want to give the title up so easily either. It was rightfully his. The money would repair his home and feed his people. And he certainly wasn't about to write anything stating that his father had never legally married his mother, not when it was a blatant lie.

But Richard stood not far away, waving the pistol like a man itching to use it, and Ewan had little choice. Dipping his quill in the ink, he tapped it to shake off the excess and then set it to the paper.

His brother told him what to write. Ewan admitted with a sensation of dread that Richard knew how to phrase things as Ewan himself would have. No one who read these letters would doubt that Ewan was indeed the author—especially when the handwriting was clearly his.

How then was he going to make them realize—make *Anna* realize—that none of it was true?

The answer came to him in a flash, and with a flourish, he signed the papers, hoping his brother wouldn't notice his error until Ewan could make his escape and perhaps even get back to Anna.

His brother looked as pleased as a cat in cream when all the papers were signed. He snatched them out of

Ewan's hand and after a quick scan, slid the papers back inside his coat.

"I'll be on my way now, brother," Richard remarked with a broad grin. "I must go home and get a good night's sleep. I'll have a heartbroken fiancée to console in the morning." He backed toward the door, keeping the pistol trained on Ewan's chest as he moved.

Ewan remained silent, but inside he was seething with anger. He was also feeling a little smug himself. His ruse would buy him some time at least. By the time his brother realized the mistake with his signature, Ewan would hopefully be free. If nothing else, Anna would notice the mistake and know that Ewan held Richard prisoner. If she went to Bow Street as he'd instructed her, they would be able to put a stop to Richard's vile plans.

Or so he hoped.

The bright gold of early morning glowed behind Anna's eyelids. With a moan, she rubbed the sleep away with the back of her fists and squinted against the brightness shining through the window. The same window where she had spent the night waiting for Ewan to come for her.

Anna grew cold despite the warmth of the sun. Ewan hadn't come.

She'd sat by the window for hours, watching the street for the sight of him. With every minute past midnight, she'd grown more and more anxious, until finally she thought she might scream. Then the anxiety gave way to dread and finally to depression. Still, she hadn't given up the hope that he might yet come. She'd fallen asleep waiting.

What had happened? Where was he? It wasn't like him not to show up and not send word.

Perhaps he had sent word. Stiffly, she rose to her feet, groaning as her muscles protested the movement. The window seat was not the most comfortable of places to fall asleep.

She splashed some water on her face from the washbasin in the corner, and after patting her cheeks dry with a towel, she smoothed her hands over her hair and gown and left her room, shutting the door behind her so no one would see the packed trunk on her bed. She would have to hide it before her maid came later that morning.

She flew down the stairs as though a pack of wild dogs was hot on her heels. She had to see if Ewan had sent her a note, anything that might explain why she was still Miss Welsley and not on her way to becoming the Duchess of Brahm or Lady Keir, whichever title he chose to use once they were wed.

"Are there any messages for me?" she demanded of the footman when she skidded to a halt in the foyer.

If he was surprised by her lack of manners, he didn't let on. "No, miss, but then the post won't arrive for several hours yet."

Numb, Anna nodded and muttered her thanks. No messages. Why had he not sent a message?

The sound of the door knocker set her heart pounding. It was Ewan, she knew it! He'd come to tell her what had happened and to reschedule their departure, she was sure of it!

Her heart plummeted when the door opened to reveal Richard. What was *he* doing there at such an early hour? It was much, much too early in the morning to be paying a social call.

He smiled when he saw her. "Anna, my dear, you look decidedly unhappy to see me. Were you expecting someone else?" His voice took on the slightest edge when he spoke—enough to make Anna narrow her eyes as she stared at him.

"As a matter of fact, I was," she replied, tired of playing games with him.

He made a *tsk*ing sound with his tongue. "I'm afraid he's not coming."

Anna's heart lurched. Apparently Richard was tired of playing games as well. "What do you mean?"

Still smiling, Richard moved toward her. "Let us take this conversation somewhere a bit more private, shall we?" He brushed past her, down the hall toward the drawing room. Anna had no choice but to follow. The nerve of him, treating her like an inferior in her own home!

"Close the door," he instructed once she stepped inside the room.

Fuming, Anna did so. Then she turned on him, her arms folded across her chest. "What's going on, Richard?"

His smile wasn't quite so bright now. "I could ask you the same thing, my dear. After all, you're the one who's been playing me for a fool for several days now."

Anna cocked a brow. "But you made it so easy." *Stop it, Anna, stop it! You don't know how unstable he is, and you're all alone with him. Don't antagonize him until you know where Ewan is.*

To her surprise, Richard laughed. "I did, didn't I? Well, I'm done with that now."

Locking her knees to keep them from trembling, Anna lifted her chin. "You said Ewan wasn't coming. I take that to mean you were aware of our plans."

"To run away?" At her nod, he continued, "Yes, I heard enough to put the pieces together when I spied the two of you in the library the other day. You really should be more careful whom you kiss, Anna. You never know who might be looking."

An angry flush crept up her cheeks. "Or in this case, 'what' might be watching."

He pursed his lips in a mock flinch. "I didn't know you could be quite so . . . abrasive, my dear. I'll have to cure you of that once we're married."

Anna started. He still wanted to marry her? What on

earth for? "I'm not going to marry you."

He smiled. "Yes, you are."

Ignoring that taunt, Anna tilted her head. "Where's Ewan?"

Richard sauntered over to the mantel and propped one elbow on it. He regarded her as though she were an unruly child. "He'll soon be on his way back to Scotland."

Anna lifted her chin defiantly. "I don't believe you."

Still smiling—Lord, how she was beginning to hate that smile!—Richard reached inside his coat and withdrew some papers. Unfolding them, he slipped one off the top and handed it to her. "See for yourself."

Coming no closer than she had to, Anna snatched the paper out of his hand and backed away until she felt there was a safe distance between them. That safe distance put her near the fireplace, where a poker sat within reach should she need a weapon. Only then did she read what he had given her.

> *My Dear Anna:*
> *By now you've realized that I'm not coming to meet you*
> *as planned. In fact, by the time you read this, I'll be*
> *preparing to return to Scotland. I think too much of you*
> *to continue on with this charade. I am not the Duke of*
> *Brahm. Richard was correct in his suspicions. I wanted*
> *the title and the money—and your dowry—to repair my*
> *home, but I cannot ruin so many lives just to benefit my*

own. I am already betrothed to a girl back home, and
honor will not allow me to treat her as shabbily as my
father treated my mother. I hope you will be able to find it
in your heart to forgive me my deception. I'm sorry to
have misled you so. I never meant to hurt you or come
between you and Richard. He is the one who can give you
the kind of life you deserve. I wish you much happiness
and hope in time you will remember me with fondness.
Yours truly, Ewan Fitzgerald.

Anna stared at the paper. Already betrothed? But he said he loved her! How could he . . .

No, he said he *adored* her, and there was a huge difference between that and love. Still, it was all too convenient. Too convenient for the man who stood to gain everything with Ewan out of the way.

She lifted her head, anger pooling deep within her. "You made him write this."

Richard shrugged. "If it makes you feel better to think that, then I won't try to stop you. But does that letter read like it was written by a man who was forced?"

He gazed at her expectantly and Anna realized he wasn't going to continue until she answered him. "It reads like he wrote what someone told him to."

Richard made a *tsking* sound as he shook his head. The look he gave her was one of pity. She was tempted to grab that poker and hit him with it.

"My dear Anna, I'm sorry to have to be the one to

deliver this heartbreak, but you know as well as I do that Ewan wanted you only for your dowry."

Anna shook with rage. "You lie."

Raising a brow, Richard eyed her knowingly. "Do I? Surely he's mentioned the sorry state of his ancestral home? I have it on good authority that he's been trying to restore it to its former glory for some time. With your dowry he would have been able to do that."

"He could have done it with his inheritance," Anna replied. She knew all about Ewan's hopes for his castle. He'd told her. Richard wasn't going to make her doubt him, not like this.

"Anna," he chided softly, as though she were a small child and not a young woman. "It would take a lot more money than what my father left him to fix that moldering pile of stone."

Anna didn't respond. She wasn't listening to this. She wouldn't!

Richard kept going, as though he sensed her hesitation. "You didn't really believe he'd fallen in love with you, did you?"

She fought to keep her expression blank, but she couldn't stop the blush that crept up her cheeks. She had believed it—she'd wanted to believe it. She still did, but Richard had played on her self-doubt and made her question Ewan's motives.

Richard smiled sympathetically, as though he could

see the direction of her thoughts. "Anna, he's known you only a few weeks. How could he possibly love you? He doesn't even know you." He stepped closer. "Not like I know you. Not like I love you."

After all these months, *now* Richard chose to tell her he loved her? It was much, much too late for that. He was the wrong brother.

But Richard was the one standing before her saying the right words, not Ewan.

Anna's heart felt as though it might break. "What do you want, Richard?"

Folding his hands in front of him, he met her gaze with eyes that looked surprisingly sincere. "I want you to marry me as we planned."

He what?

"Why?" she demanded, asking the question she'd been wanting to ask ever since he first proposed all those months ago. "Why do you want to marry me? You have everything."

Again he moved toward her and this time Anna took a step back. She had the overwhelming fear that he was going to touch her. She'd scream if he touched her.

Wisely, Richard didn't come any closer. "I just told you. I love you."

"I don't believe you." This was too easy. Too smooth. Richard couldn't fool her with his manipulation anymore. She didn't know if Ewan loved her or not, but she knew for a fact that Richard didn't.

Another sympathetic smile. How she wanted to wipe that pitying look right off his face. "Anna, I understand how upset you must be—"

"You don't understand anything."

He nodded. "Why don't I just leave you to sort this out for yourself?" He reached out to touch her cheek, but she jerked away.

He let his arm drop with a sorrowful expression. What a good actor he was. He almost had her believing he actually felt badly for her—that he felt anything for her.

"You let me know when you've reached your decision."

Anna remained silent as he turned and walked across the carpet to the door. He paused with his hand on the knob, and turned to face her again.

"I love you, Anna," he told her. "And I know you'll make the right choice."

He waited, as though he thought she might give him her answer right then.

"Good day, Richard." Her tone was so cold even she shivered at the sound of it.

She heard Richard sigh as he walked out the door. As soon as the latch clicked shut behind him, Anna sank down onto the nearest sofa and pressed a trembling hand to her mouth.

Was it true? What was real and what wasn't? Had Ewan actually left her or was something foul afoot? As sincere as

Richard sounded she couldn't shake the feeling that he'd been acting.

She didn't want to look at the paper in her hand, but something deep within her told her she had to. Yes, Richard had made her doubt Ewan in her mind, but her heart insisted that Ewan loved her as she loved him, that all was not as it seemed. And all she had to support her suspicions was the letter in her hand.

She read the words again. The handwriting and the signature were definitely Ewan's. Even the tone of the letter sounded as though he could have written it. But Anna couldn't believe he would cast her aside so easily. No, there had to be another explanation. Something wasn't right. She could feel it.

He referred to a girl "back home." Usually when Ewan spoke of "home" he called it Glenshea. It was out of character for him to not refer to it by name, but it was hardly proof that he'd been forced to write the letter.

Her gaze fell upon the signature. *Ewan Fitzgerald.*

That was it! Heart hammering, Anna checked one more time just to make certain her eyes weren't playing tricks on her. Sure enough, there it was. Ewan Fitzgerald.

Ewan's last name was MacLaughlin, not Fitzgerald. He'd taken his mother's name as part of his inheritance of her family's title. She remembered Ewan explaining it shortly after they'd first met.

Ewan did not write this letter. Oh, he might have

penned it, but someone else had told him what to write, obviously under the threat of some kind of harm. No doubt, Richard was the one who'd threatened him. And of course Richard wouldn't notice that his brother had signed the wrong name. Ewan was technically a Fitzgerald after all.

Which led her to wonder just what Richard had done with his brother. Was he holding him somewhere? Was he hurt? Was he . . . was he dead? No, she wouldn't let herself think that. She would know if Ewan was dead, wouldn't she? Somehow, she thought she'd feel it, deep down inside, she'd know if he was gone from her forever.

She had to save him. She had to find Ewan and she had to make Richard believe his plan had worked. He was much more likely to make a mistake if he was feeling overly confident, and he was less likely to do something desperate—something even more desperate than what he'd already done—for the same reason.

Hurrying across the room to the small desk in the corner, Anna pulled out a piece of parchment and hurriedly scribbled a very brief note to Richard. Lud, but she hoped she was doing the right thing!

> Richard—
> You were right about everything. I've made my decision.
> Yes, I will marry you. The sooner the better.

She sent a footman off to Brahm House with it posthaste. With any luck, Richard wouldn't receive it until later that day, but even so it didn't give her much time.

She had to find Ewan. And she had to do it before she married his brother.

"Mama, I need you to come to Bow Street with me."

Marion looked up from her breakfast with a mixture of surprise and horror. "Bow Street? Dear heavens, what has happened?"

Briefly, she told her mother about Richard's visit and the letter he'd shown her.

"Of course I'll come with you," her mother replied, pushing her chair away from the table. "Just let me fetch my cloak."

Fifteen minutes later, the two of them were in the carriage on their way to Bow Street. Anna had the letter Ewan found in Richard's room, along with the letter Richard had given her, in her reticule. She clutched the tiny purse as though it was all she had in the world.

Traffic was light at that hour of the morning and the drive to Bow Street's law office was shorter than normal. Just to be certain they weren't being followed, Marion had the driver drop them off down the street from their destination. It was easy for the two of them to lose themselves in the crowd weaving in and out along the sidewalk. Anna didn't think it would have occurred to someone as conceited as Richard to follow them, but she'd rather be safe than sorry.

Finally, they reached the Bow Street offices. Anna let her mother lead the way inside, where officers and criminals already swarmed like bees around summer flowers. How were they ever going to find someone to listen to them in all this clatter and noise?

She'd underestimated the power of her mother's boisterous nature. The woman knew how to raise a fuss that could wake the dead. Within minutes, they were in a private room with an officer, or "Runner" as they were called, giving them his full attention.

"Now," the officer, whose name was Bowles, told them. "What can I do to help you ladies?"

"I fear the life of a peer of the realm might be in danger," Anna replied.

Bowles's expression immediately lost its lightheartedness. "And who might that be?"

Anna drew a deep breath. "The Duke of Brahm." She told him the entire story, beginning with how Ewan's father had kept Ewan a secret and ending with Richard's visit to her that morning. She left nothing out, not even the fact that she and Ewan had planned to run away together. Her mother looked shocked, but said nothing. No doubt Anna would hear everything she had to say on the subject when they returned home later that morning.

By the time the Runner was through asking her

questions and getting her to repeat things, Anna was exhausted, but her spirits were lifted by the fact that the Runner seemed to think they'd be able to find Ewan just by having someone follow Richard. He kept the letters as evidence and gave Anna a card with his name on it, should she need anything or if anything else should happen.

"I think it's a wise idea for you to pretend to go along with this Fitzgerald fellow," Bowles told her. "We don't want anyone getting hurt, especially you. If he thinks everything is going the way he wants it, he's more likely to be relaxed, overconfident even, and that's when we'll nab him."

Anna managed a smile. "Thank you, Mr. Bowles. I appreciate everything you can do for us."

Bowles nodded. "I don't think I have to remind you not to tell anyone else about this, do I?"

Anna shook her head, as did her mother. "No, sir. We won't say a word."

"Good. Now, I want you to go home and get some rest. I'll be in touch as soon as I have any news for you."

And with that, they were dismissed.

As they stepped outside, her mother gave her a firm pat on the shoulder. "It will all be all right, darling. You'll see."

Anna hoped her mother was right, because if she wasn't, then Anna could very well end up married to a man she despised while the man she loved was lost to her forever.

CHAPTER ELEVEN

Thuuunk!

Ewan brought the table leg down on the chain with all his strength. Hours after Richard had left, he'd found that one of the links in the chain was even rustier than the others. It was so rusty he hoped that if he pounded on it long enough, it would break. He'd been pounding on it for several hours with no luck.

He was never going to get out of there.

Judging from what little light slipped in from the window high above his head, Ewan could tell it was getting dark. He'd been imprisoned in this cold cellar for almost twenty-four hours.

Richard had undoubtedly gone to Anna by now. What had he told her? Had she believed him? Ewan couldn't even entertain the thought. She knew how he felt about her. And she knew that Richard was up to no good. There was no way she'd believe his lies, especially with that false signature on the letter he'd been forced to sign.

His biggest fear was that she'd fought Richard. His brother was so unstable right now that any opposition could be met with violence. And if Richard harmed so much as one hair on Anna's head . . . well, Ewan would have to harm Richard.

He wiped the sweat from his brow with his sleeve. He was exhausted, and the light was too dim for him to tell if he'd weakened the chain at all.

How much longer was Richard going to keep him a prisoner here? Until after the wedding probably. He wouldn't want to risk Ewan's interference. And Ewan would interfere if he could. There was no way he'd allow Anna to marry Richard, which was why he'd better get back to work on breaking the chain.

The door opened and in walked one of the guards Richard had assigned to watch over him. He was also one of the men who'd beaten him that night. Ewan could tell because he'd suspected he'd broken the nose of one of his attackers with his elbow. This man had bandages over his nose, and every time he looked at him, Ewan could see the hatred in the man's eyes.

But the guard had made no further attempts to harm him, and hung a lantern high up on the wall, filling the cellar with warm, golden light. There wasn't much to see, but Ewan was grateful for it anyway.

"I brung you dinner," the great brute informed him in a deep, rolling voice. He set the tray on the floor and pushed it across the dirt floor. Starving, Ewan reached for it. He could just barely grab it with his fingers, even when his chain was stretched to its limit. Obviously Richard didn't want anyone getting too close now either.

"Thank you." Picking up the tray, Ewan set it on his lap. The smell of hot beef with gravy and potatoes reached his nostrils. It wasn't the work of the French chef he'd become accustomed to at Brahm House, but it still made his stomach growl in anticipation.

Grabbing up his fork and knife, he dug into the potatoes swimming in the rich, dark gravy. He closed his eyes and groaned in pleasure as the food touched his tongue. Oh Lord, it was good! He hadn't eaten since dinner the night before and hadn't quite realized just how hungry he was.

He was tearing into a chunk of thick, fresh bread loaded with butter when the door opened again. If it was the guard coming to collect the tray, the man was running a serious risk of having his nose broken again. Ewan wasn't finished eating.

It was Richard. Suddenly the food that was so wonderful just seconds ago tasted like sawdust in his mouth. Swallowing, Ewan eyed his brother warily. Was this it? Had Richard decided to get rid of him once and for all? Ewan's heart thudded against his ribs. It wasn't death that frightened him, although he had no desire to die. It was the idea of dying without ever seeing Anna again, without knowing if she believed in him. And the prospect of her marrying Richard filled him with an even deeper dread.

Smiling smugly, Richard stared down at him. Ewan kept

eating, but he set the tray aside.

"Why, brother, you look just like a filthy gypsy eating in the dirt like that."

It occurred to Ewan that his brother rarely called him by name. Why was that? Perhaps it made it easier for Richard to go through with his nefarious plan by treating Ewan more like an animal than a person.

Chewing, Ewan looked up. He swallowed before he spoke. "But I'm not a gypsy. I'm descended from the same blood as you, *brother.*"

Richard's eyes narrowed. "Only on one side."

Ewan shrugged. "But it's the side that counts, isn't it?" He meant no disrespect to Hester, but in England, it was the father's blood that counted, not the mother's. In England, Ewan never would have inherited a title through his mother.

A sneer twisted Richard's mouth. "But it's your mother's blood that shows. Her barbarian blood."

His brother had made similar disparaging remarks about the Scottish in front of Ewan before. It was a stereotype Ewan didn't quite understand, especially since Scotland boasted some of the best doctors and architects in the kingdom.

Ewan smiled. "Then I guess it's a good thing I look so much like our father, isn't it? So people will know whose son I am. Fortunately, you're pure English, so it doesn't matter so much that you look nothing like him."

He really shouldn't be baiting Richard this way, but Ewan's own temper was dangerously close to igniting. His fear for Anna and his exhaustion were wearing on him, chafing his already raw nerves.

Yes, he could tell by his brother's expression that he'd pushed him far enough. Richard looked ready to kill him.

"Why are you here, Richard?" Ewan asked, plucking an apple off his tray and polishing it on the one clean patch left on his shirt. "I thought our business was finished."

Instantly, Richard's anger disappeared, replaced with that superior confidence Ewan had come to despise. "I thought you might like to know that you will be returning to Scotland tomorrow afternoon."

Ewan frowned. "So soon?" He hoped his brother didn't hear the relief in his voice. If Richard wasn't going to kill him that meant Ewan still had a chance to stop him from marrying Anna—if he could only escape.

Richard's smile grew. "Yes. You'll be on your way shortly after Anna and I have said our vows."

Ewan fought to keep his face blank. If Richard knew how deeply those words cut him he would know his taunt had its desired effect.

"You're quite the man, Richard. Here you are, now a peer of the realm and you still have to force a woman to marry you. That doesn't say a whole lot for you, does it?"

He wasn't prepared for the kick. It hit him squarely

mid-thigh. And while it didn't hurt as much as a blow to the stomach, it still hurt.

Rubbing his leg, he glared up at his brother. "Why don't you unchain me, Richard, and the two of us can settle this on a bit more equal footing." Then, with as much insolence as he could muster, he dragged his gaze along his brother's shorter, slighter form. "Then again, with me chained up, perhaps we are equals."

Richard drew back to kick him again and Ewan surged to his feet. Richard had made the mistake of getting close enough to kick him and that put him within Ewan's reach. He snatched the smaller man by the lapels and hauled him so close their noses were almost touching. Richard's toes barely touched the ground. The shackle dug into Ewan's leg as he strained against it.

"Guard!" Richard screamed in Ewan's face. "*Guuuaaarrrd!*"

The fear on his brother's face was enough to make Ewan smile, and it would certainly be worth any beating the guard gave him.

"Where's your pistol, Richard?" He gave him a rough shake. "You're not such a big man without your weapon."

The door flew open with the guard's arrival and Ewan tossed Richard to the floor with a resigned grunt.

The man with the bandaged nose looked from Ewan to Richard.

"I want him beaten so badly it hurts to breathe!"

Richard cried, struggling to his feet.

The guard shot Ewan a dark gaze, but nodded. "All right."

Dusting off the seat of his trousers, Richard stomped toward the door. Obviously, not only was his brother a coward when it came to fighting him, he was also too squeamish to stay and watch his orders be carried out.

"You'll regret crossing me," Richard informed him, his voice shaking every bit as much as the finger he pointed at Ewan.

Ewan smiled bitterly. "Richard, I regret *meeting* you. I think you can safely assume that I also regret everything after that as well."

"Good. That will give you something to think about tomorrow morning when I marry the girl you love." With that parting shot, Richard stomped out the door.

Ewan turned his attention to the guard, who was still standing in the same spot, watching him with the same expression.

"Well," Ewan prompted, holding his arms out at his sides. "Aren't you going to beat me now?"

The guard shook his head. "Naw. You don't fight like a regular gent." His fingers went to his bandaged nose. "You fight dirty."

Stunned, Ewan watched as the big man shuffled from the room, shutting and locking the door behind him.

Well, at least he'd left him the lamp.

Sighing, Ewan rubbed his forehead with the heel of his hand. He had only until the morning to free himself. He could put only so much faith in the hope that someone would rescue him. He had to rely on himself. And so far, banging on the chain with a table leg hadn't gotten him very far.

Then he saw it. Lying on the tray not far from where he stood was his fork, glimmering in the lamplight.

He looked down at the shackle around his ankle. If he bent the tines on the fork enough that he could slip one inside the lock, then he just might be able to pick it.

Kneeling with his bound foot toward the light, Ewan grabbed the fork and set to work bending it. When he was finished, he stuck one tine into the lock and started moving it about, searching for the right spot.

If this worked, the poor guard was going to be in for a surprise when he came back to collect the tray.

And Richard would be in for a bit of a shock as well.

Anna was still awake when the sun rose the following morning. Despite Bow Street's assurances that they would find Ewan in time to prevent her from marrying Richard, she couldn't help but worry about what would happen if they didn't find Ewan in time. She would have to go through with the wedding.

The Runners had told her she didn't have to complete the ceremony, but Anna was terrified of what Richard might do to Ewan if she didn't. If Bow Street didn't find where Richard was keeping him, they'd have no evidence against Richard, and he'd know Anna had betrayed him, and he just might take that betrayal out on Ewan. So if it came to the point where Anna had to say "I do," then she would legally be bound to Richard.

She couldn't bear the thought. But if she said "I don't," then it might mean Ewan's death. And that was even worse than spending the rest of her life with Richard. She could only pray that Bow Street would find Ewan, or uncover enough evidence against Richard that they'd be able to hold him until Ewan was found.

Turning her head toward the window, she watched the sun rise through the glass from the warm comfort of her bed. Perhaps if she just stayed there everything would be all right. Maybe she could pretend to be sick. Richard could hardly force her to get out of bed if she was ill, could he?

No, Richard would know she was lying. And he'd threaten Ewan in order to get her out of bed, even if she really was sick. He wouldn't care as long as he got what he wanted.

If only Ewan's plan had worked. If only they'd managed to escape that night, then she might very well be his wife right now.

And he'd have all the money he needed to repair his castle. Perhaps then he'd decide he didn't need a wife after all?

No. She couldn't think such things. Richard wasn't

above lying to get what he wanted, she had ample proof of that. Until she saw Ewan again, Anna would believe that he had been sincere in wanting to marry her, that money had nothing to do with it. The only thing giving her the strength to go through with this charade was the promise of Ewan's love. She would hold on to that and deal with the truth when the time came.

The only hope of ever discovering that truth depended heavily on Anna's ability to continue the charade of cooperating with Richard to buy Bow Street more time. For that reason alone, she threw back the covers and swung her feet over the side of the bed. It was time get ready. The wedding was to be held at Brahm House at eleven o'clock that morning.

Padding across the carpet, Anna let out a huge yawn and shrugged into her robe. Across the room, she pulled the cord that would ring for her maid in the servant's quarters. The girl probably wasn't even awake yet, so she flopped down in a chair by the fireplace and waited.

What had Richard told poor Hester and Emily? That Ewan had up and left them? Had he shown them the fraudulent letter? Surely they wondered at the suddenness of the wedding. Originally she and Richard weren't to have married until the spring. Did the two women suspect Richard of any wrongdoing? Or were they blissfully unaware? Anna hadn't asked them. She didn't want to endanger either woman by telling them the truth, and she certainly didn't want to be the one to tell them just how evil Richard truly was.

There was no way around it; the two of them would be devastated when they learned what Richard had done, and Anna worried that the shock might be too much for poor Hester to handle, especially so soon after the death of her husband.

A knock sounded upon the door. "Come in," Anna called.

The door swung open, revealing a very sleepy-looking maid. So, she had been up when Anna rang—but just barely. She still had creases on the side of her face from the pillow pressed against her cheek.

Anna couldn't help but smile at the poor girl's appearance. "Good morning, Jane. I'm sorry to have called for you at this early hour."

The maid stifled a yawn and grinned sheepishly. "Good morning, miss."

"Will you have water sent up for a bath please, Jane? And see if my gown is ready?"

Jane curtsied in response. "Yes, miss. Would you like some breakfast sent up, miss?"

The very thought of eating made Anna's stomach roll in revulsion, but she knew she had to keep her strength up. "Just a cup of chocolate for now. I'll eat with my mother later."

"Would you like me to ask Mrs. Welsley to come to

you once she's up, miss?"

Anna nodded. "Yes. Thank you. That will be all for now, Jane. I'm afraid we have a very busy morning ahead of us."

The girl smiled, curtsied again, and left to fetch a footman to carry the bathwater.

Anna doubted her mother had slept much more than she had last night. No doubt her father had slept like the dead, blissfully unaware of his daughter's plight. His heart wasn't as strong as it used to be and neither Anna nor her mother wanted to worry him unless it was absolutely necessary. And they hadn't wanted to risk him rushing off and doing something foolish—like confronting Richard and revealing their plans.

Glancing toward the ceiling, Anna sent up a silent prayer that when her mother did come to her room she would bring news from Bow Street with her. Any news, even bad would be better than this not knowing anything at all.

A few moments later two footmen arrived, carrying buckets of steaming water. Once they left, Jane set to work, adding rosewater to the bath, placing a cake of rose-scented soap and a washcloth on the stool beside the tub. She placed several jars there as well. Jane prided herself on the quality of her beauty creams and remedies.

"Anything there for dark circles, Jane?" Anna asked as she stepped into the fragrant, wonderfully warm water. "I must look like a raccoon."

Jane smiled. "Don't you worry, miss. By the time I'm done, you'll look like your normal lovely self."

Anna smiled and leaned back in the tub. "Only as good as that? I must look positively awful now, do I?"

Jane giggled and ducked her head. "You always look pretty, miss—even if you do seem a little tired."

Still smiling, Anna rested her head against the back of the tub and let Jane work her magic. She scrubbed at her skin when one of the concoctions had to be left on for a period of time, and washed her hair during the last treatment. When Jane dumped a bucket of fresh water over her head to rinse out the soap, the cream washed off her face as well.

There was nothing quite like the feeling of being clean. Anna knew she was odd in that respect. Most young girls she knew bathed regularly, but few bathed as often as she did. And there were some people of her acquaintance who could certainly benefit from bathing more often. Augh! Even some members of London's high society smelled as though they bathed once a month—if that.

Ewan certainly wasn't among their ranks. He always smelled of sandalwood soap and that fresh, clean scent that was decidedly his. Just the thought of it was enough to cause tears to sting the backs of Anna's eyes. She couldn't bear the thought of never seeing him again, of never breathing in the scent of him, of never again experiencing the way he made her feel.

Drawing a deep breath, she tried to force herself to relax, to allow the hot water to loosen the knots in her back and shoulders. She needed to relax. She had to gather her wits and try to keep her emotions at bay. She would do Ewan no good at all if she became a bundle of nerves.

But it didn't stop her from worrying. As she climbed out of the tub and wrapped herself in the soft towels Jane offered her, Anna's mind tumbled with anxiety.

She knew she should just trust in Bow Street to find Ewan and bring him safely home, but she couldn't. And she couldn't help but wonder just what she was going to do if they hadn't found Ewan before the time came to say her vows.

They would find him. They would.

What if he didn't want her? What if he decided she was to blame for Richard's insane behavior and despised her for it?

She shuddered at the thought. Jane, mistaking the gesture for a genuine chill, built a small fire in the hearth. It was a fine summer morning and there was little need for it, but Anna was glad for the warmth.

She was sitting beside the fire, curled up in the chair, sipping her hot, sweet chocolate when her mother entered, carrying a tray. Funny how chocolate always seemed to make everything better.

"I brought you something to eat," her mother said as she closed the door behind her. "I doubt you feel like it, but you should have a little something. I brought you some eggs and some toast and jam."

Anna smiled. That sounded very much like a good breakfast to her, but to someone who loved food as much as her mother, it was a small repast indeed.

"Thank you." Anna took the tray and set her cup on it. Her stomach growled and she realized with some surprise that she was hungrier than she'd thought. Even though she didn't feel like eating, her body certainly seemed to think she needed it.

She chewed a bite of egg and swallowed. Dreading the answer she steeled herself to ask, "Any news from Bow Street?"

Her mother shook her head, a few stray curls bobbing out from underneath her lace cap. "Not yet, but they said they'd be in touch this morning, so I'm expecting something soon."

Frustrated, Anna dug into the food on her plate. "If they've been following Richard ever since we went to them, he must have surely led them to Ewan by now."

Her mother nodded. "One would think. Richard's too sure of his hold over you to think you'd betray him by going to the authorities. And he's far too full of himself to think anyone would be able to follow him."

Anna didn't remind her mother that less than a week ago she was one of Richard's staunchest supporters. While she certainly didn't like or approve of the fact that her mother had plotted with Richard to ruin Ewan, she had to admit that her mother had certainly made up for her poor behavior.

She managed to finish every morsel of food on the tray, plus her chocolate. Then, with her belly full, she leaned back in her chair and gazed at her mother. "Do you think they'll find him in time, Mama?"

Marion nodded, her jaw set with determination. "I'm sure of it. In fact, I wouldn't be surprised if the duke managed to free himself before they even get there. Knowing what he does of Richard's capabilities, I cannot imagine that he isn't trying with all his might to escape."

Anna took some comfort in her mother's resolve. "No, Ewan would certainly put up a good fight." But what if Richard's hired thugs had beaten Ewan so badly that he couldn't save himself? What if he were lying somewhere battered and bleeding? No, she wouldn't let herself think such horrible thoughts. It did no good. She had to remain calm if she wanted to help Ewan. Until she was told differently, she would assume that Ewan was hale and healthy, and on his way back to her.

As she and her mother talked, Anna dried her hair in front of the fire. Once it was almost dry, her mother helped her dress. Everything was new, except for her gown. She'd always wanted to be married in her blue satin, but given the circumstances, she decided against it. Instead, she was wearing a gown from last Season, when she'd made her debut. It was the dress she'd worn the night she and Richard met. For that reason alone Anna was loath to wear it.

It was a plain ivory gown that she and her mother had altered by sewing a few rosettes on the neckline and hem to make it a bit more festive. It had short cap sleeves and a modest scoop neckline. An ivory ribbon ran along the high waistline, just underneath her bosom. It was simple and elegant—and much better than Richard deserved.

After slipping into her stockings and shift, her mother helped her into the gown, fastening the dozens of tiny pearl buttons that ran up the back.

"What are you going to have Jane do to your hair?" her mother asked as Anna swept the heavy mass of dark waves off her shoulder to cascade down her back.

"Does it matter?"

Her mother smiled a little. "But what if the duke arrives? Don't you want to look pretty when you see him again?"

She had a point. "Maybe she could curl it a little. . . ." They discussed possible hairstyles for twenty minutes—or at least that's how long it took for Anna to realize that her mother had started the conversation only to keep her mind off of Ewan's safety.

Finally, she decided to let Jane curl her hair and pile some of it on top of her head, allowing the rest to tumble over her shoulders and down her back. It would be a very Grecian style, which was certain to be fashionable.

A knock on the door signaled Jane's arrival. Just in time.

But the maid stood in the doorway with a confused expression on her face. "Beg your pardon, Mrs. Welsley, but there's a gentleman from Bow Street here to see you—"

The poor girl never got a chance to finish as Anna and her mother both bolted from the room. Skirts hiked up around their ankles, they ran down the stairs, Anna in the lead.

Sure enough, Officer Bowles stood in the front hall, dressed in a brown coat instead of Bow Street's trademark red. Anna supposed he'd intentionally not worn the coat just in case Richard had the house watched.

"Good morning, Mrs. Welsley, Miss Welsley," he spoke as he removed his hat.

Anna and her mother both curtsied. "Do you bring us news, Mr. Bowles?" Marion asked.

"I do," Mr. Bowles replied. "Our men followed Mr. Fitzgerald to an abandoned store in the east end of the city this morning. We think that might be where he's keeping the duke. Several Runners will be on their way to the building shortly."

Knees weak, Anna couldn't help but laugh out loud, so great was her joy. "Oh, Mr. Bowles, thank you!"

He held up his hands as though he was afraid she might actually try to hug him. "Don't thank me yet, Miss Welsley. We still have to go in and make sure it's the place we're looking for. I'm afraid you still have to keep up the ruse until we have His Grace in our custody."

Anna's shoulders sagged. "Honestly?" But she didn't want to continue the deception; she wanted Ewan!

"Is that really necessary, Mr. Bowles?" her mother asked, coming up behind Anna to rest her hands on her shoulders. "It's still another hour before we have to leave for Grosvenor Square."

Bowles nodded curtly, but his expression was one of sympathy. "I understand, Mrs. Welsley, and I wish I could tell you otherwise, but we don't know for certain that the duke is in that building. And we don't know if Fitzgerald plans to return after the wedding, or what kind of instructions he gave his men. Quite frankly, I don't want to get too cocky or take any unnecessary chances with the duke's life. The more confident Fitzgerald is, the less suspicious he'll be."

He was right of course, but that didn't mean Anna had to like it. Oh well, it wasn't that bad. It wasn't as though that hour was going to be spent in Richard's company.

But it was to be spent worrying about Ewan and wondering how he was going to react to her when they met again. And that was assuming this abandoned building was where Richard was holding him.

"We'll do whatever you want, Mr. Bowles," she assured him. "Just do everything you can to ensure the duke's safe return."

His smile was warm. "We'll do our best, Miss Welsley."

He set his hat back on his head and tipped it at them. "I'll see you both at the wedding." He spoke as though everything was going to work out, but Anna suspected he had a backup plan just in case.

Once the door closed behind him, Anna turned to her mother. "I hate this."

Marion hugged her, and Anna took comfort in the gesture. "I don't like it either, dearest, but we have to be strong." Releasing her, her mother seized her by the hand and pulled her up the stairs. "Come, let us have Jane start on your hair. Perhaps His Grace will be waiting for us when we arrive at the house."

Anna hoped so too, because if he wasn't, she didn't think she was going to have to pretend to faint. She was going to do it for real.

Richard returned to the cellar that morning. Only for a few moments, though. Long enough to show off his wedding finery and to finalize plans for Ewan's return to Scotland.

And long enough to tell him how agreeable Anna was being about going through with the wedding.

It had taken all of Ewan's control not to throw off his shackle and attack his brother. He'd succeeded in picking the lock the night before, but bided his time, waiting for the guard to come back. Attacking Richard might make him feel better, but if the guard returned, Ewan would be outnumbered and he had no desire to have his own plans destroyed because he couldn't keep his temper.

Ewan knew his brother wouldn't hesitate to lie to him, but he couldn't help the sliver of doubt that planted itself in his mind. Was it possible Anna had begun to believe Richard's deception? Did she think Ewan had abandoned her? He didn't want to believe it. Surely Anna trusted him more than that? But how could he expect her not to doubt him when he doubted her?

Panic gnawed at his insides, but he pushed it aside. He had to get to Anna and make her believe he would never lie to her. But he couldn't just run up the stairs and hope that he could make it past both the guard and his brother's pistol. He had to be patient and wait for his chance.

So he waited. Long after Richard's voice disappeared up the stairwell, he was still waiting. Ewan's patience was quickly coming to an end. If the guard didn't come soon, he was going to call him in—and that was liable to raise the man's suspicions.

If he managed to overpower the guard—no, he wouldn't allow himself to think "if"—once he'd over-powered the guard, he'd lock him inside the cellar. With hope, there weren't other guards posted up above. Ewan doubted it. His brother was too cautious to hire many men. The other man who'd helped beat Ewan might be upstairs, but Ewan didn't doubt that he could handle him, provided he wasn't armed.

Bending down, Ewan fiddled with the shackle until it sat loosely on top of his foot. From a distance it might look as though it was still securely locked around his leg, but it would fall off if Ewan moved quickly, which was the plan. He'd just straightened when he heard the key in the lock.

The guard came in, carrying another tray. Ewan felt almost guilty about deceiving him. After all, the fellow could have beaten him last night and hadn't.

Then again, he'd blackened Ewan's eye that night of the attack. It was still swollen and bruised from that. Suddenly, he didn't feel as badly about what he was about to do.

The guard set the tray on the table. "The boss thought you might like something to eat before we leave."

Ewan's smile was tight. "How thoughtful."

Gesturing to the previous night's supper tray, which still sat on the floor—with a fork that didn't look as though it had been used as a lock-pick at all—the other man flashed Ewan a wary glance.

"Stand back while I pick that up," he ordered.

Ewan did as he was told, but as he did, the shackle slid off his foot to the floor.

Blast it all!

The guard's face hardened. Roaring in anger, he charged.

Fists raised, his heart and soul intent on freedom, Ewan stepped forward to meet him.

CHAPTER TWELVE

Ewan didn't waste any time. As soon as the guard came into reach, he drove his fist right into the man's bandaged nose. Hard.

"*Ow!*" Cradling his face, the man sank to his knees, moaning in agony.

"I wish I could say I'm sorry," Ewan remarked, skirting around the fallen guard. "But I'm not."

He ran across the dirt floor as fast as he could. He could hear the guard groaning as he rose to his feet behind him. Slamming the heavy wooden door shut as he raced through the opening, he turned the key in the lock and then cautiously—but quickly—climbed the stairs.

There was another door at the top. It sat wide open, and as he peered around the frame, he saw that he'd been held captive in what looked like an abandoned store.

There was no one else about, and judging from the footprints in the dust that caked the floor, the fellow he'd just locked up downstairs was the only other person in the building. Good. He wouldn't have to worry about being attacked by someone else while trying to escape.

From the cellar, he heard the guard yelling at him.

He sounded angry—only someone very, very angry used language like this man was using. Ewan's grandmother would box his ears if she ever heard him talk like that.

He left the ground-floor door open, so the guard would be easily found if anyone else came to the building. He didn't want the man to be locked up for long with only a little food and water.

But he had more important things to think about. He had to get to Brahm House and stop Richard. He didn't know if the wedding was being held there or not, but at least someone there would be able to tell him where to go.

He ran for the nearest door with hope it would lead him outside.

"Don't move!" a voice barked as he pulled it open.

Ewan froze, and found himself surrounded by several men wearing red coats. Didn't the Bow Street Runners wear red coats?

The man closest to him looked him up and down. Ewan could only imagine how he looked, his fine coat and trousers soiled beyond repair and his cravat all askew around his neck.

"Your Grace?" the man asked, his voice hesitant.

Ewan didn't know whether to relax or tense, so he did nothing. "Yes," he replied, his gaze never leaving the other man's.

"I'm Mr. Bowles," the Runner replied with a relieved

chuckle. "We've been looking for you. Miss Welsley's been very worried about you."

Ewan's shoulders sagged with relief. Thank God! Anna had gone to the Runners just as she'd promised she would. She hadn't fallen for Richard's deception! Not completely, anyway.

"Well, I'm very glad you found me," Ewan told him. "There's a man locked up in the cellar. He's been working for my brother, Richard Fitzgerald. I recognized him as a man who attacked me several nights ago."

Bowles ordered three of his men to go down to the cellar. "Your Grace, I have quite a few questions to ask you."

Ewan edged closer to the outside steps. "No doubt you do, but I'm afraid they're just going to have to wait. You see, I have a wedding to stop." Brushing past the officer, he practically jumped off the steps to the ground.

Bowles was hot on his heels. "Allow me to accompany you." His tone clearly told Ewan that he wouldn't accept no as an answer. Hailing a hackney cab, Bowles held the door so that Ewan might climb in first. "I also would like to be there when Mr. Fitzgerald discovers that he's been caught. You can answer my questions along the way."

Leaning back against the seat, Ewan sighed in frustration. "If I answer your questions, will you promise to arrest my brother on sight?"

Bowles smiled and leaned out the door. "Grosvenor Square," he ordered the driver. "And if you know what's good for you, you'll hurry!"

How much longer was she going to have to maintain this farce?

Anna sat in a parlor just down the hall from the drawing room where the ceremony was to be held. Her mother waited with her, both of them chewing on their fingernails and pacing as the hour drew closer and closer to eleven.

That was how Hester and Emily found them when they came in a few moments later.

"Nervous, my dear?" Hester asked with a smile when she saw Anna.

On the verge of hysteria, Anna nodded. "A little," she managed to squeak.

Hester sat down on a nearby cream brocade-covered sofa. "I was nervous on my wedding day too. It's only natural. I only wish I knew what Richard's hurry was." Her gaze locked with Anna's. "Has something happened that I should know about?"

Oh, so many things had happened that Hester should know about, Anna wouldn't even know where to start! "I suppose he's just eager," she lied.

Emily toyed with the fingers of her gloves. The young girl looked so blue-deviled and depressed it wasn't funny.

"I wish Ewan was here."

Hester covered her hand with one of her own. "So do I, dear."

So did Anna. Here was the opening she'd been looking for. "Where is Ewan, anyway?"

Emily's wide blue eyes were glassy with unshed tears. "We don't know!"

Hester patted her daughter's hand. "He left me a brief note thanking me for our hospitality but that he was leaving for Scotland immediately."

"And he didn't say anything but good-bye in mine," Emily interrupted with a sniff.

"He left Richard a letter saying that Richard was the true heir to the dukedom, but that just doesn't make sense." Hester looked up. "I *know* Ethan and Maureen were married, Anna. I've seen the marriage certificate. Ethan believed it to be valid and so do I. Why would Ewan write such a letter?"

Oh, how badly Anna wanted to tell her the truth, to tell her just what a lying monster her son was, but she couldn't. She couldn't hurt Hester like that.

"I don't know," she lied. "Perhaps he knew how much the title meant to Richard."

Hester's expression was pained. "Even so, he can't just *give* it to Richard. It's not legal, especially if the marriage was valid."

Anna struggled to remain calm even though her heart was pounding. Hester knew the truth! Richard would not be able to prove his false claims to the title when his mother knew they were lies. How she wished she could tell Hester that.

"I just don't know, Hester. It makes no sense to me either."

Hester's jaw tightened and Anna was shocked by how stern she looked. "I don't think so. I think you know more about what's going on than you're telling me, Anna. Do you know where Ewan is?"

Swallowing hard against the words that threatened to spill out of her, Anna shook her head. As guilty as she felt for not telling Hester the whole truth, she couldn't bear to be the one to explain everything to her. At least she wouldn't be lying this time. "No, Hester. I can honestly tell you I have no idea where he is. I wish I did."

Hester sighed. "So do I. I'm sorry for being so short with you, my dear. I'm just so worried. Even though he's not my son, I've come to care for Ewan in the short time I've known him."

Anna understood how she felt all too well.

"We all started to care for him!" Emily blurted, the tears in her eyes giving way to anger. "We deserve more than an impersonal note in farewell!" She turned away as a sob burst forth.

The weight of her friend's sorrow pushed heavily on Anna's shoulders. She couldn't keep silent much longer.

Hester's gaze was pained as it turned from her daughter to Anna. "I know there was some tension between him and Richard. Richard took his father's death so hard, and then to find out that he wasn't the heir after all . . . well, you can imagine what an upset it might be to a young man."

"Yes," Anna replied, almost choked with bitterness. "I can imagine." She didn't have to imagine. She *knew* how hard Richard had taken his father's death—it had driven him insane.

Rising to her feet, Hester smiled her kind, sweet smile. "I'm sure you and your mother would like a little time alone before the ceremony. Emily and I will leave you now." She came to Anna with arms outstretched, wrapping them around her in a delicate embrace. "You're bringing so much joy to our family, Anna," Hester whispered against her ear.

Horror seized Anna by the heart. Joy? Good heavens, joy was the last thing she was going to give poor Hester. When Bow Street arrived and took Richard away, Hester was going to be heartbroken. But there was no other way. Richard had to pay for what he'd done.

Plastering a bright smile on her face, Anna returned the hug and when Hester released her, embraced Emily as well. Then the two women took their leave, and left Anna and her mother alone again.

"That poor woman is going to be crushed when this is all over," Marion remarked softly.

Anna shook her head. "I really don't know if I can do this to her."

"You're not to blame for any of this."

Anna pinned her mother with a sharp gaze. "Am I not? If I hadn't fallen in love with Ewan, Richard might have contented himself with my fortune and left his brother alone!"

"Do you honestly believe that would have been enough to appease Richard's greed?"

Wearily, Anna shook her head. "I don't know, but at least then I wouldn't be lying to two people who have never been anything but kind to me."

Her mother's gaze was narrow. "Do you want to save Ewan?"

How could she even ask? "Of course I do!"

"Then you must do this in spite of the pain it will cause Hester."

Her mother was right, of course. Anna might not like the situation, but she would do whatever she had to in order to ensure Ewan's safety.

She glanced at the grandfather clock in the far corner. Only fifteen minutes left.

"They're not going to make it in time," Anna said, her voice hovering dangerously close to panic.

Crossing the carpet with three impatient strides, her mother took both of Anna's hands in hers and stared deep into her eyes. "Anna, you must relax. Bow Street knows where Ewan is. I'm sure they have him now and are on their way here as we speak."

In her heart, Anna wanted to believe her mother, but she couldn't fight the awful doubt and fear that simmered within her. "And if they aren't?"

Her mother's mouth tightened. "Then right before you are about to take your vows, I will throw myself on the floor and pretend I'm suffering an apoplexy."

Anna laughed, much of the tension leaving her body with the mental image of her mother pitching her round body to the floor and pretending to have a seizure in front of Hester and her family.

"You'd do that for me?" Pulling her hands free, Anna wiped her eyes.

Marion smiled sadly. "I am not without my share of the blame for this situation going as far as it has. I should have known from the beginning that Richard was unstable, but he played on my greed and my determination that you would marry well. I could never forgive myself if I actually allowed him to hurt you or Lord Brahm. So yes, I will throw myself on the floor and make an idiot of myself if it will keep you out of his clutches."

More tears filled Anna's eyes, and this time they weren't from laughter. Her throat and chest were tight with emotion.

"Thank you," she whispered, reaching out and squeezing her mother's hand. Her mother nodded, as though she didn't dare speak for fear of making them both burst into tears.

It was five minutes to eleven. Oh, why did time go so fast when she didn't want it to?

"They'll come," her mother said in a firm, yet hoarse voice. "They have to come."

It felt like only seconds had passed when a knock came upon the door. Heart pounding, Anna stared at her mother as she bade whomever it was to enter. Was it Bow Street? Was it Ewan?

It was a footman. Anna's heart sank.

"They wanted me to tell you that it's time, Mrs. Welsley, Miss Welsley," the young man told them.

Oh please, no! She couldn't do this! Her mother met her horrified gaze with a sympathetic one. Turning to the footman, she said, "We'll be ready in just a moment."

The footman bowed and left. Marion took Anna by the shoulders. "I can't do this, Mama," Anna whispered.

"You can, and you will. You don't have to say 'I do.' Just go along with everything right up until then." She squeezed. "I'll be there with you, ready to humiliate myself if necessary. All right?"

Anna nodded, drawing a deep breath for strength. Of course she could do this. She had no choice.

"Good." Her mother released her. "I have to go take my seat now. I'll send your father in."

Left in the room by herself, Anna could fully face her fear. She knew Ewan hadn't meant to jilt her that night. She knew he'd been serious about taking her to Scotland and marrying her, whatever the reasons behind the offer. What she didn't know was if he would still want her.

The letter Richard had shown her was obviously a fake, but Ewan had had plenty of time since then to reconsider his offer. What if he wasn't with the Runners when—*if*—they stopped the wedding? What if he didn't want to see her? What if it had been just a plan to get at her fortune and he didn't care about her at all? What if his kisses—kisses that had turned Anna's world upside down—had meant nothing to him? Nothing whatsoever.

Marrying Richard was easier to face than the idea that Ewan might not care for her.

Squaring her shoulders, she pushed the awful thought aside. She had to concentrate on the moment, not what might or might not happen. She was not going to marry Richard and she would deal with whatever happened with Ewan afterward. If she thought about it now she would just break down and then Richard might do something that would hurt more than just Ewan or herself.

Her father barely had time to give her a kiss on the cheek before the music started. *Poor Papa.* He still didn't know what was going on.

Anna's knees shook as they made the short walk to the drawing room. Everyone turned to watch her as they stepped inside the door. Thankfully there weren't very many people there—Hester, Emily, Anna's mother, and a school friend of Richard's. Hardly the big church wedding Richard had originally wanted.

The groom stood near the mantel with the vicar. Anyone who saw him might believe his smile to be one of happiness at the sight of his bride, but Anna knew better. It was his smug victory smile. He thought he'd won, that he'd outsmarted them all.

At that moment, Anna realized that she'd never hated anyone in her life as much as she hated Richard Fitzgerald.

Her father walked her right up to Richard and the minister, and then he left her. She wanted to cling to him, beg him not to give her to such a vile man, but she couldn't. As cowardly as she felt, she knew she had to trust that everything would be all right.

"You're lovely," Richard told her, loud enough for everyone to hear. Anna winced when she heard Hester's happy sigh. How could his mother not see that Richard was putting on an act? He was a remarkable actor.

Unable to stand the sight of her groom any longer,

Anna turned to face the vicar, who took that as his sign to begin the ceremony.

"Dearly beloved, we are gathered here today . . ."

Oh God, she was going to be sick. Sucking deep breaths through her nostrils, Anna closed her eyes and willed her stomach to stop churning.

It will be all right. It will be all right. . . . Over and over, she repeated the words in her head until her stomach calmed and the hot dizziness swarming her mind disappeared. It would have been awful if she'd cast up the contents of her stomach all over the poor vicar.

Then again, it certainly would have put an end to the ceremony. The thought made her smile—almost.

Oh God, where were the Runners? Why hadn't they arrived? Shouldn't they have been there by now? Had something happened? Something to Ewan?

The room swam around her and she closed her eyes. She concentrated on her breathing. She concentrated on remaining upright. She concentrated on everything but what was going on around her.

How long she stood there, staring at her flowers, she had no idea. She thought of Ewan, of their first kiss, their first dance. She even went so far as to pretend it was him standing beside her and not his lunatic brother.

". . . husband?"

Anna looked up. The vicar was looking at her. Richard was looking at her. She glanced over her shoulder.

Everyone was looking at her. She turned back to the vicar. "I beg your pardon?"

The vicar smiled. "I asked, do you take this man to be your lawfully wedded husband?"

No! No, she didn't! "I—"

From behind her, she heard her mother moan. Oh Lord, she was really going to fake a seizure!

"Answer the man," Richard hissed, grabbing her arm in a painful grip. "Say 'I do.'"

"You're hurting me!" Anna hit him with her bouquet, scratching him with a thorn. He jumped back with a curse. The vicar raised his brows.

"I do *not!*" she cried as Richard fixed her with a glare of pure hatred. "I wouldn't marry you if you were the last man on earth!"

Hester gasped, her father snored, and the vicar watched the whole thing with blatant interest.

Fists clenched at his sides, Richard stepped toward her, his face flushed with fury. "You will marry me. You'll marry me or your dear Ewan will never make it back to Scotland alive."

Another gasp. Poor Hester.

"Now, see here, young man—" the vicar began.

Richard turned on him. "That's 'my lord' to you. I'm the duke, do you hear me? I'm the Duke of Brahm and I will be treated with all the respect that title demands!"

"You don't deserve the respect that title demands,"

boomed a familiar voice from the doorway.

Now it was Anna's turn to gasp.

It was Ewan.

Happy as he was to see Anna, it was Richard whom
Ewan kept his gaze locked on. His brother was a powder
keg right now, and he looked ready to explode.

"You!" Richard cried in disgust. "What are you
doing here?"

Ewan turned to Bowles. "That's him." He watched as
the Runners converged on his brother. He knew he should
feel something—anger, even sympathy—but he couldn't.
All he felt was relief that it was finally over.

"No!" Richard shouted as the Runners tried to sur-
round him. He ran behind the vicar. "You can't do this!
I'm the Duke of Brahm."

Hester stood, her face white with shock. She turned to
Ewan. "What's the meaning of this?"

But it was Bowles who answered. "I'm afraid your son
kidnapped His Grace and tried to force him to sign over
his title."

Hand pressed to her heart, Hester sank back into her
chair. Emily wrapped her arms around her shoulders. The
two of them looked completely shocked.

"Why?" Hester whispered.

Ewan felt the anguish in her voice. Reaching out, he laid

a hand on her shoulder. "I'm afraid Richard has amassed some significant debts, Hester," he said in the softest tone he could manage. "He was desperate for money."

Hester paled as she digested the information. Choking on a sob, she turned away, slipping away from Ewan's hand and into the arms of a very confused-looking Emily.

Richard struggled as two of the Runners grabbed him by the arms and pulled him toward the door. "You can't do this to me!" he cried. "I'm a peer of the realm!"

Stepping to the side, Ewan tried to get out of the way as his brother was dragged forward. Richard dug his heels into the carpet every step of the way, struggling against his captors until his pale blue coat tore and his hair stood on end like a wild man's. He pulled up short in front of Ewan.

"I'm the Duke of Brahm!" he insisted, his blue eyes bright as they met Ewan's. "I have the paper to prove it! It proves you're illegitimate. You signed it!"

Slowly, Ewan shook his head. Pity was an awful thing to feel for one's brother. "You should have paid more attention to that signature, Richard. My last name's MacLaughlin, not Fitzgerald."

Disbelief flickered across Richard's face. "No."

Ewan nodded. "Yes."

"You tricked me!"

Surely Richard couldn't find it that hard to believe?

After everything Richard had done, did he truly believe he and Anna wouldn't try to fight back? Did he think they'd give up so easily just because he thought the title should be his and not Ewan's? Apparently, yes.

Ewan met his brother's gaze. "Yes, Richard. I tricked you. I'm still the Duke of Brahm, and I always will be." He turned his attention to Bowles. "Please get him out of here."

"No!" Richard cried as the Runners started pulling him again. "*No!*"

Two other Runners shut the doors as the others hauled Richard through it, muffling his angry shouts.

"What's going to happen to him?"

Ewan's heart broke when he looked at Hester. Clinging to Emily, she looked as fragile as a china doll.

"I'll make certain he gets the help he needs, Hester. He'll be looked after." And he meant it. He knew of at least one doctor who might be capable of helping Richard put his mind back to rights. His brother had been driven to madness by grief and greed. Surely a young man could be brought back from such a thing.

But Ewan had more important things to think about than his brother's sanity.

Anna still stood near the back of the room, clutching a bent and broken bouquet of white and yellow roses. She was the most beautiful thing he'd ever seen in her long white gown with her hair and lace veil cascading down her back. She stared at him with big brown eyes brimming with tears, and suddenly his own eyes felt as though they were burning.

He'd worried that he'd never see her again. He'd been terrified he'd lost her forever. And now all he could do was stand there and stare at her like an idiot gazing upon a goddess.

"Ewan." Her voice was choked with emotion. "You came."

The next thing he knew, he was standing in front of her. How he'd crossed the room that quickly he had no idea, and he didn't care. Sweeping her off her feet, he crushed her against his chest, twirling her around in a circle as he kissed her like a thirsty man given a drink of water.

"Of course I came," he murmured against her lips, reluctant to stop kissing her. "I couldn't let you marry Richard, could I?"

"What the devil is going on here?" he heard Anna's father demand.

Chuckling, Ewan set Anna back on her feet, and turned to face her family and his own. "I'm in love with your daughter, Mr. Welsley, and with your permission I'd like to marry her."

Anna's mother clapped her hands in glee. Even Hester and Emily managed to look happy for them, despite their shock over Richard.

Mr. Welsley definitely looked confused, but he

shrugged. "Certainly, my boy. Certainly."

Ewan turned back to Anna. Her smile was hesitant. "You're not just doing this for the money to repair your castle, are you?"

If she'd slapped him he wouldn't have been more shocked. "You think I just want your money?" He couldn't keep the incredulity from his voice.

A dark blush crept up her cheeks. "You said you needed a lot of money."

He stared deep into her eyes and saw the insecurity there. What had Richard told her? He tried not to be hurt by her doubt. After all, he'd doubted her as well.

"I have a lot of money," he informed her. "I have all the money I need. Anna, I love you."

Tears filled her eyes. "Do you mean it?"

Ewan nodded, a slow smile curving his lips. "Marry me?" he asked, running the tip of one finger down her cheek.

She nodded, a tear trickling down that same cheek. "I'd love to."

Anna turned to the old man beside her. "Vicar? Would you marry us?"

The vicar nodded, seemingly unbothered by the morning's events. "Certainly."

Still Ewan protested. "Now?"

Anna's smile grew. "Right now! I'm not letting you out

of my sight until we're married."

Ewan laughed at her eagerness. It warmed his heart to know she was in such a hurry to become his wife. "But we don't even have a license."

"Yes we do," Anna informed him. "Richard purchased a special license several days ago. It would be a shame to let all that money go to waste when we can use it."

Ewan couldn't help the laughter that bubbled up in his throat. A special license allowed people who could afford them to marry quickly. They were very costly. What fitting revenge on his brother than to marry Richard's intended with his own special license! There was a certain justice to it. He hadn't even filled in the names.

"All right." He chuckled, finally giving in. "I'll marry you right now."

Stepping up beside her, he took both of her little hands in his. Staring deep into her eyes, he saw all the love he felt for her reflected back at him in the chocolate-brown depths. She hadn't told him she loved him yet, but he didn't need to hear the words to know how she felt.

"Would you like me to start the ceremony again or just skip to the good part?" the vicar asked cheerfully.

Ewan and Anna both burst out laughing. "Just skip to the good part," Ewan replied.

"Do you, Anna Elizabeth Welsley, take this man to be

your lawfully wedded husband?"

Anna grinned. "I do."

"And do you—" The vicar paused. "What is your name, young man?"

Ewan glanced at him, hating to take his eyes off Anna for even a second. "Ewan James MacLaughlin."

"Do you take this woman to be your lawfully wedded wife?"

"Oh, yes," he replied, both breathless and determined.

The vicar shrugged. "Then I now pronounce you married. You may kiss the bride."

And Ewan did. Thoroughly, deeply and with all the love in his heart, until the vicar cleared his throat and brought him back to earth.

Three hours later, after a thorough washing up on Ewan's part, a leisurely breakfast, and much explaining to Hester, Emily, and Mr. Welsley about what had happened, Anna and Ewan once again prepared to leave for Scotland. This time, however, there was no one to stop them.

Ewan's trunk, which the Runners had found in the abandoned store, was loaded onto the carriage along with Anna's. The rest of her belongings would be packed and sent on later in the week.

They said their good-byes somewhat tearfully. Both of

Anna's parents cried as they kissed their only daughter good-bye. Mr. Welsley shook Ewan's hand and Mrs. Welsley crushed him against her impressive bosom with a rib-cracking hug that surprised Ewan almost as much as it surprised Anna.

"You take care of my little girl," she insisted tearfully.

Ewan nodded, his breath coming in painful gasps. "I'll do my best, ma'am. I promise."

But it was Hester and Emily whom he hated to leave. With Richard gone they had only each other, and he feared losing both his father and brother might be too much for either of them.

He'd underestimated their strength.

Emily hugged and kissed him and made him promise to come back for a visit soon. Then she moved on to say good-bye to Anna.

Hester took his hands in hers and rose up on her tiptoes to kiss his cheek. Her eyes shone with tears but she held them at bay.

"I'm so sorry for what happened, Ewan."

He squeezed her fingers. "You're not to blame for any of it. I don't want to hear you say you are." He smiled. "Write to me and let me know how he's doing. He'll need you once he comes to his senses. He'll need you to forgive him."

They'd dragged their good-byes out long enough.

After a few final hugs, a footman held the carriage door open while Anna and Ewan climbed inside. They waved from the window as they rolled down the lane and, finally, out of sight.

Ewan wrapped his arm around his wife's—*his wife's!*—shoulders as she snuggled against him.

"It's nice to sit beside each other and not care if anyone sees," she said.

Ewan chuckled. "Yes, it is."

She gazed up at him, her head tucked against his shoulder. "I was so scared I'd never be with you again."

His smile faded as his throat tightened. "I know." He squeezed her shoulders, suddenly needing to lighten the mood. He didn't want to think about what could have happened. All he wanted to think about was their present—and their future.

"You haven't told me you love me yet," he remarked, teasing her.

Her eyes widened. "Of course I love you! I married you, didn't I?"

He grinned. "You did. And rather forcefully I might add."

She blushed. How he loved her blushes!

"Are you happy?" she asked. At his nod, she continued, "Are you sure we don't need my dowry to fix the castle? I don't mind if you want to use it for something that will make you so happy. Our home is worth every penny."

Ewan smiled. Already she was saying things like "we" and "our." He loved it.

"The money is a godsend," he replied, slipping a finger beneath her chin. He tipped her face up as he slowly lowered his. "But all I want—all I've ever wanted, my sweet, wonderful Anna—is *you.*"

And as the smile lit her face, Ewan touched his lips to hers and gave himself up to the first of a whole lifetime of kisses.

DEAR READER:

Did you really think Ewan wouldn't save Anna from marrying the dastardly Richard? Please. Our hero came through, of course.

Ewan isn't the only hero out there, you know: In SAMANTHA AND THE COWBOY there's a blue-eyed cattle hand who'll make your knees go weak. BELLE AND THE BEAU features a dedicated freedom fighter, a young man full of the promise of his people. And could there be a more charming medieval rascal than Gavin of GWYNETH AND THE THIEF?

Read on for an introduction to these three heroes . . .

Abby McAden
Editor, Avon True Romance

FROM
SAMANTHA AND THE COWBOY

by *Lorraine Heath*

Sweeping his hat from his head, the young man squinted at the early morning sun. Samantha's heart very nearly stopped. His eyes were a stunning blue. But it wasn't the color that snagged her attention as much as it was that he seemed to be a young man with an older man's eyes. A young man who had seen much that he might have wished he hadn't. A thin white scar creased his left eyebrow, parted the tiny black hairs there.

The scar made him seem mysterious, dangerous.

He leveled his gaze on her. Her stomach quivered.

"You shouldn't have lied to Jake," he said quietly. "Telling him you knew how to herd cattle when you don't didn't sit too well with him," he added.

"I *do* know how to herd cattle," Samantha insisted.

She grew uncomfortable under his harsh scrutiny as he captured her with his intimidating gaze.

"All right." She relented. "I know how to herd *one* cow. Our milk cow. To pasture and back."

His lips twitched, and for a heartbeat, she thought

he was going to smile.

"It's not exactly the same," he said.

She jerked up her chin. "But I could learn."

"Why did you lie?"

"I need the hundred dollars. Bad. I'd do just about anything to be part of this outfit." And that was the honest-to-gosh truth. "Besides, I'm a fast learner."

Nodding, he settled his black hat back into place. "The herd's camped about ten miles north of town. Just follow the road and you can't miss us. Report to Jake there at dawn tomorrow if you're serious about being part of the outfit."

Startled, she took a step back. He couldn't be saying what she thought he was saying. He couldn't be hiring her on. "But he said no," she reminded him.

"You just leave the trail boss to me. If you truly want the job, it's yours. Just don't ever lie again." He turned to leave. "We'll see you in the morning."

"Wait!" she called out.

He glanced back at her over his shoulder.

"I-I don't even know your name."

"Matthew Hart."

Matthew Hart. He disappeared around the corner, and Sam sank to the ground as her legs finally gave out.

✦

FROM
BELLE AND THE BEAU
by Beverly Jenkins

"Are you warm enough?" Daniel asked Belle.

Wrapped in the heavy cloak, she nodded shyly. Her sixteen-year-old heart warmed at his concern. "Have your parents been helping runaways a long time?"

"Since before Jojo and I were born. Mama freed herself by running away from Virginia when she was twelve."

"Your mother was a runaway?"

"Yes."

Belle found that information surprising. It had never occurred to her that Mrs. Best was slavery born, but the knowledge gave Belle hope that one day she too could become as polished and confident as Mrs. Best. Right now, she didn't feel polished at all, but she was a free young woman.

In the silence that followed, Daniel said, "Well."

Belle felt shyer and more unsure than ever. "Well."

"Guess we should get going."

Belle nodded.

He then asked, "You sure you're warm enough? I know

it's warmer where you're from."

Belle nodded, again too overcome by being alone with him to form words. *He probably thinks you're a simpleton,* she scolded herself. "How far is the station?"

"Another few miles."

Back home, because there'd been no call for Belle to travel, or to be anywhere but sewing for Mrs. Grayson, she'd never seen a train except in pictures. "I've never seen a train station," she said without thought, then immediately wanted to take the words back.

A simpleton and *ignorant!*

Daniel sensed her discomfort, so he said gently, "That's nothing to be ashamed of. Lots of things will be new here. Think of yourself as a traveler in a strange land, and whenever you need help or have a question, remember we're all here."

Belle hadn't thought about being up North in those terms, but realized Daniel was correct; she was a traveler in a strange land.

"So will you let me know if you need anything?"

Belle looked him straight in the face. "I will."

"Promise?"

Holding his eyes, she said, "I promise."

"Good, now let's take you to see the station."

Belle wondered if she'd ever breathe again.

꒜

FROM
GWYNETH AND THE THIEF
by Margaret Moore

"I thank you for your generous hospitality, my lady,"
Gavin said in a low tone that seemed to make something
inside her quiver, "but I really must be on my way. I have
urgent business to attend to for my master."

Gwyneth planted her feet and crossed her arms, determined to act upon her plan. "You have to stay."

He frowned, his dark brows lowering. "*Have* to?
Nay, I dare not. If I feel well enough to travel, I must,
or my master will be angry."

"No, he won't. You have no master."

Gavin's frown deepened. "Why do you think that?"

"Because I saw you in the woods *before* you were hurt."

His expression grew stern as he grabbed her shoulders
and pulled her close. His lips curled into a sardonic smile
and his brown eyes seemed to flash with scorn. "A fine
game you've been playing, with me the dupe. What will you
do, lady? Turn me over to the king's justice? If you think to
do that, you had better have more than ropes here."

She reached into her belt and pulled out her brother's

dagger which she had hidden there, putting the tip of the blade against his throat. "I have a use for you."

"Indeed?" he asked, one brow quirked in query as he eyed the dagger in her hands. "So that is why you put me here in this room and that fine bed. What is this use you have for me that requires you to house a thief in a fine chamber and give him such expensive clothes? You've treated me like a guest, except for the locked door. And the dagger at my throat, of course."

Before she could answer, a look of sudden comprehension dawned in his brown eyes.

"Somebody undressed me and combed my hair," he murmured as he circled her. "And I would have to be a fool not to know girls find me handsome. Since I am not a fool, I believe you do, too. Is that why you took pity on me, my young and pretty lady? Is that why you combed my hair and gave me your brother's clothes? What use have you for me here?"

She blushed hotly as she answered him. "You are an insolent rascal!"

"Sometimes." He smiled as he halted in front of her. "Don't you like rascals, my lady? Don't you find us . . . exciting?"